WINGS OVER IRAQ

Eric B. Forsyth

is the author of:

An Inexplicable Attraction: My Fifty Years of Ocean Sailing (2018),

available in the U.S. in full color, black and white, and e-book, through:

Amazon.com,

BarnesandNoble.com

and other online booksellers,

and in black and white and e-book in the U.K. through:

www.YPDbooks.com

WINGS OVER IRAQ

A NOVEL

BY

ERIC B. FORSYTH

WINGS OVER IRAQ

Copyright ©2020
Eric B. Forsyth

Published by:
Yacht Fiona Books
www.YachtFiona.com

Edited by:
Margaret Daisley
Blue Horizon Books
www.bluehorizonbooks.com

Cover and design by:
Jay R. Pizer
Imax Productions
www.imaxproductions.com

Publisher's Cataloging-in-Publication data:
Forsyth, Eric
Wings Over Iraq
ISBN 979-8-9853220-5-7

Table of Contents

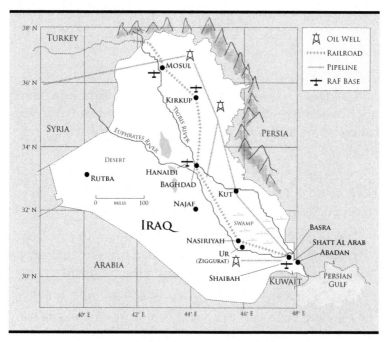

Iraq as it might have been in the 1920s

Chapter One

Chadwick was due to fly on a routine patrol one afternoon when the plane captain, Flight Lieutenant Harris, was called to the adjutant's office. When he returned, he looked troubled.

"Change of plans. Here's a new route. It's the one Flight Lieutenant McGregor flew this morning, but the plane hasn't returned. We're going to take a shufti, a look-see."

It was most likely the plane had landed on an emergency strip due to engine trouble, but if it had been brought down by unfriendly fire, the crew were in serious jeopardy.

They found the bomber in the desert about a mile from the pipeline. Harris dropped to a couple of hundred feet and flew slowly parallel to the line of disturbed sand that marked the track of the crash.

There was no sign of life, but the upper wing obscured most of the fuselage.

They dropped lower. Harris passed a note: *Landing— look for obstacles*. On another low pass Chadwick looked carefully for boulders but spotted only small stones.

Harris brought the plane down with a loud crash and taxied to within ten yards of the downed bomber. All was quiet, apart from the engines ticking over.

Chadwick was scared. He'd heard horrifying stories from other pilots of what happened to downed crew caught by the Arabs.

Harris yelled in his ear, "Go take a look. And take this revolver." He passed Chadwick a Webley.

Chadwick climbed onto the wing. As he took the gun, he was puzzled. "I don't see any wogs."

Harris looked at him pityingly. "It's not for you. You might need it for them," he said and nodded at the wrecked bomber. "There's no help out here and it'll take a day to get an armored car here."

Chapter Two

On a late afternoon in January 1928, Professor Kurt Scharf trudged along Leipziger Strasse in Berlin. There was a cold, biting wind that blew from the river, and a relentless rain produced halos around the dim streetlights. His nose dripped, and he cursed under his breath as he searched for a small entrance door in the massive edifice of the War Ministry. He was following instructions received by telephone the day before.

It was all a little mysterious, but he was curious. And that morning he had travelled to Berlin by train from Bonn, where his university was located. Finally, he spotted the number 17 on a small metal plaque next to a recessed door. He pulled a large knob and the door opened almost immediately. A burly man in a servant's uniform stood in the half shadows.

"Yes?"

"I am Professor Doctor Scharf. I have an appointment with Herr Weiss."

"Please wait," the man said brusquely and then turned to enter a door behind him.

The professor was left standing in a bare corridor. At least the outside door was closed, and he was out of the rain. *Be thankful for small mercies*, he thought as he struggled to extract a handkerchief from an inside pocket.

The doorman returned. "Follow me, please."

He climbed two flights of stairs and entered a long corridor. He noticed the floor had changed from linoleum to parquet. His guide tapped softly on a door, which he then opened and with a nod of his head indicated Scharf should step inside.

Scharf entered a spacious room that was furnished austerely in government style, with a desk, a large wooden filing

3

cabinet and three chairs. In a corner stood a large steel safe. A portrait of Chancellor Hindenburg hung on the wall behind the desk. There was a large map of Europe and the Middle East on one wall, and nothing on the other walls. A tall man of middling years rose from the desk to greet him. He was immaculately dressed in a double-breasted suit and an American dress shirt with a military tie. Scharf suddenly felt old-fashioned; he was wearing a wing collar.

"Welcome, Professor Scharf," the tall man said. "My name is Heinrich Weiss." He held out his arm and vigorously pumped the professor's cold hand.

"Good day," said the professor. "Is there somewhere I could hang my coat?"

Weiss pointed to a coat tree. "Over there. Please take a seat."

"Vile weather," said the professor as he eased into a hard chair.

Perhaps Weiss detected a hint. "Would you like a little something to warm the insides?" he asked.

"That would be very acceptable," the professor replied.

Weiss produced two glasses and a bottle from a drawer in his desk. He poured two generous shots of Schnapps, passed a glass to the professor and raised his own. "*Prosit*."

"I'm sure you're curious to know why I asked you here," Weiss started.

"*Naturlich*," said the professor. "I take it I'm somewhere in the bowels of the War Ministry?"

"Precisely," said Weiss. "I represent a very small cog in the army machine. Intelligence Department." He saw a fleeting smile cross the professor's face. "You were in the army during war, at the front?"

"Yes," replied Scharf, "Infantry, mostly at the Somme. Perhaps that's why I like digging."

"And you didn't have a high opinion of Army Intelligence?" pursued Weiss.

Scharf did not reply but smiled and spread his hands. "I'm sorry," said Weiss," I forgot to ask if you would like a cigarette."

"I don't smoke," the professor replied.

Weiss took out a case, extracted a cigarette, put it in an amber holder and carefully lit it with a lighter. "Are you a patriot?" he suddenly asked. "What do you think of Germany's present position?"

"That's a very difficult question to answer. At the moment, things are so unstable," replied Scharf.

"Precisely."

It became obvious to Scharf that this was a word Weiss was fond of.

"It is the army view that from this instability will arise stability and the iniquities inflicted on the Fatherland can be redressed."

"You mean another war?" asked the professor, his eyes widening. The prospect of another war seemed incredulous to him, beyond reason.

"Not necessarily. It is simply that from a position of strength, changes can be negotiated. This bears on why I asked you here today." He paused. "Professor, I understand you are an archaeologist with an interest in the Middle East, and it is my understanding that you have approached the British for a permit to excavate at Ur."

"That's true," replied the professor. "I made some useful contacts at the British Museum when I dug at Nineveh a few years ago."

"Ur is in southern Iraq," mused Weiss. "It's an area we have some interest in."

"May I ask why? Obviously, I don't need to know any military secrets, but it is a fairly blighted region."

"Are you familiar with progress of the Berlin to Baghdad Railway?" asked Weiss.

"In general terms. It's not finished."

"True. Work began in 1903 in Turkey, and it has been a huge engineering challenge, carried out entirely by German companies, as it is considered of immense strategic value to Germany. At the moment it is held up in the French mandated territory of Syria, but that will be corrected, and the line will be complete within a few years."

"So, Baghdad is a long way from Ur."

"Precisely," said Weiss, again. "What I am going to tell you must be held in the strictest confidence. Will you give your word as an officer and gentleman?"

Scharf smiled to himself at Weiss's quaint phraseology but with a straight face said, "*Naturlich.*"

"When the line is completed as far as Baghdad," Weiss continued, "it is the plan of the General Staff to ensure several lines are extended south, branching to the Persian Gulf and the Gulf of Aqaba. These lines will bypass the Suez Canal, England's vital link to India and the Far East," said Weiss, his voice sharpening. "In a nutshell, professor, I am going to suggest that I add one of my men to your team at Ur. The army needs up-to-date maps and topographical details of the area. This would be the perfect cover to perform a surveillance."

Professor Scharf was quiet for a moment, turning Weiss's words over in his head. "A few problems come to mind," he said. "To begin with, the project is not fully approved, and certainly not funded. Anyone affiliated with the work would have to pass as an archaeologist and I suspect even the British would become suspicious of somebody traipsing around southern Iraq with a theodolite."

"Good points," said Weiss. "This needs some careful planning. I think I can help with funding. I would like you to give some thought about a suitable person to join the team. Please think this over. Could you come up with the initial cost of an expedition and the annual cost within a week?"

Professor Scharf was at once elated but also concerned about the level of effort needed. He groaned, "I'm fairly busy, Herr Weiss. I present eight lectures every week. I'm preparing a paper and I have two graduate students to supervise. A week is very tight."

"Please do your best," commanded Herr Weiss. "Shall we say the same time and place in seven days?" He rose to indicate that the interview was over.

"If you insist," replied the professor. He hesitated. "There is also the small matter of the travel costs. A return ticket costs me five marks, although I plan to save money by staying with a colleague when in the city."

"Ah, yes," said Weiss. "I can reimburse you for receipted expenses from a small office expenditures fund. *Auf wiedersehen*, Professor."

Professor Scharf slogged along the sidewalk in the rain towards the U-Bahn station. He felt excited. If Weiss was on the level, he could fund his expedition with army money and even achieve some solid archaeological results with money that might otherwise have been wasted by the military, at least in his opinion. He had little faith in Weiss's justification—probably all lies—and besides, the British were firmly in control of Mesopotamia with a mandate granted by the League of Nations after the war. He would have to tread carefully if he wanted to avoid jeopardizing his work.

Still, the chance was too good to miss.

Chapter Three

For the next few days, Scharf worked furiously when time permitted on a revised submission to the Berlin Museum describing the proposed dig at Ur. He prepared a preliminary cost estimate and discreetly sounded out colleagues about other archaeological sites in southern Iraq. His wife, Lisa, grew increasingly exasperated.

"What the hell are you up to, Kurt?" she demanded. "You come to bed looking like a dog's dinner, not even a kiss."

His wife was an attractive woman who was somewhat lonely and bored without the companionship of her husband, who travelled frequently. She was conscious of her position as the wife of a full professor. She dressed well and wore modest make-up. She often put her flaxen hair up in a braided crown, a traditional German style that her husband liked. She carefully watched her diet and stayed fit. At heart she was bitterly disappointed that the marriage had not been blessed by children. She was in her late thirties and she felt time was running out. In her husband's opinion, she had a strong sexual appetite, although he was no judge. His wife was the only woman he had ever slept with.

"I'm trying to get some funding for a new dig. If I get the money, and that is a big if," he said. "I would only be away for a few weeks. I don't like the place any more than you did, *verdammt* sand and bugs."

His wife had made a visit to his last dig, and he suspected her major complaint was the rickety camp beds and the mosquito nets separating them.

At the appointed hour, Professor Scharf made his way to the small door at the War Ministry and was soon laying out several documents for Herr Weiss's approval.

"Firstly," he said, "here is a preliminary financial estimate. This includes the purchase of equipment and transportation to Mesopotamia in order to set up the camp. The yearly costs include two full-time academics, two full-time professionals, the stipend for two graduate students, all Europeans. The native staff would consist of eight full-time workers based at the camp and up to twenty day-laborers, as needed."

Weiss glanced at the paper without any obvious reaction. Professor Scharf handed him a second document.

"This is an amended description of the proposed work to be submitted to the Berlin Museum," Scharf said. "I think I've found a way a way to justify the presence of your man and give him some leeway to travel around southern Mesopotamia."

Weiss raised his eyebrows, clearly interested in what Scharf had to say. "Continue."

"One of the largest ziggurats in Mesopotamia is located at Ur. It is thought ziggurats were the massive foundations of temples which are now gone. The one at Ur is over four thousand years old. Since it was built sea levels have changed significantly."

Professor Scharf droned on. Weiss showed signs of impatience, waving his cigarette and tapping his foot.

"Please get to the point."

"Four thousand years ago, the shore level was higher than today, but over the centuries the water has receded. It would be extremely interesting, from an archaeological point of view, to track the way habitation, towns and villages originally clustered near the ziggurat, and then moved to follow the shoreline. This would give a timeline showing the waning power of the priests who ruled Sumer back then. An excavation and delineation of ancient sites would make a good Ph.D. thesis and would require a lot of travel in the area."

Professor Scharf paused triumphantly.

"Excellent," cried Herr Weiss. "Professor, I congratulate you, but we have to find a good man for this job."

"That's your problem," said Scharf. "If you find a young officer with the right surveying credentials, I could provide a crash course in the archaeology, enough to get by as a graduate student."

"Please leave those documents with me," demanded Herr Weiss. "I will bring a candidate to pose as your graduate student to our next meeting. Now, there is the question of your travel costs. Do you have receipts for the railway tickets?"

"Yes, here they are." Professor Scharf laid them on the desk. "I have to say, Herr Weiss, that I am surprised you require them for my petty ten-mark expenditure but accept without question my estimate for the dig of nearly four hundred thousand marks!"

Weiss laughed heartily. "Ha, ha! You see our accountants simply do not understand the functioning of the intelligence department, but they know what a railway ticket is. At our next meeting we will discuss your estimate, however."

A week later Professor Scharf made his way in light snow to the familiar rendezvous. He shook off the snow as he hung up his hat and coat.

Herr Weiss greeted him cheerfully.

"Schnapps?"

"Please, thank you."

Standing by Herr Weiss was a young man in uniform. "Let me introduce Leutnant Felix Goelz. Professor Doctor Scharf."

The professor extended his hand as he appraised the man. He was a well-built fellow of above-average height with blonde hair. They all sat down, and Herr Weiss started the interview.

"Leutnant Goelz was commissioned two years ago. He holds a baccalaureate degree in mechanical engineering, and in the past year has completed the army surveying course for engineering officers."

"I am pleased to meet you, Leutnant. Tell me, have you any interest in ancient history?"

"To be frank, sir, my studies have been directed at our modern technology, but I understand that I may be seconded to your expedition. You can be assured I'll try my best to assimilate what knowledge I may need."

He was very formal and stammered slightly. Scharf could see that Goelz was nervous, but decided he liked him, and addressed Herr Weiss. "Leutnant Goelz seems most suitable. And now, I would like us to discuss the papers I left last week."

Weiss turned to the young man. "Thank you, Leutnant Goelz. That will be all for the moment. I'll be in touch."

Goelz rose, saluted Weiss and left the room.

"If the expedition is funded," said Professor Scharf, "I think he should spend a month at my university before departure."

"Agreed," said Weiss. "On that subject, the wheels have been turning at the highest levels and I am fairly confident we will be successful. The project proposal has already been submitted on your behalf and you should hear from the museum shortly."

The professor was surprised that events were moving so swiftly.

Weiss continued, "All financial arrangements will be made through the museum. On the surface, your expedition is one of many they are funding in the field."

"When will the funds be made available?"

"I hope you can ship all the equipment to Basra this summer and have the site set up by winter. Staff will join the expedition for the start of digging in the spring of 1929."

"But that means I will have to travel to Ur this year."

"Precisely."

"I'll have to scout the area and decide where the camp will be situated— and I've already made arrangements for this summer."

"Change them," said Herr Weiss airily. "That, I am afraid, is the price you must pay for a little army support."

Professor Scharf groaned inwardly. Explaining this to his colleagues, and even more so to his wife, was not going to be easy. He began to realize that he was not in fact really in charge of the expedition.

"There is the small matter of the financial estimate you prepared," continued Herr Weiss. "Most of the expenditures seem to be reasonable, but you listed a small truck, new, to be shipped from Germany.

"A vehicle of that sort is essential," explained the professor. "Supplies have to be run to the camp almost every day—food, kerosene, bracing for the trenches."

Herr Weiss lifted his hands. "I don't dispute your experience in this sort of thing. Probably the Somme was good training." His smile reminded Scharf of a wolf. "Yes, you need a vehicle, but I would prefer a local truck, a few years old that draws no attention to itself. I think it is likely that my man would also need the use of motor transport on occasions. You can buy one when you are there this summer and have it thoroughly overhauled before the dig begins."

Professor Scharf felt slightly overwhelmed. "My costs may need to be revised if the camp is set up before the end of year.

It will have to be manned, watchers appointed, and we'll need a driver it seems."

Herr Weiss didn't disagree. "Please keep me informed of your progress, especially your planned departure this summer. By the way, you'll need a contact in Nasiriyah, which I believe is the nearest town to the ziggurat. I'll look into that."

Scharf had arranged to stay with friend for the night. He caught a tram heading west to the Potsdamer Platz, where he had to change lines. As he descended from the car, he found to his surprise that the square was mobbed with protestors. He pushed his way through the crowd and suddenly a wave of humanity carried him into the middle of a furious fight between rough-looking men, some wearing military steel helmets. He ducked as an empty beer bottle flew through the air and smashed into fragments on the cobbles at his feet. A man next to him swore and waved a fist. On his coat was a red armband with a hammer and sickle.

The clamor rose to a crescendo at the sound of police whistles. He spotted a phalanx of policemen pushing their way to the center of the fight, freely using their batons. Scharf elbowed his way behind them to where the crowd was thinning. His heart was pounding. Eventually he was able to board another tram and make his way to his friend's apartment.

When he described his ordeal, the friend dismissed it. "Happens almost every day," he said. "The communist thugs fight the Nazi thugs. The damned country is coming apart."

True to his word, Weiss telephoned the professor a few days later. "I have a name for you in Nasiriyah. This person will be useful in recruiting workers and providing local information. I will send you a letter, but it will not be headed 'War Ministry.' I think our relationship must be discreet. Expect a letter at your university addressed from the Berlin Travel Bureau."

The letter arrived on the same day as the one from the Berlin Museum, which congratulated him on the approval of his dig at Ur. When Scharf told his colleagues in the department, they were astonished.

"My God, Kurt," said one of his friends, "What did you do? Seduce Frau Meister!" Meister was the forbidding secretary of Professor Doctor von Braunsburg, the distinguished Director of Antiquities at the Berlin Museum.

"It's a tremendous honor," he told his wife. But she was not amused.

"Kurt, you will be away for months. I'm going to be so lonely, and we have made holiday reservations at Karlsbad."

"Well, we'll have to cancel them. Perhaps you can accompany me to Iraq if we pay for your ticket."

Professor Scharf entered into the whirlwind of preparations needed to get the expedition under way. When he embarked on a steamer at Hamburg for the voyage to Basra in early July, he was accompanied by Frau Scharf.

His ship left the Elbe River and butted a southwest wind in the English Channel. A day after leaving Hamburg, the White Cliffs of Dover were just visible on the starboard bow. Professor Scharf stood on the after deck grasping the rail cap and watched as the sun glinted off the wings of a biplane heading for the English coast.

Chapter Four

Pilot Officer Allan Chadwick graduated from the Royal Air Force College at Cranwell in early June of 1928. His admission to Cranwell was due to his exceptional showing in school math and science exams. However, although he was very intelligent, he lacked self-confidence in social settings.

He was a little above average height with a wiry build. He came from Liverpool and three years at Cranwell had only slightly mellowed his Lancashire accent. He received his commission and pilot's wings at the same time and after a brief leave, he was posted as a supernumerary officer to 74 Fighter Squadron stationed at the RAF base at Tangmere, on the English south coast. On arrival at the station he reported to the commanding officer.

"How many flying hours have you got, Chadwick?" the C.O. asked.

"A hundred and thirty-five." Chadwick replied, "Mostly on an Avro 504K, including twenty-two hours on a Bristol Fighter.

"Good. You're posted to my squadron as a supernumerary pilot, which means you're not on the permanent strength. You're probably in limbo until the great brains in London decide what to do with you. I suspect you'll be en route to the Middle East or Far East before long. In the meanwhile, you must keep your hand in, report to A Flight when you're settled in—that'll be Flight Lieutenant Munro."

Munro was a busy man. He talked briefly to Chadwick, ascertained his flying experience and told him to go down to the flight line and draw a flying suit and helmet.

"You can crawl over one of our Siskins, but before you fly it, sign out a 504 and get familiar with the area."

Chadwick was delighted. The Siskin was a front-line fighter, equipped with a radial engine. It could exceed one hundred and fifty knots and climb to ten thousand feet in less than ten minutes. In the end, he made three flights over several days in a 504, a training plane he was very familiar with, and noticed that the wind was usually southwest. He was impatient to fly a Siskin, but they were too much in demand for a newcomer to expect to get some air time in soon.

On his last flight in a 504, he spotted a large black car on the road to Newhaven. He dropped lower to take a closer look and saw that it was a Bentley. He was thrilled; a four-and-a-half-liter Bentley had just won the twenty-four-hour endurance race at Le Mans. This car was being driven rather sedately and Chadwick debated whether to drop even lower and buzz it—and then rejected the idea. He was the "new boy" and needed to stay in the good graces of the flight commander if he was to get a flight in a Siskin.

The next day Chadwick was ordered to go over the technical features of a Siskin and discuss flying characteristics with an experienced squadron pilot. He approached a pilot he had become friendly with, Pilot Officer Gubbins.

"I say, Nick, how about walking out to the crate that's over there and going over a few things?"

"Jolly good. Let's go."

The pair walked out to a stationary plane. Chadwick climbed into the cockpit, and Gubbins stood on the wing. They discussed engine starting and take-off.

"Swings a bit to the left if you're quick on the throttle," explained Gubbins. "Just be ready with some right rudder. You can get the tail up about thirty knots and climb away at fifty. Depends a bit on how much extra stuff you're carrying. Climb speed is about eighty-five to ninety, gives you about a thousand feet a minute. Pretty good, eh? Aerobatics are real fun; you can pull a lot of 'G.' The plane is all metal. Enter a loop at about one hundred and twenty knots, full power to the top and Bob's your Uncle."

Later in the afternoon Chadwick was called to Munro's office. "You've been assigned 3127. Take it up for an hour," Munro told him. "No flying in cloud. Be back before seventeen hundred."

Chadwick quickly donned flying gear, did a quick external examination, grabbed a parachute and clambered into the waiting Siskin. He churned with excitement. An airman swung the propeller, Chadwick waved away the chocks and taxied to the take-off point on the large airfield. After a last-minute check of the controls he slowly advanced the throttle and smoothly lifted off the field. What a delight!

At five thousand feet over the English Channel, he checked around, made sure nothing was loose in the cockpit, and began a barrel roll. This was followed by a loop-the-loop. At the top, inverted, he could see the horizon. He brought the wings level with quick movement of the stick and cut engine power. As the Siskin swooped to the bottom of the loop, centrifugal force pushed him hard against the parachute he was sitting on. When there was nothing but sky ahead, he applied full power, the engine roared and he climbed to ten thousand feet. He levelled off and glanced around.

Where the hell am I? he thought. On his left, the coast was a faint smudge. He put the nose down and started a speed run. The plane rapidly accelerated to one hundred and sixty knots, the stick force grew, and he had difficulty keeping the nose down. The noise and vibration were overwhelming.

That's enough, he decided and throttled back. Nothing seemed amiss. Oil pressure and engine temperature were normal. He felt almost euphoric. On his right he could see a steamer leaving a long wake. On the left was Beachy Head. Tangmere was about fifty miles to the west.

Damned wind has carried me east, he thought as he swung the plane round and headed for the coast.

When he landed, the Flight Sergeant told him the adjutant wanted to see him. He signed the duty log and dumped his gear in the crew room. He walked quickly to the adjutant's office.

"Ah, Chadwick. Your posting has come through. You're going to 314 Squadron at RAF Hinaidi, Iraq."

Chadwick felt as if the ground had opened under him. His euphoria quickly evaporated. He had been posted to a bomber squadron.

"I'll give you a chit for tropical gear and a tin trunk. You can pick them up at the quartermaster's. You may want to buy some personal gear too. I believe Hinaidi can be hot in summer." This was a personal joke, as the temperature at Hinaidi could reach 130 Fahrenheit in summer. "I suggest you talk to someone who's been there. I think Flight Lieutenant Munro spent a couple of years in Iraq."

After leaving the adjutant's office, Chadwick tracked down Munro in the officer's mess. "Thank you for the ride in the Siskin," he started to say. "It was spiffing—." He hesitated, not wanting the officer to sense his disappointment. "I just got my posting, bombers in Iraq."

Munro picked up on Chadwick's lack of enthusiasm. "Chin up," he said. "You'll have a lot of fun, even though it is a beastly place!"

Chapter Five

Pilot Officer Chadwick signed out of the base and made his way home to Liverpool, in the northwest of England. He was informed by telegram to report to the military movements officer at Liverpool dock in two days. He had been assigned a berth on a troopship heading to India and would disembark at Basra.

Chadwick bid farewell to his parents at their house in Liverpool. His mother was tearful, and his father said he looked "grand" in his uniform. It was not far to the docks and so he took a taxi, which drove underneath the overhead railway connecting all the docks.

On board he shared a cabin with two other junior officers, both in the army. Discipline was fairly tight. The quarters for enlisted men were inspected by junior officers every day. When it was feasible, there were exercise classes on deck. In bad weather officers attended lectures on British military organization in the Middle East and India.

Crossing the Bay of Biscay, the weather was rough. The smell of seasick vomit permeated the cabins and gathering rooms. Officers were excused attendance for meals if they were too sick, but if they did show up for a meal, they were expected to wear best dress uniform. Grit from the funnels got everywhere, but Chadwick and his cabin mates were assigned a batman who did his best to keep their clothes clean and made the beds.

No passengers were allowed ashore at Gibraltar, but word leaked out that they would get shore leave in Port Said, Egypt. At one of the lectures given before they arrived in Egypt, they listened to sage advice from a grizzled Squadron Leader who was returning for a third tour.

"You've been trapped on the ship for a couple of weeks," he said. "Naturally you'd like some female company. Under no circumstances engage in carnal activities with native women. The ones you'll meet will all be worn-out professionals, and you'll get a dose of clap, a court martial offence," he warned them. "In clubs and hotel bars you'll meet a better class of women, usually Europeans, but they're just as dangerous. They're after your money. They work in cahoots with the club and persuade you to buy champagne at outrageous prices. When their glass is poured, it's ginger beer or something similar. They get a rake-off, depending on how much they've conned you to buy. They're very charming. Offer to buy them a beer and they'll up and go. They know you're wise to their little tricks."

Chadwick listened to the squadron leader with slight bewilderment. He had very little experience of women. He was a virgin and secretly ashamed of his gauche manner with the opposite sex. Women were a mystery to him, and the squadron leader's comments served to reinforce his own conviction that he would never pay to solve the mystery.

The Squadron Leader went on to describe the climate and seasons at the usual British bases. "Tailors are cheap, but don't buy anything here, as you'll be pestered by gully-gully men to do so. They'll offer you everything, including their sister. You may want to consider buying a Bombay Bowler, a pith hat. Offer them a quarter of their asking price and be firm! Pith hats can be a blessing in the heat. They work best if you soak then in water for a minute, particularly if there is a breeze. If you go ashore at Port Said, you'll be given a pass you have to show at the gate. Access to the docks is strictly controlled, and you'll be logged in and out. This is to make sure you don't go AWOL," he said with a laugh. "Wear civvies ashore," he added.

When the ship tied up at Port Said for three days, selected groups of enlisted men and officers were permitted ashore on each day. Passes were made out for eight hours, and no one was allowed to stay ashore at night. Most of the men on board had never left the British Islands before, let alone visited a foreign country.

Due to the strategic importance of the Suez Canal, British troops were stationed at the Canal and major cities. Egypt was nominally independent but there was an "understanding" with Britain. The arrangement was not popular with Islamic nationalists, who were often encouraged by the Germans to foment riots. The situation was often tense.

Pilot Officer Chadwick was given a pass for shore leave on the second day, along with one of the army officers he shared a cabin with, Lieutenant Roy Kershaw. They were allowed to leave the ship at noon.

Officers used one gangplank and other ranks used a second gangplank further forward. The heat was oppressive. As they walked towards the dock gates, Chadwick noticed the men leaving the ship doffed their hats and a military policeman dropped something into each one.

"What's going on there?" he asked Roy, nodding at the crowd at the foot of the forward gangplank.

Kershaw had been talking to the men in his platoon before disembarking. "If they want one, the MPs drop a French letter into their hats," he replied. "A condom."

"Fancy that," Chadwick remarked, "The army is encouraging loose behavior."

"Don't be a prig, Chadwick. They're being realistic. Better spending a few pennies up front than have a man out on sick leave," retorted Kershaw.

Outside the gate they were besieged by touts, but they worked their way to a taxi and asked the driver to take them to the Casino Palace Hotel. Men from the ship walked in groups down the Shariel Gumhuriyah, a main street lined with impressive buildings, each with elaborately carved balconies running the full length of each floor. The street was crowded with horse-drawn carriages, cars and trucks and overburdened mules. The taxi windows were all the way down, and the pungent smells of horse manure, gasoline fumes and spice wafted on the warm air, along with a clamorous noise.

They soon arrived at the hotel, a solid structure with a large advertising sign for Dewar's Whiskey on the roof. Kershaw paid the taxi driver and they sauntered into the crowded lobby. They were soon seated in the dining room, where they both ordered a beer and studied the menu. It was very hot, but large fans in the ceiling kept some air moving. Kershaw settled for a fish, while Chadwick stuck to traditional English fare and asked for Shepherd's Pie.

They discussed their first impressions, and it became clear that Kershaw was the more worldly-wise. His father was a lawyer and Kershaw had been brought up in an upper-middle-class home. He often heard his father recounting legal points over dinner. Chadwick's father was a butcher who had done well during the war and opened a small chain of shops.

After coffee, they retired to the hotel bar. It was fairly crowded, but they squeezed in and ordered more beer.

"This should keep the houris away," joked Chadwick, referring to the talk they received on the ship. "Watch out for a champagne-bearing Mata Hari."

Kershaw looked at him and decided the next few hours with Pilot Officer Chadwick promised to be dull. And then his hopes were lifted. A pleasant feminine voice with an English accent rose above the hubbub. "Excuse me, I'm awfully sorry to bother you, but I can't get near the bar. Would you be a dear and order me a pink gin?"

Kershaw turned to the person behind him, a slim woman in her thirties. She held out a ten-shilling note.

"A pleasure," he said, and got the attention of the barman. When he had her drink, he turned. The woman was sitting down at a small table that had just been vacated. He walked over, saying "Here's your pink gin and change, miss."

"Thank you so much." She looked at him appraisingly. "Would you like to join me?"

"Delighted," he said. "I'll just get my beer. He walked back to the bar and said to Chadwick, "Excuse me, Allan, I just met a friend. I'll see you back on board."

Chadwick was startled. He watched Kershaw walk back to the small table and murmur something to the woman sitting there, and she smiled. *My God*, he thought, *Roy's a fast worker. I could probably learn a lot from him.*

"I hope you don't think me forward," the woman said to Kershaw, "but I couldn't just sit at a table by myself. I'd be pestered to death—this place is ninety-nine percent men."

Kershaw said, "A pleasure to meet you. My name is Roy."

"Sheila," the woman replied. "What regiment are you with?"

"Actually, I'm just passing through. I'm on a troopship heading for India. They just let us rats off the ship for a few hours, in case it's sinking."

She chuckled. "I'm staying at another hotel, but I'm so fed up with the bar there I came here for a change."

"Are you army?" asked Roy.

"My husband is a major in the engineers. He's gone on ahead to deal with some problem that arose while we were on the ship. He's going to find living quarters when that's dealt with and I'll follow him. Simla, I think. So, I've been left to molder here alone."

She made a small moue. They looked at each other.

"I'm afraid I have to be back on the ship by eight p.m. Doesn't leave much time to do anything interesting."

"I could show you a few things this afternoon, if you like," said Sheila. There was a loaded silence that coalesced into an unspoken agreement.

"What hotel are you staying at?" asked Roy.

"The Grand," she said, "Room 210." She finished her drink. "Give me ten minutes and you might like to pop over."

She rose. Kershaw gave her a mock salute. "Duty calls," he said. He watched her make her way through the crowded room to the hotel lobby. *The Squadron Leader was right,* he thought. *You do meet a better class of women in hotel bars.*

Twenty minutes later he knocked on the door of room 210. Sheila opened the door, let him in, and then locked it.

"You were going to show me some of the Port Said sights," he said.

Sheila let her dressing gown fall open, "How about this?"

Chapter Six

When the German ship carrying Professor and Frau Scharf arrived in the Persian Gulf, the temperature in the shade was forty centigrade at noon—over a hundred Fahrenheit. Lisa Scharf complained bitterly. "I'm going to melt," she said.

A seaman standing close by overheard her. "Oh, this isn't too bad," he explained. "In another month it could hit fifty degrees. You get used to it."

The ship anchored some distance from the Basra waterfront, and a lighter deposited them on a landing. They were the only passengers leaving the ship. The professor engaged a horse-drawn carriage to take them and their luggage to the Shams al-Basra Hotel. On the way to the hotel, Scharf looked at the ancient buildings, and could see the town was clearly very old. Some structures had been abandoned. Rotting beams could be seen through gaping windows. In local folklore it was said to be the port that Sinbad the Sailor sailed from.

Once they settled in their room, he asked the concierge the best way to get to Nasiriyah. He discovered there was a train and a ferry along the Euphrates. The train was quicker, but more expensive. At this stage the professor was goading himself to keep expenses to a minimum so that more money would be available for the digging. Later on, worn down by the local inefficiency and downright corruption, he would pay without too much thought just to get a job done.

The ferry to Nasiriyah was slow and hot, even under a large awning, but the steady progress brought a gentle breeze. The river wound through the center of town, where scores of small native boats were moored along both banks.

Professor Scharf took a carriage to the Zamzam Hotel, a modest establishment. At dinner, he heard several diners speaking English, and guessing they were involved with the archaeological digs, he walked over while they were sipping coffee. He introduced himself, self-conscious of the fact that his English was slow and not quite fluent, although it was functional. But he was warmly welcomed and invited to sit down to share coffee with them.

"Is Dr. Rawlins around?" he asked, enquiring after the chief of the British team.

"He's not here tonight," he was told. "He'll be at the dig tomorrow. Come out with us."

He arranged to meet them for breakfast, at six a.m. The day began early to avoid the heat. They drove out to the digging site in a rented car. It was about ten miles from the hotel. The great ziggurat dominated the horizon.

The professor was soon seated in a tent with Dr. Rawlins. After chatting over the activities of mutual friends, Dr. Rawlins said, "There have been some small changes to the site originally selected for your dig, Kurt."

"Oh, tell me."

"I know you planned to excavate some of the town built to house workers that erected the ziggurat. A very interesting idea, but a complication has arisen. Believe it or not, the air force wants to build an airfield that would cut across some of the areas we've surveyed for a later dig. From their point of view it makes sense, as the ground is slightly higher and not prone to flooding in the rainy season."

"Why do they need an airfield here?"

"I'm afraid I'm not privy their military plans, but I think it's connected with the discovery of new oil fields."

They sat silently for few moments. "This is what I suggest," offered Dr. Rawlins. "I believe the old town extended to the west, an area that will soon be part of the airfield. If you start there, we'll have some knowledge of what lies under the ground before the air force takes over and digging will be impossible. You may even find remains of the ancient harbor."

After some thought Professor Scharf said, "That means I'll be under some time pressure. You know, I've just now arrived. Equipment from Germany is on the way, but nothing is ready." Still, the professor's interest was piqued. Discovering remains of the old harbor when Ur was near water would be a real coup.

Chapter Seven

Chadwick arrived at Basra two weeks after the professor and his wife. The troop ship anchored off in the Shatt-al-Arab. No other officers were leaving the ship at Basra. The RAF put him up at the Shams al-Basra Hotel, and he was told to wait for further orders.

One night in the bar of the hotel, he chanced upon Frau Scharf. Still envious of Lieutenant Kershaw's success at Port Said, he asked her if she would like a drink. Frau Scharf had a poor command of English, but she understood his invitation.

"*Ja*, yes, thanks you." She ordered a glass of wine.

"Allan" he said.

"Lisa," she said, adding, "I am sorry, my English is very poor."

"You're forgiven. Do you live here or just visiting?" asked Chadwick. He looked at her. She was an attractive woman, well-dressed, and she had a certain poise. When Frau Scharf was served her wine, he tipped his glass towards her. "Cheers."

"I am from Deutschland. *Ich wart, vait for mein mann.*"

Although Chadwick did not quite grasp her full meaning, he got the picture. He said, "I wait here," he explained, "to go, *fahren*, to Baghdad." A vestige of the German learned in school had come back to him.

After a few stilted sentences she thanked him again and rose to return to her own room. As he watched her go, a phrase from a book he had once read came to mind. *Lucky is the man whose first love is an experienced woman.*

The next day orders came through for him. He was to be the officer commanding a detachment of airmen travelling to Baghdad by train. He received a travel warrant for a first-class, one-way ticket to Baghdad. He met an RAF bus at the station and was formally put in command. The men traveled second class, but both classes had couches for sleeping, as it was a two-day trip. Fortunately, the detachment came with a sergeant who sized up Chadwick immediately.

"Don't worry, sir, I'll look after things."

A Crossley tender picked up Chadwick at the railway station in Baghdad and dropped him off at 314 Squadron Offices, RAF Hinaidi. He entered the orderly room and asked for the adjutant. An elderly officer emerged from a side office.

He saluted and said, "Chadwick, sir. Just arrived from Basra."

"Welcome aboard, Chadwick. I'm Flight Lieutenant Wiltshire, adjutant. Come along. I'll introduce you to the C.O."

They went a few doors down a corridor and Wiltshire knocked quietly.

"Come in," a booming voice shouted.

"Sir, this is Pilot Officer Chadwick, joining us from Cranwell College, just entrained from Basra."

The C.O. was a tall, big man. On his chest was a DFC ribbon and several wartime campaign ribbons. He came around a desk and grasped Chadwick's hand, "Pleased to have you join the squadron. Have a seat." He nodded to Wiltshire, who retired. Chadwick was delighted to detect a northern accent. "I'm Squadron Leader Welch. Where are you from, Chadwick?"

"Liverpool, sir," replied Chadwick.

"You attended Cranwell, eh? How long did that take?"

"Three years, sir."

"Well, I must say, I've never met an officer who attended Cranwell. How much flying time have you got, Chadwick?"

"About one hundred and thirty-nine hours, I did a little flying with 74 Squadron before I was posted."

"Any two-engine time?"

"No, sir, all my time is on single engine aircraft."

"Well. You're going to get a lot more multi-engine time in the next few years."

Welch went on to tell Chadwick that the squadron had two flights of Vickers Vimy bombers, three planes in each flight. "We also have a passenger version," he said. "It's really a Vimy with skin. We do the odd transport run when needed. And we have an armored car company, manned by pongos."

Chadwick was puzzled. "Excuse me, sir, why do we have armored cars, pongos?"

"Cut along now and find your flight commander. He'll explain just what we're trying to do here."

The next day Chadwick was introduced to his new flight commander, Flight Lieutenant Frank Lattimer. They shook hands. Chadwick looked keenly at the man who would be his immediate superior for the next couple of years. He was of average height with slight build. He had sandy hair and a small mustache. On his uniform were three campaign ribbons. Lattimer was intrigued to find he had a pilot educated at the college level.

"I had hoped to go to university myself," he said to Chadwick, "but the war got in the way. You know there are some damned interesting digs here in Mesopotamia. Abraham, him of the bible, was born just down the river."

"Anyway," Lattimer continued, "here's a booklet that explains what the RAF is doing in this Godforsaken spot. In a nutshell, Air Marshall Trenchard needed a peacetime job for the RAF, or the politicians would have disbanded it. When Mesopotamia was seceded from Turkey and given to Great Britain after the war, the army said it was too expensive to run because thirty-six regiments would be needed. Trenchard saw his chance and said the RAF could control the place with twelve squadrons from the air and a few armored cars on the ground. So here we are, although with only six squadrons. The pongos run the armored cars, the army. Any questions?"

Chadwick shook his head.

"When it comes to the flying," continued Lattimer, "we usually fly two or three patrols a day. The main job is to look after the oil wells, refineries and the pipelines. Every so often we have to deal with the naughty Bedouins, Arabs or Wahabis. They attack isolated settlements, road convoys to Baghdad and sometimes do a little sabotage in the oil fields. The Wahabis cross the border from Persia, but the others are local pests. We have a way of dealing with each, you'll find out. At the moment we have eleven qualified plane captains, and nine odds and sods pilots like you, flying as second pilots. Each plane usually carries a front gunner who also acts as bomb aimer. The rear gunner has two Lewis guns mounted on Scarff rings, one pointing up and one down. Any questions?"

Again, Chadwick shook his head. He felt a little overwhelmed.

Lattimer went on. "Our machines have been modified from the old planes used in the war. Then they carried one pilot. They must've been tough bastards. Now the Vimy has a dual cockpit. The captain sits on the right. Engine instruments are on the engine nacelle on each side, flight instruments are in the center cockpit. The C.O. mentioned you have no multi-engine time. I'll arrange for you to get some dual flying with one of the captains. Mainly this involves flying the Vimy on one engine in an emergency, totally different than anything you've experienced before. Draw some flying gear from stores and read the booklet I gave you. Also find a copy of Pilot's Notes for the Vimy and get familiar with that."

Breakfast in the mess was 0530 hours and flying started at 0600. Chadwick was introduced to Flying Officer Brian Holmes, who was to take him up for his first ride in a Vimy. Holmes had a nonchalant air about him. He had straight black hair combed back and was slightly taller than Chadwick.

"We're going to fly without crew today," said Holmes. "It's getting pretty warm already, temp is ninety-five. The engines don't like too much heat and the air thins as it gets hotter. I'll just show you the area and let you feel the controls. It's difficult talking up there. The props' tips are only three feet from the cockpit. I'll take a notepad and scribble messages."

They examined the exterior of the plane and climbed into the open cockpit. Airmen swung the propellers on command from Holmes, left and then right engine. They settled into a steady roar. To Chadwick the noise seemed deafening. Holmes checked the magnetos, one engine at a time, and then waved away the chocks. They taxied to the edge of the field, using one engine or another to help make turns, as the plane had no wheel brakes. Airmen helped by pushing on the wings. Heading into wind, Holmes revved up the engines and the Vimy lumbered into the air. They climbed away, ascending about two hundred and fifty feet per minute. At an altitude of five thousand feet, Holmes tapped Chadwick on the shoulder and pointed to the stick.

Chadwick grabbed it and immediate found that some force was needed to keep the plane flying level. Holmes indicated a turn to the left, and Chadwick banked slightly and then leveled out. Holmes pointed to his notepad. *Steer 180,* he wrote.

Chadwick found it was extremely difficult for him to steer a steady course on the Vimy, compared to the small planes he was used to flying. It was a very heavy plane, and during a turn, inertia caused it to swing through the heading he was trying to hold. Holmes pointed to the altimeter. The plane was slowly descending and had lost about three hundred feet of height. Holmes pointed up. Chadwick advanced the throttles and the Vimy slowly gained height. He found that trying to hold a heading of one-eighty and keep the airspeed steady for a climb took all his concentration. He was sweating profusely.

Holmes pointed to the left, and on his pad he wrote, *Lost? Head east to the river.*

Chadwick flew the plane for a few minutes, then Holmes pointed to his own chest and took the stick. Twenty minutes later they touched down with a loud bump, crossing the airfield boundary at about forty-five knots. Chadwick climbed out of the plane, unbuckled his chute and leaned on the fuselage.

"Not as easy as it looks," said Holmes, with a grin.

Chapter Eight

Hamid Mustafa was born in 1890 in Basra of Sunni Arab parents. At that time, the Turks ruled Mesopotamia. The family was very poor, and at age fourteen, in 1904, Mustafa signed on as a boy on a German freighter. It was a rough and tumble life, but he was quick-witted and by the time he was eighteen, he spoke fluent German and passable Spanish and English. From the German crew he picked up an anti-British bias that would remain all his life.

He qualified as an able-bodied seaman when he was twenty. He worked hard to help the bosun and learn the ropes. When that old seaman was badly injured by the failure of a defective wire rope and left the ship, the Captain promoted Mustafa to bosun, a signal honor for an Arab and a measure of his intelligence and common sense. He soon discovered the captain had a little racket going on the side which needed the bosun to store certain cargo with great care so that it could be expeditiously removed from the hold in a short time and swung overboard to a waiting small boat. He decided to emulate the captain and within a few years he had accumulated enough money to make him wealthy by Mesopotamian standards.

On a boiling hot summer's day in 1914, Mustafa entered the bridge house when the ship was riding at anchor at Basra Roads. The Captain was talking to the company agent.

"Hamid," the Captain said, "Herr Richter here says there is going to be war between Germany and other European countries. The company will probably send the ship to the Far East."

"If it's all the same to you, Captain, I'll sign off here while I am home and sit it out."

War broke out while he was living with his parents. Mustafa figured the British would go for the oil controlled by Turkey and he invested in a number of modern, efficient ferries that plied the waters of the Euphrates and Tigris Rivers, and a string of barges. He was not surprised when the company agent, Herr Richter, stopped by his office late one afternoon. Richter told him that German Army Intelligence was building a network in Mesopotamia to help the Turks and ferment anti-British sentiment among Arabs. Richter asked Mustafa to take some serious responsibilities for the network.

Mustafa was able to negotiate a handsome monthly fee and he entered whole-heartedly into the game of espionage. When the British attacked Kut, about halfway between Basra and Baghdad, he was able to play both ends. The British paid him handsomely to move equipment up the rivers and the Germans paid extra to make sure it was mostly damaged in transit, late or lost. When the war ended Mustafa was rich.

In the post-war years, Mustafa became a senior player in the effort to gain independence for Iraq, the new name for the conglomeration of Mesopotamia and Kurdish and Arab lands. He also continued to make money and built himself large houses in both Basra and Nasiriyah, the limits of his business empire. When the rail line was improved, he could make the trip between the two cities in a few hours.

The German defeat had removed their financial support for Mustafa, but he continued his association with German intelligence, in the form of Herr Weiss. By fortunate chance he was sitting in his office in Nasiriyah when Professor Scharf telephoned. He had been alerted by Weiss to expect the call. The next day they sat in cushioned comfort sipping coffee while Professor Scharf introduced himself.

"Herr Mustafa—," the Professor began.

"Call me Hamid," interrupted Mustafa

"Hamid, then. I'm in charge of a dig at Ur financed by the Berlin Museum. I've just arrived from Germany and hope to start work early next year. A good deal of equipment is coming by sea and should arrive in Basra shortly. I will also need to procure some gear here, especially a light truck."

"I can help you with the arrangements," said Mustafa.

"There is also the question of labor. Although I haven't examined the site in detail, I believe the excavations will be deep."

"The English seem to get by with fairly shallow trenches near the ziggurat," said Mustafa.

"True, but I was told the site approved for my dig has been moved west where the sediment is deeper. For some reason the British plan to build an airfield so my site will be out of bounds in a couple of years."

Mustafa was very interested to hear that and decided Herr Weiss should be informed. But he made no comment.

"Professor, if you give me the manifests of the gear coming from Germany, I can arrange for it to be delivered to your site. Laborers should not be a problem. The permanent staff may be more difficult, as good cooks are hard to find who are used to European tastes."

"Another thing," said the professor, "I'd prefer a foreman who speaks German."

"I'll see what can be done. Where are you staying?"

"I'm at the Zamzam. Which brings up another point. At the moment my wife is staying at a hotel in Basra, while I am busy at Ur. I think she would prefer to be here in Nasiriyah. However, bringing my wife to Iraq is a purely private arrangement, not part of the Museum expedition. Over time, the expense of a hotel would be onerous. Are there any decent private pensions here?"

"I will happy to look into it for you. Would you accept my invitation for dinner tonight at my house?"

"Only too pleased."

"Eight o'clock then. I will send a car to the hotel for you." This grandiose gesture on the part of Mustafa was quite unnecessary, and only offered to show his affluence and standing. It was only five hundred yards from the hotel to Mustafa's house.

Chapter Nine

Pilot Officer Chadwick assiduously read the material suggested by his flight commander and spent time with a sergeant fitter carefully going over a Vimy in the hangar. He was surprised to find the plane had two small propellers mounted near the main engines—one drove a pump which transferred fuel from the main tanks to a small tank over the engine; the other turned a generator which kept the batteries charged. Before Flying Officer Holmes took him for another flight, they had a long discussion about single engine operation.

"Frankly, it's damn tricky, Chadwick. If you lose an engine, get the crate on the ground as soon as possible. If one engine dies, the plane will swing violently towards the bad engine. You must quickly apply the opposite rudder. If you try to maintain height you'll slow down, and the rudder will become less effective. Unless you act very quickly the plane might stall and probably spin. Your only option if you lose an engine is to descend, keep the speed up and hope to God there is a clear piece of real estate ahead. When you crash and survive, pray to God there are no Bedouins around, especially women. I'll tell you about them someday when I'm drunk. There's another thing, do you know how big the props are?"

"Ten feet diameter," said Chadwick.

"It was a rhetorical question. Anyway, the damn things are big and heavy. Four massive blades. They have terrific momentum. If the engine seizes up, the prop will break into pieces and fly through the cockpit. It's happened. There's not much left of the pilot."

"I'll try to remember that."

With that, they climbed into flying gear, examined a plane on the flight line and eventually climbed away into the hot air. It was bumpy with thermal currents shaking the plane. Chadwick took the controls for forty-five minutes and executed a few gentle turns while endeavoring to maintain a constant altitude.

"Not bad," said Holmes when they returned to the crew room. "Maybe tomorrow we'll try landing and a touch and go."

For a few days Holmes was busy flying operational sorties. When he had time off, they practiced together, and Chadwick became more proficient, but shaking off his fighter type flying was hard. After ten hours of dual, Holmes pronounced him fit to fly as second pilot.

Squadron Leader Welch took him up for a check flight. At five thousand feet, flying straight and level, he suddenly pulled the throttle of the left engine shut. Chadwick immediately clamped on full right rudder and advanced the throttle of the right engine. He adjusted the Vimy for a gentle descent and checked the fuel valves to make sure they were fully open. Welch took control, executed a hard-descending turn, at the same time advancing the throttle of the left engine, which came to life with a couple of loud bangs.

As they walked across the sand carrying their chutes, Welch said, "All right, lad, you'll do."

The equipment ordered by Professor Scharf was slowly unloaded on the dock at Basra and, when fully accounted for, Mustafa had it put onto one of his barges and shipped to Nasiriyah. The camp was duly set up at the dig site. The professor managed to get to Nasiriyah most days to have dinner and stay with his wife. The English contingent were duly impressed with the speed of progress.

In November Leutnant Goelz showed up and the professor and his wife sailed back to Germany. All was set for a good digging season in 1929.

Chapter Ten

In the final days of 1928 there was a top-level, secret meeting of military and civilian leaders of the Weimar Government in Berlin. The aim was to make sure there was a consensus on foreign policy in the Middle East.

The Foreign Minister kicked off with a summary. "Great Britain has established a firm hold on much of the former Ottoman Empire that now supplies them with oil. The French control Syria, which does not appear to have much oil. The Americans have great influence with the Saudi royal family in Arabia and are helping them absorb the small tribal kingdoms. Germany has no direct control over areas producing oil. We have influence over the Turks and get much of the oil we need from Baku. The Turks are very resentful of the semi-independence of the Kurds in Northern Iraq. A good deal of oil has been discovered in that region, centered on Mosul. In the south of Iraq, oil from the region is refined at Abadan." He paused to let this information sink into those assembled.

"Our actions in Iraq should be aimed at stirring up hatred of the British and the establishment of an independent country," he continued. "Once that is accomplished, we can back the Turks in an invasion of northern Iraq. Control of the oil fields will go to Germany. In the south, nationalization of the oil industry by an independent government could terminate the British contracts and instead allow a contract with German companies. General von Hollen, would you care to comment on our activities to secure these aims?"

The general rose the address the group. He was a little put out that the minister used his military rank, rather the name he used with the many secret agents that reported to him: Herr Weiss.

"Naturally I have to be very discreet. Even the walls have ears." Weiss looked around the room, as if expecting to see spies peering from the doors and windows. "We have established networks in place. At the lower level they support acts of harassment against transportation and oil facilities. At a higher level we support parties aimed at securing independence. This is not straightforward—there is a good deal of animosity between Arabs of different sects. I cannot give more details in such an open forum."

After more discussion, much of it pointless, the meeting closed. Within two days a summary lay on the desk of British Intelligence in London and of the OGPU in Moscow. Neither agencies learned anything they did not already know.

Felix Goelz was not idle in Nasiriyah. He learned to drive the truck that Mustafa had bought for the expedition and made two trips a week to the camp site at Ur to ensure the skeleton staff were keeping up the facilities. Professor Scharf had left him some books on archaeology and his own report on the digging at Nineveh, which he had excavated a few years before. On his own initiative, Herr Goelz started to learn spoken Arabic. There was only one British archaeologist staying in Nasiriyah because the rainy season made digging impossible. Goelz cultivated him to improve his English and pick up some excavator's lore. He was helped by having the truck, sometimes giving a ride to the Briton, who otherwise had to take a taxi.

Hamid Mustafa occasionally asked Goelz over to his house for a meal. He was aware of the young man's dual role and even suspected that he might be reporting on him to Herr Weiss. When Goelz confessed he was trying to learn some Arabic, Mustafa suggested he may combine business with pleasure by meeting a lady friend of his who loved Germans. Mustafa himself, of course, was simply ensuring he had another entre into the expedition. The more he knew, the better.

"Perhaps the next time we have dinner together I should invite her?" Mustafa said. "She is a German lady whose husband was unfortunately killed just after the war. She is fluent in Arabic."

Felix Goelz was non-committal.

The weather in Baghdad was somewhat drier than further south, but nevertheless, 314 Squadron's flying activities were hampered by overcast skies and rain. When flying was scrubbed, Chadwick spent a good deal of time in the hangars. He was particularly friendly with the flight sergeant in charge of engine maintenance, Evans, a Welshman.

He discovered Evans had entered the RAF through Halton, a school for apprentices started by General Trenchard. These trained technicians were the backbone of the ground staff in the RAF. Trenchard believed if you repaired a plane you should fly it. When the fitters and mechanics completed the course at Halton they were then trained as aerial gunners. This also had the advantage that an aircraft forced down by engine failure or a structural problem, had a man on board who may be able to repair it.

Chadwick was fascinated by the Rolls Royce Eagle engines that powered the Vimy. They were the ultimate development when the engines were first built for the Schneider Trophy competitors in the early 1920s. Chadwick spent a lot of time with Evans examining engines that had been stripped for a rebuild.

When the weather was suitable, Chadwick flew with most of the squadron captains on training exercises. These usually involved gunnery or bomb aiming practice. A Crossley tender would leave the airfield early and drive twenty miles into the desert. For bombing practice, they pegged out a twenty-foot diameter circle made of canvas with a black ring in the center. When the ground crew was clear they fired a green flare. The Vimy was flown at about seventy-five knots and one thousand feet above the ground. The pilot had to maintain a steady heading which took the plane over the target. As the plane approached the target it disappeared under the nose and the pilot could not see it. The forward bomb aimer would do his best to hit the target with a fifty-pound bomb, which had detonators but was filled with flour.

When the run was finished, the second pilot fired a red flare. The ground crew made an accuracy assessment and then set up a smaller target vertically on poles. On sighting another green flare, the Vimy would start a strafing run. This continued until they ran out of ammunition or the guns were jammed. A red flare from the Vimy closed out the session.

After the Crossley left, Arabs would materialize as if by magic to salvage scrap metal and bullets. Brass cases were particularly sought after, as they could be reloaded. The Arabs even scooped up the flour.

If a captain was in a good mood and the air was stable, Chadwick would be allowed to land the plane. When the Crossley returned to base, the targets were laid out for all to view. Sometimes the canvas targets displayed no damage. There was stiff competition between squadrons to get the best scores when two units shared the same airfield.

Chadwick was disappointed by the poor accuracy of the bombing runs. He went to a Vimy in the hangar and sat in the forward cockpit. To the right of the mounting for a Lewis gun was the bomb sight, simply a tube like a rifle barrel with a peep sight and a V-notch at the rear. The angle of the tube could be adjusted by an arm clamped by a knurled screw. To Chadwick's mathematical turn of mind, the problem was simple. The aimer viewed the target through the sight, and when it lined up, he pulled the bomb release lever on his left. Chadwick reviewed the set-up in his mind. When the bomb left the aircraft, they were both travelling at the same speed. The bomb was retarded by air resistance but continued to accelerate downwards under gravity. If it was released at the right point, it would strike the target just as it hit the ground. Accuracy depended primarily on setting the bomb sight angle which depended on the height and speed of the bomber, and of course, on the pilot flying directly over the target, without left or right error.

Chadwick thought about the problem in his quarters and eventually went to talk to his flight commander, Lattimer. "I'd like to talk to you about bombing accuracy, sir," he began. "I know I'm just a new boy, but I think some improvements wouldn't be difficult to make."

"Go ahead, Allan. That's why the RAF sent you to Cranwell."

"Well, as the aircraft approaches the target, the pilot loses it under the nose, and a drift left or right before bomb release causes an error. A simple periscope pointing down could be installed so the pilot can see the target all the time. It would be quite simple, two mirrors at forty-five degrees with a cross-hairs."

"Sounds good," murmured Lattimer.

"If I have your permission, sir, I'd like to have a fitter make one and install it. Then we can evaluate it."

"Let me think about it," said Lattimer. What he really wanted was a chance to discuss it with the C.O. "By the way, Allan, what about height and airspeed errors?"

"I have some ideas about that too, sir, but I need to think about it a bit longer."

"Cut along, old chap, and I'll be in touch."

Flight Sergeant Evans introduced Chadwick to the chief airframe rigger. They made a sketch and the sergeant said it could be knocked together in a couple of days. A young fitter who was also a Halton graduate made some measurements and cut the pieces for the tube from thin plywood. The two mirrors were made from a larger mirror which was sacrificed for a good cause. The crosshairs were made from copper wire soldered together. Chadwick was on tenterhooks when they cut a small rectangular hole in the cockpit floor and lined up the sight. The first flight was a disappointment, however, as the lower mirror vibrated in the slipstream. They glued a frame holding a plain glass window in front of the lower mirror and when the bombing range was open again, made several runs. Without question, the lateral errors were significantly smaller.

Lattimer was impressed and congratulated Chadwick. "What about longitudinal errors?" he asked.

"I'm thinking about it," was Chadwick's guarded reply.

Chapter Eleven

Hamid Mustafa was as good as his word and when he invited Felix Goelz to dinner, he also invited a German lady he was friendly with, Maryana Koepka, who preferred to be called "Schuttzi." She was in her early thirties; her husband had been killed by a stray bullet in the 1920 uprising against the British rule imposed by the League of Nations. He had been a quantity surveyor employed by a German firm that was rebuilding the docks at Basra. He was a prudent man and had been well-insured, leaving an annuity payable in pounds sterling, which was why Schuttzi stayed in Iraq where the living was cheap, at least until something better showed up.

Mustafa liked her and he felt a little guilty about her husband's death, as he was involved in the organization of the uprising, although few persons knew that.

They all enjoyed a delicious meal prepared by Mustafa's excellent chef. Goelz and Schuttzi were well-lubricated with brandy but Mustafa abstained, though he was not a devout Muslim and did not give a hang for religious strictures. In his youth he had seen fellow sailors blow a month's pay on booze and women. Even as a boy, he decided he was too smart to do that.

Goelz was mostly quiet and a little reticent, while Schuttzi chattered away, pleased to speak German. She was an ebullient person. When Mustafa first met Schuttzi, he was attracted by her plump figure and open ways. She didn't need much persuasion to climb into bed with him, but when he saw her undress his passion deflated like a punctured balloon. She had not shaved her body hair, something Muslim women were very particular about. Throughout the Arab world, the parts covered by hair such as armpits and groin, were considered unclean and could not be washed properly unless shaved. Mustafa apologized and blamed his impotence on the heat, and they had remained friends. Mustafa sometimes asked her to act as a hostess if he was entertaining visiting European businessmen.

They finished the meal with a local delicacy, sweet Basra dates stuffed with nuts. When Goelz and Schuttzi made their *"auf wiedersehens,"* Hamid was not sure if the dinner had been a success.

Now that Chadwick was considered a competent second pilot, he began to fly routine patrols with various plane captains. The planes were manned by two gunners and two pilots. They carried full armaments including Lewis guns and a number of bombs ranging from twenty-five to one hundred pounds. The flights often began early, shortly after sun-up, and lasted two to three hours.

Flights were classified as routine or reprisal. Reprisals were in response to incidents investigated by the armored car patrols. The most common incidents were attacks on road convoys to smaller settlements such as Rutba, an old fort with a well. It had expanded as bus companies opened up routes across the desert. Usually the bus passengers were robbed, but there was no loss of life. In that case, as soon as the marauding tribe was identified, an armored car would pay a visit to the tribal village. After a discussion with the sheikh, the car commander would order a strike for the next day which destroyed buildings or tents. An effort was made to avoid loss of life if the robbery itself had not resulted in deaths. Because they were warned, the tribal members stood a mile away as their habitation was destroyed. Flight crews were under orders to minimize the chances of killing a civilian.

Sometimes the young men in the tribe, incensed by the raid, would open fire with rifles. As the plane held a height of one thousand feet they always missed. They saw their attack on a convoy as a right, an ancient sport they had practiced for centuries. The gunners would give them a burst of machine gun fire without hitting anybody, and everyone was satisfied.

Until he had more experience, Chadwick flew routine patrols. On a patrol along a pipeline, the captain passed him a note—*Look down. We're passing an emergency landing strip. They're every 50 miles.* Chadwick glanced at the strip. It had been cleared of stones and the edges were marked with bitumen.

The patrols usually ended by lunch and the afternoons were free. Chadwick spent a lot of time on a design for a bomb aiming sight and he discussed his ideas with the technical sergeants. He had a sketch of the device he envisaged. The sergeants were skeptical. The sighting tube was unclamped during a bombing run, and the sergeants were practical men.

"It will vibrate too much, sir. Wouldn't be no use," one of them said.

Chadwick guessed they were right. He went to discuss the problem with Frank Lattimer, explaining his design. "The idea, sir, is to move the adjustment arm of the sighting tube during a run on the target so as to allow variation in height and airspeed, which would in turn change the angle of the tube. An aneroid capsule would adjust for height and a flat plate in the airstream working against a spring would compensate for speed."

"Very ingenious," said Lattimer. "Why won't it work?"

"I talked to some of the tech sergeants. Without the clamping screw on the adjustment arm they think it would vibrate all over the place. They're probably right. I think it could be made but the whole assembly would have to be separate from the plane, maybe on springs."

"Too much for us to tackle on the base, Allan?"

"Yes, I think so."

"Never mind. You'll be pleased to hear all the squadron planes are to be fitted with periscopes."

Later, Lattimer went to talk to the C.O., Welch, about Chadwick's idea.

"Bright chap, that," Welch said. "Ask him if he'd like to sketch it up and I'll send it in to HQ with the next squadron report."

Chadwick's sketch and notes were indeed sent along to Iraq Air Command, and his sketch was ultimately sent to Bomber Command in England. Someone there sent it to the Royal Aircraft Establishment at Farnborough, where RAF Research and Development was carried out. Ultimately, a letter thanking Welch for *his* idea made its way down the command chain.

One day just before Christmas, Chadwick saw on the Duty Roster that he was flying with Flight Officer Holmes on a reprisal mission. Before they left, Holmes briefed all the crew. "We are to destroy some rat hole. They've been warned to expect our attack. They killed a policeman. If they shoot, we are to return lethal fire. The pongos are shit scared we might attack the wrong encampment. They'll have an armored car, stationed exactly five miles to the north of the target. That's our landmark."

"Pilot Officer Chadwick is responsible for navigation," Holmes continued. "We'll follow the pipe to Sammara, turn west and if we should find the pongos, they'll shoot red flare when they hear our engines. From there we fly due south for exactly five miles. Bring a stopwatch, Allan."

They took off at 0600 hours and ninety minutes later found the armored car. The flare rose into the sky and Chadwick carefully timed the run as Holmes steered a steady course. The encampment appeared on schedule. No animals or people were visible. They flew over the target at one thousand feet, made a turn a mile away and Holmes tapped the forward gunner on the shoulder. He dropped two fifty-pound bombs, and then they made a turn to inspect the damage, which was very little. Two large tents were lying on their side.

They made four more runs and reduced a few more tents to ruin. Holmes tapped the gunners on their shoulders and pointed down. He dropped to two hundred feet and made another run, and his time the gunners poured lead into the ruins. Suddenly there was a flash of white on the right side. Several men had emerged from underneath a tarpaulin covered with sand. They leveled rifles and began shooting.

Holmes made another low-level pass and the gunners blazed away at the knot of men. One went down and the others disappeared into the sand. When they turned and flew back for a look, Chadwick could see a Bedouin lying on the sand, his white burnoose stained red. Chadwick's heart beat with excitement, but he felt sick as they passed the pathetic corpse. He had never seen a man killed before.

Several hours after they landed, the word came back from the Armored Car Corps—mission successful.

Chapter Twelve

Preparations for Christmas were in full swing at Hinaidi station. There were three Vimy squadrons based there. Chadwick was informed he was to represent his squadron on the welfare committee—*Whatever that is*, he wondered. He attended a meeting of the committee on the afternoon of the day they had attacked the Bedouin camp. Arrangements for the season were discussed.

The officers planned a formal dance on Christmas Eve in the mess, music by the station band, who would receive suitable compensation funded by a whip-round. Nurses from the local hospital had been invited. The N.C.O.s looked after themselves; they received fifty pounds from the welfare fund which came from discretionary monies the station commander possessed. The main purpose of the afternoon meeting was to finalize arrangement for the airmen. Their party would be in the dining room. Music by a Victrola. Female students from a Teacher's Training College would be bussed in. Beer, juice and soda would be paid for with the welfare fund.

Someone asked about the French bus. The flight lieutenant chairing the meeting looked a little embarrassed. "We had one last year and it was very popular," he admitted.

A spokesman for the airmen had suggested to him before the meeting that maybe the fund could run to two buses. Fortunately for Chadwick, who was too shy to open his mouth, another young officer who was newly arrived asked, "What's a French bus?"

"Ah, well, the chap running this committee last year made arrangements with the French madam of an establishment in town to park a bus they had, which was sort of a mobile extension of her house. It was well set up inside and a few of her girls came with it. He was posted soon after Christmas. Not sure if there was a connection. He was a real card."

Someone asked the name of the madam's place. "I believe it is The Sky's the Limit Bar," the flight lieutenant said. "The Committee records have a bill from the madam for last year's—er—expenses."

After some discussion there was general agreement that such an arrangement would be impossible this year. Chadwick began to feel that the airmen, who were paid the least, were also getting the least support for their party. He was emboldened to speak, asking the chairman, "Was that bill you have for the time the men spent with the girls?"

"Yes, I think so," replied the chair.

"Do you remember how much it was?" asked Chadwick.

"It was a little over twelve pounds, I think. Yes, twelve pounds, six shillings. I believe an, uh, encounter was a pound and the six shillings covered petrol."

"I have a suggestion," said Chadwick. "I think the men deserve a Christmas bonus, a present, perhaps you could call it. I'm sure the fund could afford fifteen pounds to buy fifteen vouchers, good at The Sky's the Limit Bar. Those that might want to participate could draw lots from a hat at the party."

The officer chairing the meeting thought it over. "Not a bad idea. Someone with a voucher could buy drinks at the bar or anything else they wanted. Nothing prurient about that."

Chadwick's suggestion was adopted by the meeting. When it was over, several officers gathered around to congratulate him on a masterly compromise.

After dinner Chadwick went to the bar in the mess. It was unoccupied apart from a fellow pilot, Bill Smethurst, who had been quite friendly to Chadwick. He ordered a beer and turned to face Smethurst. "Can I get you a beer too, Bill?"

Smethurst pointed to his half empty glass. "I'm fine for the moment. Did I hear correctly that you had a bit of a shoot-up this morning?"

"It was my first time on a reprisal patrol. We killed a Bedouin. A group were shooting at us. It was sickening."

Smethurst sensed the mixed emotion in Chadwick's reply. "I must say, Allan, I've often wondered what gives us the right to kill a fellow for something he, or his family, have been doing for centuries."

Chadwick looked at him in surprise as he took a long pull from his glass. "I haven't thought about that before."

"We must do our duty, eh, no matter what?" Smethurst said ponderously. "Sometimes obeying orders isn't easy, but where do you draw the line?" He went on. "The Bedouin lead a poor, hard life. I feel sorry for them. They don't understand us and vice versa."

Chadwick finished his beer and patted Smethurst on the shoulder as he left the bar. "Bill, you worry too much."

Word of Chadwick's contribution to the airmen's festivities got back to Welch. When they ran into each other in the crew room, the C.O. asked Chadwick if he had ever been to The Sky's the Limit Bar.

"No, sir," said Chadwick.

"You're a funny lad. The field is standing down at Christmas for three days. Maybe you should take a bus into Baghdad and pay a visit."

Chadwick put on his best blue uniform on Christmas Eve and reluctantly made his way to the Officer's Mess. He was not a good dancer and felt awkward in mixed company. He had found at Cranwell that a couple of stiff scotch and so-das eased the tension. When he arrived, he discovered the bus with the nurses was late. Several senior officers were dancing with their wives to a waltz. While he was sipping his second drink the nurses arrived. They were outnumbered by the men about three to one.

The Master of Ceremonies tried to bring in some variety. After a couple of modern dances like the Lindy Hop and a Tango, the M.C. got four lines of three couples formed and the band broke into the Dashing White Sergeant, a Scottish reel. After that, the band took a break. Knots of men collected around the edge of the room, with one or two nurses in the middle.

Chadwick wandered over to a group that Brian Holmes was standing with. He used his greeting to worm into the bunch and found himself standing next to a pretty girl with a Lancashire accent. "Where're you from?" he asked her.

"Bury," she answered.

"I'm from Liverpool. Allan," he said and shook her hand.

"I'm Margaret." The band started up again.

"Would you like to dance?"

"Delighted." She grabbed his hand as she walked onto the dance floor.

The band was playing a foxtrot. They danced slowly. It was very hot, and both were sweating. He smelt her heavy perfume as they danced close together and he could feel the straps of her underwear under her light frock. When the dance finished, they moved back to the side.

"Thank you," she said. "That was very nice."

And then another pilot grabbed her and waltzed her away before Allan could reply.

At midnight the M.C. glanced at his watch and then shouted, "Merry Christmas, RAF Hinaidi."

Everyone turned to the person next to them, and if they were the right gender, they got a hearty kiss. Allan had made a point of standing next to Margaret as midnight approached. She kissed him full on the lips and gave him a push from her pelvis. He rather liked it.

Chapter Thirteen

Most flights were scheduled for an early morning take-off, but a few took place in the afternoon. The idea was to introduce an element of randomness, so that watchers, of which there were many, could not be sure when a plane would happen by.

One day about a month after Christmas, Chadwick was in the crew room talking to the captain of his flight, Harris. They were listed for a 1 p.m. departure. Afternoon flights were not so popular with crews. The air was bumpy and if they were late, the approach was made in the twilight with the sun low on the horizon, sometimes in their eyes.

Suddenly Harris was called into the adjutant's office, and when he returned a few minutes later he said to Chadwick, "Change of plans, here's a new route. It's the one McGregor flew this morning. They haven't returned. We're going to take a shufti, a look-see. McGregor was ordered to inspect a remotely operated oil well. Follow the pipeline for about fifty miles to a valve station. From there he followed a major pipe for about one hundred miles."

Harris debated whether they should follow the route in reverse, but decided to fly first to the oil well, as presumably McGregor had done.

An hour after leaving Hinaidi, they arrived at the well. Harris dropped down for a close look from three hundred feet and then headed along the pipeline. Half an hour later they saw the Vimy. It had come down in the desert, about a mile from the pipeline. The wing was tilted at an angle, suggesting the undercarriage had collapsed.

They dropped lower and slowly flew on one side of the wreck. There was a still figure in the rear cockpit, but their view of the other cockpits was blocked by the upper wing.

Suddenly, the forward gunner pointed to the right. A prostrate body was lying on the sand.

Harris faced a dilemma. He wanted to get his plane on the ground to see if the men in the wreckage were wounded and needed help. Standing orders for a situation like this called for him to fly back to base and let the armored cars deal with it. That would have meant losing the rest of day and another night before anyone could get back to the downed bomber. He passed a note to Chadwick: *Going to land, look out for obstacles.*

Harris flew parallel to the downed Vimy, about one hundred feet above the ground. There were a lot of small stones but no large ones. After another pass, he positioned the plane for a landing so that it would come to rest near the other Vimy. They landed with a crash and the plane skidded noisily towards the wreck. Harris had judged it well. They stopped about ten yards from the wreck. Harris left the engines running at tick-over and shouted to the gunners. The front gunner was directed to keep an eye on the right and the rear man on the left. Both guns were cocked.

He yelled into Chadwick's ear, "Go take a look. And take this."

He passed a Webley revolver to Chadwick, who carefully climbed out of the left-hand side of the cockpit. The propellers were still turning. Chadwick slid off the back of the wing and ran to the wreck. There was a strong smell of petrol.

Chadwick stood back for a good look. It appeared that the plane had caught a sustained burst of machine gun fire. The gunners and McGregor were all dead from bullet wounds. The right engine nacelle was riddled, which probably explained why the Vimy came down. Bullet holes in the fuselage in line with fuel tanks were the cause of the leakage. Fuel still dripped to the ground. Both Lewis guns were missing.

He ran back to his plane and climbed on the wing, squeezing close to avoid the spinning propeller. He yelled into Harris's ear, "Three dead there. Second pilot missing. Petrol everywhere. Miracle it hasn't burnt."

Harris pointed to the body lying a few hundred yards away. "See if you can help him."

Chadwick ran to the prostrate figure. As he got close a dense cloud of flies rose from the body. He stopped and looked at the lifeless figure at his feet. The face, streaked with blood, was frozen in a hideous grimace. The pilot's throat had been cut from ear to ear. Chadwick recognized the fellow pilot, Bill Smethurst. He had been posted to the squadron a few months before Chadwick and had always been friendly. Chadwick could scarcely bear to look at the corpse, but suddenly he realized the thing in the middle of the bloody mess was the man's penis, stitched between his lips by heavy black thread.

Vomit jetted up from his stomach. He turned away, fell to his knees and puked on the sand. He forced himself to look again. The pilot's flying suit had been cut open, his crotch was a tangle of blood and flesh, on which the flies were trying to settle. Chadwick waved them away and looked again at the pilot's face. The eyes bulged, and he realized the pilot's eyelids had been cut away. The horror hit him like a blow, and he retched again into the sand, his eyes full of tears and his mouth and nostrils burning from the salty vomit. "Oh! God, Bill, Oh! God," he cried.

There was nothing he could do. He ran back to the plane. Grasping the side of the cockpit he shouted to Harris what he had seen.

"Christ," Harris said, "I hope he was dead."

"No. They cut off his eye lids, so he had to watch. Then they cut his throat."

"Bastards. It's the bloody women that do that. The men do the shooting, then it's the women's turn to have fun—if anyone is left alive."

Chadwick told him that the plane was saturated with petrol. Harris passed him a Very pistol. "Burn it."

As soon Chadwick climbed back aboard, Harris gunned the engines and bounced into the air. He took off straight ahead, which was dangerous. They had not surveyed the ground there before landing, but he had looked carefully while Chadwick was at the wreck and decided it was worth a shot. He wanted the armored cars to be alerted as soon as possible. Chadwick sobbed quietly as they flew back to Hinaidi.

When they had landed and taxied to dispersal, Harris cut the engines and turned to face Chadwick. "Look," he said, "you joined the Air Force and you thought you were going to have fun flying. So far, you've had the fun. That's the easy bit. Today you started to learn what it's like to be a professional. The only reason you're flying is so you can drop a bomb or fire a gun where the government wants you to. I don't want to sound hard but stop blubbering. Clean yourself up, go to the bar, and get drunk."

The next day Chadwick talked to his flight commander, Lattimer, who knew all about the previous day's flight and the deaths of the four crew. "I know it was tough on you, Allan," he commiserated.

"But I want to know what happened."

"The armored car pongos will clean things up and bring the bodies back for burial."

"It looked to me like machine gun fire," Chadwick said. "The bullet holes in the fuselage, where the tanks are, were evenly spaced. You can't do that with a rifle. Could you ask the pongos while they're cleaning up to find some bullets and brass cases?"

"Why, Allan, that's what the wog scavengers go for. We don't need the money," Lattimer joked.

"But if we had a few samples I think our armorers could make a good guess about what kind of gun fired them."

"I'm sure they'll be British, 303. The wogs have stolen a few Lewis guns over the years."

"Still," Chadwick persisted, "we should check."

Lattimer was so impressed by the young man's persistence that he passed on the request to the army and was rewarded a few days later by getting a handful of lead and brass cases. The cases had been found near Smethurst's body.

A funeral for the dead men was held the same day. The bodies of the three airmen in the plane had been reduced to skeletons by the fire. The weight of the coffins was made up with sandbags. Smethurst's body was autopsied by the station doctor, who completed a confidential report for an officer of British Intelligence who appeared in his surgery one day. All the coffins were labeled "Closed" and could not be opened except with special authorization.

The doctor mentioned Chadwick's concern about the bullets to his visitor. "Damned interesting," was his response. "Anything come of it?"

Chadwick had taken the pieces picked up by the army to the Master Armorer, who told him, "I don't need a gauge to tell you what those are. German, eight-millimeter, light machine gun. I think the Huns called it an MG15."

Chadwick relayed this news to Lattimer. "The rounds were German. You told me the Army chaps never found the location of the gun used to hit the Vimy, so they must have blazed off a few rounds while those bastards were torturing Smethurst."

Lattimer duly passed on this information to the intelligence officer.

When the word of the Vimy's downing reached Hamid Mustafa, he was furious. He had smuggled a few cases of German guns left after the war into the country, at some risk to himself. These had been given to leading sheiks on the strict understanding they would not be used until there was a co-ordinated plan of attack. Curiously enough, Mustafa was not planning to use this force against the British. He was deeply involved in plans to declare a republic and have the British mandate cancelled. His problem was that several tribes felt the new President should be one of them, and a civil war looked likely.

He pondered for a while and then called his chauffeur, Ahmed. When Ahmed appeared, he said, "Get the car ready. We're driving to Baghdad tomorrow. Have it fueled and a picnic basket on board by seven."

Mustafa walked into the parking space behind his house early the next morning. He gazed fondly at the gleaming Mercedes Benz tourer and then climbed in. Ahmed was a good driver and kept his foot down, narrowly missing the horse-drawn carts, camels and swaying mules that packed the road. He made good use of the strident horn and deposited his boss at the entrance to the Cristal Grand Ishtar Hotel as the sun was setting.

Mustafa was soon ensconced in a palatial suite, and busy on the telephone as he nibbled on a chicken leg. The next day, Ahmed drove him to a large Bedouin encampment on the outskirts of the city. Sheikh Muhammad al Sadir greeted him solemnly. After preliminary courtesies, Hamid got down to business. He briefed the sheikh on the shooting down of the British Vimy and told him he was fairly confident he knew which tribe had violated the trust he had made with them when he gave them guns.

The sheikh listened carefully. "They must be punished in some way. We need discipline. When the time comes to declare a republic, we must be sure of our men."

Mustafa remained silent. The Sheikh continued, "We must arrange for the British to punish them. This will make them martyrs, and at the same time, it will further the hatred of the British. In any event, I suspect the British are already searching for the perpetrators. We must give them a little help. Letting a lion kill a jackal helps the shepherd."

He smiled, and Mustafa retreated, clear in his own mind what he had to do. He decided to drive back to Basra the next day. He was tempted to stay a few nights in Baghdad, and he let his thoughts wander over the delights he might enjoy, but he firmly put them away. It was essential to put events in motion. The trip back was a nightmare; the road was damaged by heavy rain and the blaring horn gave him a headache.

Chapter Fourteen

A meeting of squadron commanders was called at RAF Hinaidi. They were to be briefed by an intelligence officer.

"Some Bedouin tribes have got hold of old German light machine guns. We're not sure how these entered the country. They have a range of over a thousand yards, which means that our practice of maintaining a thousand feet during patrols is clearly dangerous if the use of these guns becomes widespread. However, the downing of 314's Vimy is the only incident to date in which the German guns were involved. We'll adopt a wait and see posture for the time being." He looked around the room to make sure he had everyone's attention.

"In order to discourage any more attacks," the intelligence officer continued, "the wogs involved in this one must be given a good hiding. Our armored car patrols are searching for the encampment of the tribe responsible as I speak. When we find it, it will be attacked without warning. We're reluctant to order a mission that could result in the loss of life of innocent people, including women and children. But in this case, one officer was tortured to death, almost certainly by women, so they may not be so innocent after all. Any comments or questions?"

Welch rose. "It was my squadron that suffered this terrible loss. It was one of my pilots who died in such a horrible way. If the encampment is found within the range of our operations from Hinaidi, I would like to be at the spearhead."

"Another thing," Welch continued, "we've all conducted so-called reprisals. The wogs are warned and we bomb their encampments. If they're Arab and the place is made of mud brick, then you can see some damage that's going to take a while to repair. But the Bedouin tribes live in tents and are nomadic. Apart from knocking them down, there doesn't seem to be much damage that can't be repaired with a needle and thread. What's the point?"

"I know it must feel frustrating sometimes," the intelligence officer responded, "but the political situation here in Iraq is very tricky. Britain can't afford to lose the oil. If widespread unrest develops, some countries that are not so friendly may try to get the League of Nations to revoke the mandate. Thus, we must rule with kid gloves. The loss of the Vimy has not been publicized, and any retaliation will also be under wraps. There are factions in this country that would make hay from a public fight."

"Now turning to the Bedouins," the intelligence officer went on, "if we attack without warning they would lose livestock, a serious matter for them. The camels and sheep represent the wealth of the tribe. The animals would be target for machine gun fire. The message would certainly get around to other tribes, who might be reluctant to suffer the same fate if they provoke a major retaliation."

There was more discussion, with one squadron leader suggesting using incendiary bombs. "If the tents were close together that would make some sense. But the encampments are not too crowded. What's your verdict?"

Most attendees thought the flames would spread, given a fair wind. The intelligence officer digested their opinions and said he would recommend the use of incendiaries, at ten percent of bomb load.

Chadwick had a free day when the senior people were meeting with the intelligence officer. He arranged to bus into Baghdad with a fellow pilot, Phil Loper. They dismissed the idea of visiting The Sky's the Limit Bar as unworthy and spent most of the day in the Baghdad Museum, admiring the carved stones and artifacts that went back four thousand years. Their airfield was at the very center of the "Golden Triangle," where settled civilizations arose from nomadic hunter-gatherer cultures. It was fascinating, but by the middle of the afternoon they had had enough.

They left the cool museum building and stepped into the street, where the hot, humid air hit like a dragon's breath. "We have to find a bar and sit down," Loper said.

They spotted a sidewalk café a few hundred yards down the street and made a beeline for it. They ordered some beer and the waiter placed a complimentary dish of sweetmeats on their table. The sidewalk was quite wide. Their table was some distance from the edge and the passing throng of pedestrians was entertaining. Beggars approached them and the waiter shooed them away. They ordered another beer each. Then in the distance they heard a faint racket that got louder and louder.

The waiter appeared at their side, "You must go upstairs," he demanded in passable English.

"Why? We're not doing any harm."

"Effendi—you are English! Bad men coming!"

He hurried them inside and upstairs to a room on the balcony. Through the delicately carved latticework, they could see the street clearly. The clamor reached a pitch as a ragged procession came into view. The leaders banged on drums and behind them men clashed cymbals. Then, to the astonishment of Chadwick and Loper, almost naked men, each wearing only a loincloth, followed, brandishing whips which they used to flog their own backs, sometimes flogging the backs of the men in front of them. They were covered with blood and wailed piteously.

When the waiter reappeared, the Englishmen asked what was going on. "They are Shits, bad men," he told them.

"Shits," repeated Chadwick. "Ah, yes—She-ites. It's a branch of the Muslim religion. I've read about them."

When the street was quiet, or relatively so, they made their way back to the bus.

Welch had a briefing for the officers and N.C.O.s of his squadron the next day. "Intelligence has discovered which Bedouin tribe brought down our Vimy and Flight Lieutenant McGregor and his crew," he told them. "When they pinpoint the tribe's encampment, we'll be the first to get a crack at them. We'll carry H.E and some incendiary bombs. The main thing is to kill the animals—that is, the non-humans, the camels and sheep. But don't worry if any Bedouins get in the way. Keep firing. We'll probably carry five ammo pans per gun. Once we have a location there will be a final briefing."

The final briefing happened the next day, when Welch told the crews of both flights that they would be the first instrument of revenge. Three armored cars would be stationed about two miles from the Bedouin camp and about four miles from each other. The lead car would be due west of the camp. It would fire a red Very to start the operation, A Flight first and then B Flight would join in fifteen minutes later. Welch would lead the attack, followed by Harris and then Holmes. Chadwick was to fly with Holmes. The planes would fly line astern, one thousand feet apart.

Welch picked up the western armored car and started a run-in when the flare floated up. It took about a minute and a half to reach the camp. The Bedouins had clearly been alarmed by the Very flare and the camp was full of running figures. Welch came in at about three hundred feet and the gunners opened up on sheep in an enclosure made of bushes, and on camels tied to lines.

When Chadwick's Vimy got into a firing position, the sandy terrain was already red with blood and animals writhed on the ground. Welch's plane made a slow turn and climbed to five hundred feet. As it crossed the camp boundary, they released four bombs, which landed squarely in the center of the camp. Ahead of Chadwick the second plane dropped a cluster of H.E. bombs and the aimer in Chadwick's plane released all their bombs. After they turned and flew back, the small encampment was in shambles. Smoke rose from the still-burning incendiary bombs. The gunners let fly with their Lewis guns, and the remaining bombs were unloaded, but the Bedouins had fled well beyond the camp's boundaries by then. As they headed home, B Flight appeared and started to add to the carnage. Chadwick felt exhilarated, but for few minutes he could feel himself shaking. He was devastated to see the animals killed.

Mustafa soon heard about the raid. He realized the British had been subtle, that they had killed a lot of camels and sheep but no humans, and they had inflicted a serious financial loss on the tribe. The tribe was an important part of the force he was accumulating to deal with Shiite forces in the south, where they were stronger, centered on Najaf. As for the impetuous tribesmen who shot down the Vimy, he passed word to the tribal leader, Sheikh Hatim al-Faris, that he expected punishment to be meted out for jeopardizing the plans to bring independence to Iraq.

As he pondered these issues, he was contacted by Professor Scharf. Spring was bringing better weather and the professor was eager to start digging. Mustafa realized that the camp was well placed as an assembly point for his group that would cover the Shiite tribes in Najah. *Why not have two dozen men stationed at Ur to act as workers until they were needed for finer things he had in mind?* After some negotiation over pay, the sheikh agreed that twenty to twenty-four tribal men could stake out a satellite camp near the German dig.

There remained the question of the foreman who would supervise the tribal workers, liaise with Professor Scharf, and keep in touch with him. He finally chose the captain of one of his ferry boats, Yusuf Ismail, who was a practical man and fiercely loyal to him. Yusuf spoke passable German, learned when he worked for the German company building the docks at Basra.

Felix Goelz was delighted to learn men were available, as he was beginning to get bored by the inaction, although he had managed to use the expedition truck for some initial surveys of the area.

Mustafa sent a telegram to Professor Scharf, telling him that all was ready for the arrival of the European staff.

Professor Scharf arrived within the month, leaving his wife in Germany with the promise she would join him when things were going smoothly. The British had also arrived to start the season's dig at their own site. Professor Scharf discussed with Dr. Rawlins, the lead archaeologist on the site, exactly where they should start and prepared a rough map which Goelz used to lay out the lines of the first trench.

Chapter Fifteen

At Hinaidi the weather brought the first really hot days of the year. The Vimy was fundamentally underpowered and long flights at nearly full throttle brought engine overheating problems. To help with cooling, the upper nacelle of each engine was removed. In an ironic turn of fate, this change saved Holmes and his crew from an almost certain crash. However, events after that threatened to put their lives in greater danger.

The routine patrol commanded by Holmes consisted of Chadwick, as second pilot, and two gunners, both sergeants. Sergeant Bostick, front gunner and bomb aimer, was a qualified engine mechanic. For the first hour the flight went smoothly. Chadwick gazed at the Iraqi countryside as it floated by a thousand feet below. Every two minutes he scanned the engine and flight instruments. Holmes did most of the piloting.

They were flying parallel to a long pipeline and had passed an emergency landing strip about twenty minutes earlier, when Chadwick's eye was caught by a long, black ribbon of oil coming from somewhere on the cylinder head of the left engine. This was serious. His thoughts flashed to the talk he had with Holmes weeks earlier. If the engine seized up, the great wooden propeller would probably disintegrate and pieces would fly though the cockpit, killing both pilots.

He tapped the pilot on the shoulder and pointed to the engine. Holmes strained to get a good look, and then sat back and mouthed, "Shit." He wrote on the pad, *Nearest strip?*

Chadwick wrote, *Halfway between, suggest continue on course.*

Holmes nodded, then throttled back on the left engine and pushed the right engine throttle to full power. He applied corrective rudder and kept the Vimy flying along the pipeline. The plane began to descend at just under a hundred feet per minute.

When the engine noise changed, the front gunner swiveled round and looked at Chadwick, who pointed to the left engine and drew a hand across his throat.

The plane was down to one hundred feet when the front gunner glimpsed the emergency landing strip ahead. He waved furiously and pointed, slightly to the left.

Holmes shut down the left engine and bounced onto the strip a few feet from the boundary marker. When the plane came to a halt, the crew disembarked and Sergeant Bostick climbed onto the wing. He peered at the engine and wiped the oil off with a rag.

"Good landing, sir," said Chadwick. "Close call."

"It's the oil feed pipe to the rocker box, sir," Bostick called to Holmes.

"Can it be mended?" Holmes called back.

"Dunno, sir. I'll take the union nut off, then I can see the pipe better." Bostick rummaged in the front cockpit and emerged with a pipe wrench. He climbed back to the engine, managed to get the union nut free, and then his face fell. "I thought the pipe might have cracked," he explained, "but it's the nut."

They all joined in a debate about a possible repair. The mechanic thought that strands of wool taken from the rag he had used might be wrapped under the nut as it was tightened. They tried this over the next hour or two, but each time they started the engine it leaked badly. The oil level in the tank was near the bottom of the dipstick. The mechanic was of the opinion that they would not make it back without repairing the leak and an oil refill.

Holmes addressed them. "By now we'll have been posted missing. A plane will be along before sunset. Get the Aldis lamp ready for a chat when they show up. Gunners, stay by your Lewis guns, we might have visitors."

Four hours later, a Vimy appeared and circled the party on the ground. Chadwick aimed the Aldis lamp at the plane and flashed in Morse code, *Left engine US*—unserviceable.

The plane overhead signaled, *Will return AM. No wogs near*.

The sun was low as the plane departed. The crew shared some water from a canteen.

"We'll stand one-hour watches," Holmes said. "Three hours off. Wake up everybody at the first sign of visitors."

Chadwick was scared. He knew firsthand what could happen if Bedouins caught the British on the ground. But he felt reassured by the Morse message from the reconnoitering flight, no wogs near. Unfortunately, that wasn't true.

Seven miles away, sheltered in a low wahdi, four young Arabs from a Bedouin tribe boiled water over a dung fire. Their camels were tied to stakes in the ground. They had been out all day hunting game. They had not been very successful. They had killed four hares, which they planned to eat for supper, along with some flat bread. They had hoped to come across wild boar. One of them looked attentively to the east. A glint in the sky caught his attention.

"There's a plane circling over there," he said, pointing. His Arabic name, in English, meant, "Lion with eyes of a falcon." He had earned this title because he could make out seven stars in the Pleiades Constellation.

The Arabs discussed what the circling plane implied. "They must be looking at something," one of them said. "There is a pipe over there."

"Maybe a leak," another one offered. That sounded interesting. Oil was a valuable fuel. If they could collect a few liters, it would boost the success of their hunting expedition. They decided to ride over to the pipe in the morning.

After a leisurely start the next day, they rode a few miles and then stopped. To their amazement, they made out a plane on the ground. They all knew the value of a British plane. The guns alone were worth a small fortune. They were still debating whether they had the slightest chance of killing the airmen and capturing the plane when, to further their amazement, a second plane approached and then landed near the object of their attention.

The rescue plane was piloted very skillfully by Welch. The air was still, and he elected to land in the opposite direction of that taken by Holmes. He stopped near the stricken plane so that his guns covered the dead spot formed by the tail of the first plane. Now the two planes had an effective three-hundred-sixty-degree coverage.

The second pilot stepped down and passed out some orange juice and a pile of cheese sandwiches. Fastened between the upper and lower wings of Welch's plane was a spare Eagle engine.

Welch walked over to the Holmes, saying, "Let's have a look at your duff engine." Bostick stepped onto the wing and showed the C.O the broken securing nut.

"I've brought you a new engine," Welch said. "Engineering would like the old one back."

Holmes looked at him with surprise. "We're supposed to switch two engines, just like that?"

"We're going to get some help," the C.O. told him. "An armored car will be here by lunch time. They're bringing along a few extra goodies, like oil and water, tools, and a cart that can take the weight. Before they arrive, we need to dismount two propellers and rig them as sheer legs. Also, Bostick is a mechanic. He can disconnect the controls, fuel pipes, and so on."

"By the way," Welch added, "there are a few of our wily oriental friends watching the proceedings from a couple of miles over there." He pointed in the direction of the Bedouins.

Within two hours, using a small block and tackle, the gunners had the new engine suspended from two propellers lashed together. The rig weighed too much for them to attempt to move it. At this point, the armored car showed up. All the Britons surveyed the situation. They needed to move the sheer legs a few feet so the cart could be positioned under the engine.

"We just need manpower," Welch said.

The army captain in charge of the armored car spoke up. "That's it? You just need some muscle?"

"Yes," Welch replied. "We'll have to keep the guns manned. That leaves six of us."

"I'll go and have a little parley with those wogs over there!"

Before anyone could object, he and the driver roared off towards the watching Bedouin, who didn't have time to mount their camels before the armored car reached them.

"Greetings, fellow travelers," the captain said in Arabic.

The Bedouins looked at him warily. The driver remained in the car and idly spun a machine gun round to cover the group.

"My friends over there," the captain said, pointing to the two planes, "would like to meet you, and if you help them, I can put a little money your way."

"How much?" one of the Bedouins asked.

"Two pounds."

"No, no paper money, gold," bargained the Arab.

The army man was quite used to providing baksheesh. He always carried pieces of gold made by dividing a British sovereign. He briefly went into the car and returned with something in his hand. He opened his palm to show a quarter sovereign piece. "A quarter sovereign." The Arab nodded.

"Come with me," the captain ordered. "When we are finished the gold is yours."

The driver drove slowly back to the planes. The Bedouin followed. The RAF men looked at the little procession with surprise.

"Here you are, sir. All the muscle we need."

They all went to work, but a problem immediately arose. They had enough muscle to lift the rig so that the engine could be suspended over the cart, but it was unstable.

"We need hand ropes attached to the top, one forward, one aft," the mechanic pointed out.

They had used all the rope brought by the armored car to secure the top of the sheer legs and cradle the engine beneath the block and tackle. The army captain went up to the Arabs and explained the problem waving his hands to mimic the rig toppling over. The Bedouin looked at the engine, which was suspended, the propellers leaning against the aircraft's wings. He was quite intelligent and immediately grasped what was needed.

He said to the army captain, "I have thongs, one quarter sovereign more."

The captained decided the engine was worth a great deal more than that and he nodded his head. "Agreed."

The Arab turned to the camels and removed the reins, which were made of leather. After tying on the reins, they lowered the engine onto the cart and, with some pushing and pulling and some holding of the reins, they moved to the other Vimy. The spare engine was quickly removed, as there were no controls or pipes to deal with. Within two hours both engines were securely fastened between the wings. The mechanic added water and oil and was watched with great interest by the

Bedouins. They asked the army captain for the water which was not used. They emptied the surplus into goatskin flasks.

Welch climbed aboard, fiddled in the cockpit and called, "Contact!"

Two gunners grabbed a blade each and turned the engine. It didn't start.

"Switches off," Welch called.

The gunners rotated the propeller through a revolution. They were sweating now from their exertions, and maybe with a little concern.

"Switches on. Contact!"

They swung the engine again and it fired with a roar. They loaded all the gear into the armored car.

Chadwick sought out the army captain. "I must say, I really appreciate what you pulled off, sir. To be truthful, I was damned scared the Bedouins would attack us."

"Never a chance," the captain replied, "You had 'em outgunned. They're not stupid."

The planes taxied to the end of the strip and the army captain walked over to the Bedouin, who had watched the proceedings with great interest while they waited patiently. The captain slipped two quarter pieces into the hand of the senior Arab, saying, "Peace be with you and many thanks."

Holmes took off first. Welch then taxied to the very edge of the strip and swung into the light wind. Taking off with a nine-hundred-pound engine on one wing was going to need extreme flying skills. He had accomplished it earlier in the day, but the strip was much shorter than the field at Hinaidi. The army and the Arabs watched him loft into the air at the far end of the emergency strip.

The Arabs salaamed and loped away on their camels.

Chapter Sixteen

It required a great deal of work to get the German dig up and running. The sun was relentless. Professor Scharf ordered dozens of bamboo poles and many bales of thick cotton cloth. These were positioned to shield the men working on the trench.

Probes had shown that the old ground was covered by ten to fifteen feet of sand. Professor Scharf predicted the sand was the result of a tidal wave occurring much later than the epoch in which the ziggurat was built. He was mildly encouraged; the remains of a tidal wave could indicate they were digging near the old shore and possibly in the vicinity of the ancient harbor.

Besides sunshades, they constructed tables for sifting the soil brought from the strata of old ground. Each bucketful had to be carefully examined after the sand was filtered away. Soon they began finding pottery shards. This was a signal to proceed more carefully. The soil and sand were brushed away; a careless shovel might damage a precious artifact that was in pristine condition.

Professor Scharf began to realize the work was far more difficult than at Nineveh. There the buildings were mostly stone, but the common building material at Ur was mud brick. Over the thousands of years since Ur was built, the mud had reverted to its natural form and the clue they had reached a building was a change in color of the soil. The original shape had been lost. Eventually they traced out the layout of streets and buildings. It was painstaking work that took weeks, even for a small area. The street they exposed was meticulously drawn by Felix Goelz, who began to develop a great interest in the work.

Felix Goelz was also kept busy by Hamid Mustafa, who commandeered the truck once or twice a week. These were night runs from Nasiriyah to outlying villages and sometimes to abandoned buildings. Goelz asked Mustafa what was going on. He pointed out, quite reasonably, that he was paid by Herr Weiss, who required fairly detailed reports of their activities. These he compiled at night, after the run was over, using a one-time code pad given to him by Herr Weiss before he left Germany. The coded letters were sent by normal mail, a fact that amused Goelz, as the postal system was run by the British.

Mustafa was stockpiling caches with weapons in preparation for the anticipated civil war when the king was deposed at the start of the rebellion "When will this happen?" questioned Goelz, who was ignorant of Iraqi politics.

"No one knows," replied Mustafa, "but almost certainly within a year."

Mustafa had been under the eyes of British Intelligence for many years. He was not regarded as dangerous, more of a facilitator, and his close contact with Felix Goelz put the German archaeological expedition under the British microscope.

One day, a very smooth-talking Englishman from military intelligence ran into the British archaeologist, Dr. Rawlins, at his hotel in Nasiriyah and over a glass or two, steered the conversation to the German expedition.

"Are they in competition?" the Englishman inquired.

"Goodness no," replied the doctor. "In fact, they're digging just where I suggested. I wanted a feel for the terrain before the RAF occupy the area with a new airfield. But they are well-financed. They've moved a small bunch of Bedouins into a camp nearby, just to act as diggers and laborers."

"Is that usual?" inquired the visitor.

"No, we hire men when we need from Nasiriyah. It's considerably cheaper. But of course, we've been here for a few years, so we have contacts and often get the same men, men who are familiar with the job."

His curiosity aroused, the intelligence agent filed a report which recommended a visit by the Armored Car Corps to the new Bedouin encampment. Later, an armored car arrived at the camp. The soldiers discovered the men were from the same tribe that had shot down the Vimy earlier. It made sense. The tribe had sustained a great loss in the retaliatory raid, and they had many mouths to feed. The men were usually kept busy at the German dig, and the encampment was home for all their families, wives and children.

The armored car captain asked where their food was coming from, and was told they bought sheep carcasses in Nasiriyah, often dropped off by the site truck.

The captain left. He had soldiered in Iraq for many years and had a sense that things didn't seem quite right, but he couldn't put his finger on why.

At the site the laborers had moved tons of the overlying sand. Professor Scharf had the difficult decision of where to put it. It wasn't practical to move the sand too far, but wherever it was placed it might block a future digging site. He bought a dozen wheelbarrows and had the Arabs make a small hill, fifty feet high.

Digging in the outlines of the former building, they soon hit pay dirt. One area yielded three cylindrical seals. The professor was very familiar with these Mesopotamian artifacts. They were made of fired clay and heavily incised with symbols. By rolling them across soft clay, the Mesopotamians left an official seal. These would have been in constant use at a port, he exulted, and thought that perhaps the harbor was directly underneath them.

On most days the sifting tables brought up pottery shards but no metal objects. When the professor took the finds to the British site, Dr. Rawlins was very impressed. "You must have seen seals like this at Nineveh, Kurt," he said.

"Yes," Scharf replied. "Usually they were near offices, temples—the active commercial part of a town, not houses. You suggested a good place to start."

"An element of luck," said Dr. Rawlins. "Keep digging!"

Professor Scharf looked at a sketch of the building outlines they had exposed so far, prepared by Felix Goelz. *Suppose we've found the office of a warehouse,* he mused. *Where would other buildings be located with reference to that?* He decided to start two new areas under the supervision of the two archaeologists attached to the expedition. His two graduate students, the genuine graduate student and Felix Goelz, would supervise the sifting tables.

At Hinaidi, the flying continued as the summer heat climbed. Allan Chadwick still found flying the lumbering Vimys rather boring and he lusted after a fighter squadron posting. Perhaps when his tour was up on 314 Squadron, he could request a change. In the meanwhile, he tried to master some eccentricities of the old plane.

Sticking well forward between the front wheels was a sturdy wood and steel skid. This had been added as a later modification when ham-fisted pilots landing too fast had tipped the nose far enough down that the propeller tips touched the ground, usually with disastrous results. One of the captains he flew with showed him that, with a delicate touch, the skid could be made to just touch the ground and dramatically shorten the landing run. It might be a skill that would come in useful one day.

On a patrol two days later, Chadwick and Flight Lieutenant Harris, flying together with two gunners, encountered a sky that darkened very quickly. A few miles away the sky met the ground with a churning, turbulent curtain of sand—a sandstorm. Normally, a Vimy could outrun a sandstorm. Harris turned away from the curtain and pushed both throttles open. Suddenly dark shapes filled the cockpit. They had collided with birds also escaping the sand onslaught. A large hawk, in a panic, threshed in the cockpit and sliced with its talons. The captain's goggles were ripped off and sharp claws tore flesh off his face. Chadwick grabbed the stick and eased the plane into a climbing turn. With one hand he managed to push the screaming bird clear of the plane.

At two thousand feet they were above the boiling sand. Chadwick leveled off and headed for the airfield. Harris was bleeding badly, and blood from a deep cut on his forehead covered his eyes. There was a first-aid kit clipped to the inside of the cockpit, but it was on the captain's side. Chadwick couldn't reach it, but the rear gunner had seen the accident. He unclipped, climbed onto the wing and inched up to the cockpit on the captain's side. He reached into the cockpit and grabbed the first-aid kit. Holding the coaming with one hand, he got the lid off and pushed some pieces of the cloth inside into the pilot's hands. When the captain nodded, he backed away and climbed into the rear cockpit. Chadwick landed the plane forty-five minutes later. Harris was unconscious.

After the ambulance crew had rushed the captain to the hospital, Chadwick seized the rear gunner by the hand. "Good work, McIntyre! You should get a medal."

While the ground crew washed down the plane, Chadwick told the story to his flight commander, commenting, "Sergeant McIntyre should get a medal!"

Lattimer shrugged. "Sounds rather routine, actually. People walk on the wing all the time, at least in America!"

British Intelligence began to take more of an interest in Mustafa and the German dig. They started around the clock surveillance of Mustafa's warehouse in Nasiriyah and soon discovered the midnight deliveries using the expedition truck. Finding out the destination of the deliveries was more difficult. Traffic was sparse at night and it was not possible to shadow the truck without being obvious. It took a while to identify Felix Goelz; sometimes he was the only driver. He had taken to wearing a burnoose and keffiyeh when making the runs. In the dark he could pass for a native.

The British decided that they needed a man in the inside of the German expedition. One day the Armored Car Corps paid a visit to the Bedouin camp. The captain talked to the Arab leader and said there were repercussions from the attack on the Vimy. The authorities in Baghdad demanded names. The captain asked if any of the men currently working for the Germans had been involved in the downing. There was an explosive denial. Those villains were part of another family, he was told, and now the whole tribe was suffering.

The captain was sympathetic. He asked casually if the men sometimes helped with deliveries made by the truck. As it turned out, Goelz sometimes took a man along. "I'd be interested in knowing where the deliveries were made," the captain said. "Just between us."

The Arab understood at once. Deceit between factions was a way of life, and the British and the Germans were just big tribes to him. A sovereign changed hands. The Bedouin leader at the encampment began to collect chitchat from the Arabs working at the expedition concerning Felix Goelz. The next time the Corps captain stopped by, he mentioned that the German spent a lot of time writing letters and often copied things from a small book.

Several young boys from the encampment worked around the expedition camp, helping the cook, running errands and cleaning up in the tents. Very little went on that they were not aware of. The boys were often busiest in the evening, when the dig for the day had finished and the Europeans were relaxing after dinner and discussing the day's progress or the state of the world.

Fairly late one night a boy, Abdul, who looked after Felix Goelz's tent, entered it to find Felix masturbating. Goelz was embarrassed, rather than angry.

"Master, I understand," said the boy quickly. "No women here, let me help," and bent over Felix.

Against his better judgement, Goelz permitted Abdul to come to him late at night a few times a month. Inevitably word of the German's weakness spread among the gossipy community and reached the ears of the leader, who passed it onto the British Armored Car captain. Eventually the information reached British Headquarters in Baghdad. The intelligence section had a meeting to discuss the development.

"Just who is he?" asked one of the attending officers.

"According to the passport information with immigration, he's a student," was the reply.

"What was he before that? We must do some digging."

It took over a month to find Felix Goelz's name on the Field Strength List of the German Army. The British were delighted; a serving officer guilty of homosexual activity was liable to a court martial and would probably serve prison time. Goelz was easy to blackmail into complete cooperation.

Professor Scharf was busy at the German dig. The season was drawing to a close. He was still optimistic that they might expose remains of the ancient harbor. He had an idea that possibly the tidal wave that had deposited so much sand on the site had swept smaller objects inland. Heavier structures might lie in the direction of the old waterfront.

He called Felix Goelz and explained his theory, and asked Goelz to make a map of the site showing the exact location of each artifact they had unearthed so far. When this was done, they both studied it carefully. It was difficult to make any sense out of the random pattern. Then Goelz pointed out that the finds were clumped. Often several artifacts were found close to each other, and in-between was a blank space. The clumps could be where eddies formed as the wave receded. They connected the clumping areas with straight lines, and the lines were roughly parallel.

"That's the wave front," declared the professor. "We'll dig on a line at right angles to that." How far to move the new dig was purely a guess, but he chose five meters.

A few days afterwards, they started to excavate the new site. When their spades struck something solid, the mud-colored sand gave way to a brick made of terracotta, baked in a fire and impervious to water. For over a week the workers carefully shoveled away the sand with trowels and stiff brushes. They exposed the top layer of what appeared to be a three-sided room about two meters wide.

"It's a shrine," said Professor Scharf, pointing out the three-sided construction. "We must dig between the two parallel walls. There may be an object of veneration down there."

During the next few days, they slowly exposed a terracotta plaque about fifty centimeters high, forty centimeters wide and five centimeters thick. On one side was sculpted a figure of a beautiful woman wearing a large crown of bull's horns, a symbol of very high rank. That was all she was wearing. She stood on the backs of two supine lions, and by her side were two large owls.

Professor Scharf examined her before she was moved from the ancient matrix she was lying in. He brushed her gently with his fingers. A steady rain helped to wash away the mud. "*Mein Gott,*" he said. "Who are you?" This was obviously a world-class find. They worked all night to excavate around the plaque and gently lift it out of the shrine.

A day later, when the plaque had been cleaned up and stored in the professor's tent, he had himself driven over to the British dig. "Dr. Rawlins," he cried out, as he saw the British archaeologist at the bottom of a trench. "Can you spare a few minutes? I have something to show you." He was bubbling over with excitement.

Dr. Rawlins sensed his mood, climbed out of the trench, rubbed his hands together and headed for the truck, saying, "Let's go."

The professor guided the old British leader into his tent and dramatically pulled back the sheet on his bed. "Look at the lady I have in my bed!"

Rawlins was visibly affected. He had started to make a witticism in response to the professor's joke but as soon as the plaque was exposed, he dropped to his knees besides the bed and peered intently at the figure. "Wonderful," he breathed. "She's Babylonian, about the era of Hammurabi, at a guess."

"Who is it?" asked the professor.

"I think she's the goddess of love and war, Ishtar," replied Dr. Rawlins. "But I'm no expert. Professor Masud at the Baghdad Museum is the man to ask." He rose to his feet and scrutinized his colleague. "What are you doing about security, Kurt? I know collectors who would kill for a Babylonian relief sculpture in this condition."

Professor Scharf had given no thought to that problem. In the meanwhile, Ishtar stayed with him. The team continued to excavate the shrine. At a lower level they found many corroded copper plates, just green dust, far too fragile to remove. *They're prayers*, thought the professor, *wishes, hopes, hatreds, inscribed on thin copper and dedicated to Ishtar*. Unfortunately, none of them had a legible text, and so the lady's name remained a mystery.

Outside the shrine they found broken pieces of amphora, large pottery vessels used in ancient times to hold wine, olive oil, and fruit paste. In the hands of an expert, Scharf thought, the patterns on these shards would yield a reliable date, accurate to within a few hundred years.

Chapter Seventeen

In Baghdad and London, British Intelligence pondered the next move in Iraq. The British had established a puppet monarchy in the early 1920s under a hereditary Hashemite tribe. King Faisal ruled a strip along the Tigris and Euphrates rivers, but the majority of the country—the deserts—were under the control of a disparate collection of sheikhs, owing little allegiance to the king. The Iraqi army was too small to be a significant factor but was loyal to the king. Clearly the intent of the Germans was to remove Faisal and substitute a powerful sheikh, but which?

A British Intelligence assessment was that the arming of Arabs in the south was to prevent British forces landing by sea. Presumably a thrust would then be made towards Baghdad, the King's palace and the Iraqi government buildings. The decision was made to move two squadrons of bombers and four corps of armored cars to the south. When in position, the Arab threat would be neutralized, and it would be made clear to the local sheikhs that a move to support an uprising in the north would be dealt with ruthlessly.

A heavily armed truck convoy carrying a thousand British troops left Cairo bound for Baghdad to reinforce the garrison there. It was planned to move a Vimy squadron from Mosel to Hinaidi to replace the planes that would fly south. On the political front King Faisal was assured that a new constitution would be drawn up to further integrate the country and increase the size of its army.

Chadwick heard that the squadron was to be moved south but his mind was on a notice posted in the officer's mess. A Hospital Hop was coming up in Baghdad, in celebration of autumn. He signed up for the bus and got his batman to press his good pair of slacks. They drove over to the British hospital about eight in the evening and found that, at this dance, the men were in a minority.

Allan was hoping to see Margaret again and he soon spotted her. He walked over to her side. "Now then," he said with a deliberately heavy Lancashire accent.

She picked up the joke right away and mimicking his accent said, "Weir asta bin sin I saw thee?

They both giggled "How about a dance?" he asked.

"Luuvely," she said and walked him onto the floor.

They danced together for a while. She was shorter than Allan. He pressed his nose into her hair, which smelt faintly of perfume. It was another world from the masculine smells that permeated squadron life. It was hot and humid and when she asked if he would like a walk outside to see the grounds, he readily agreed.

She showed him a detached building that she said was the isolation ward and then they came to a long, two-story building. "This is the Nurses Nookery," she said, and taking his hand, led him in between double doors and then marched them towards a wide staircase.

"Am I really allowed in here?" he asked.

She flashed him a look of disdain. "You're an RAF pilot," she said. "Nothing is supposed to daunt you!" After a pause she added, "Surely you want to see how us poor nurses are treated, daughters of the empire, serving king and country, just like you."

Upstairs she opened a door in a long corridor, and they stepped into a spacious room with a tall ceiling. There were two single beds, made of painted iron pipe. Around each was a mosquito net suspended from a hook on the ceiling. There was a dresser and a small sink with a solitary tap. "I share this with Kate. She's on shift, won't be back until midnight."

In fact, she had negotiated quite deliberately with her roommate to make sure Kate would be at work. *Luck only comes if you prepare for it,* was one of her mottos.

Allan stood by a bed a little unsure of what to do next. She looked at him. "Undress!" she said sharply in a nurse's voice. Suiting her action to the word, she slipped off her frock and ducked under the mosquito net onto one of the beds.

In fact, Allan was embarrassed to disrobe in front of a woman. At Cranwell the men swam and showered at the playing fields completely naked, but he had never stood naked in front of a woman. Margaret looked at him, "I'm a nurse," she said. "I don't think you have anything I haven't seen a hundred times before." She gave him a kiss.

"The bed's a bit narrow, but we can manage." Then she said, tenderly, "This is your first time, isn't it?"

Allan blushed, and whispered, "Yes."

"Well, we'll make it something you're familiar with. The RAF taught you to fly, I'm going to teach you how to fuck. What's the first thing you do when you're going to fly a plane?"

Puzzled, Allan said, "We walk around the aircraft, making sure no covers have been left on, that the control surfaces are free to move, that sort of thing."

"Perfect. Look." Margaret unhooked her brassiere and flung up her arms. Rotating her waist, she said, "No covers. I'm free to move. Are we ready for take-off?"

Allan, fascinated by her breasts, managed to say weakly, "We should start the engines."

She shed her knickers and, grabbing a wrist, pushed his right hand between her legs. "Wiggle your fingers, hard." She adjusted her position and sighed, "Don't stop."

After a minute Allan's hand ached and he nearly fell off the narrow bed. "I'm falling off the bed," he said, unromantically.

Margaret opened her eyes. "All right, the engine is running, ready for your first solo. Prepare for take-off. Climb on top." Her expert fingers guided him in.

They left the Nookery just in time for Allan to catch the bus back to the base. "Margaret," he said, "I don't even know your last name. The squadron may be moving soon. Would you like me to write?"

"You can if you want," she said. "My name's Kaufman. I'm Jewish, but I'm not very religious."

Word of the discovery of Ishtar's plaque rapidly spread around the dig. The Bedouin workers were particularly keen to see it. Bearing in mind Dr. Rawlins' warning, Scharf decided to clean up the shrine and put Ishtar back. He assigned the job of making an iron gate for the shrine to Felix Goelz. After making careful measurements, Goelz drove into Nasiriyah to find a blacksmith, who made iron bands which completely encircled the shrine so that hinges and locks could be mounted without damaging the original terracotta brick. The gate was secured by a large padlock for which only Professor Scharf had the key. A sturdy roof was added.

To the surprise of the archaeologists, the Goddess was of great interest to the Bedouins, who gathered around the shrine every night. Professor Scharf went to find the foreman, Yusuf, to ask him why the workers were so interested in the plaque.

"It's strange," he explained, "they feel she's appeared at this particular time to give guidance."

"'Guidance to what?" asked the professor.

"There's a lot going on," said Yusuf uneasily. "You should ask Herr Goelz."

When Professor Scharf caught up with Goelz, he first congratulated him on the fine job of restoring Ishtar's shrine. Then he asked what was happening to the Bedouin workers. "Is it connected with your mysterious truck journeys?"

"In a way," replied Goelz. "I just follow the orders from Mustafa, who presumably gets his from Herr Weiss."

"What are the trips for?" asked Scharf. "Do you know?"

"Yes, I have a good idea what's going to happen, but I don't know when."

"And what is it?"

"Are you sure you want to know?" asked Goelz. "It might be better for you if you're just a simple archaeologist, if the British come nosing around."

"Damnation," said the professor. "We have just made one of the most important finds in the excavation of Ur, and it may be jeopardized by some silly local squabble."

"Herr Weiss may see it the other way around," said the somewhat embarrassed Goelz.

Two days later, the Imam from the Bedouin tribe showed up at the encampment. He had ridden by camel with a phalanx of guards from the main settlement near Baghdad. He was the religious leader of the sheikhdom, a Sunni Muslim. He spent a lot of time at the shrine and talked frequently with Bedouin workers. Then he came to see Professor Scharf, bringing along Yusuf Ismail as an interpreter.

Standing in the professor's tent, he bowed slightly. "Salaam," he said in Arabic. "You have brought great and wonderful tidings to us, professor," translated Yusuf.

"I am glad you approve."

"She is one of the old gods," the Imam said. "They were very powerful and far-sighted. I would not even think of the impertinence of trying to communicate with her. Her priests were highly educated and often of royal blood. But the symbols are clear. She determined victory and defeat in war."

"Ah, yes, of course," said the Professor, somewhat at a loss.

"She is supported by two lions," translated Yusuf. "These are the symbols of the British Empire. We must respect that. Her wings are symbols of the great mechanical birds that the British fly. The owls confirm the wisdom of not raising arms against the British. They will soon be gone anyway. I will talk to a Mufti. Perhaps if he agrees he will issue a fatwa."

"What is that?" asked the professor.

"It is a binding ruling, based on Islamic law."

The professor thanked him, offered some tea, which was politely refused, and sat on his bed to think things over when the two men left.

Yusuf Ismail knew that Hamid Mustafa would want to know as soon as possible about the chance of a fatwa forbidding action against the British. It was four days before he could get to Nasiriyah and telephone Mustafa, who was in Basra.

At Hinaidi airfield, 314 Squadron made preparations to move en bloc to Shaibah, near Basra. Several flights were made using the passenger-carrying version of the Vimy. Equipment for service and maintenance of the planes was carried by truck. They were told it would be a one-month assignment before returning to Hinaidi.

Before the squadron moved, a major in charge of a group of armored cars arrived to talk over tactics with Welch. "I've been briefed by the intelligence gentlemen," he told Welch. "Basically, our job is to clean up the gun-running to Shiite tribes in the southern part of the country so that they are discouraged from supporting a planned coup in the north. I have the location of numerous sites where guns and ammunition are known to be stored. We'll bring a truck with a pair of armored cars and remove what we find."

"The problem will be in walled towns like Najaf," he advised. "We're likely to be sniped at and the trucks will be unable to negotiate the narrow streets. But once we're there, we'll inspect the site. If guns are found, we'll mark the place with a smoke pot. If we coordinate properly there'll be a plane nearby. On the cue via an Aldis lamp, you chaps drop a couple of two-hundred-pound bombs."

It seemed rather make-shift to Welch. "Are you going to warn civilians?" he asked.

"Believe me, old chap, as soon as our cars show up the population will run."

"We'll need a strict timetable for this kind of operation so that we're on hand when the smoke pot is lit. How far will your chaps withdraw from the target?"

"About two hundred yards. How good are your bomb-aimers?"

"I suggest we bomb from three hundred feet altitude. That should get us close."

"The armored car crew can monitor the site after the first run and communicate if more attention is needed."

"I suggest we try a run at Najaf before we move entirely to Shaibah. It's nearer to Hinaidi and we can get our tactics refined."

"Good idea," said the major. "I'll go through the intelligence tonight and phone with a proposed strike date tomorrow."

Three days later Welch, with Holmes as second pilot, flew to rendezvous with two armored cars north of Najaf. As they circled over the town at one thousand feet, they watched the cars enter the wall and make their way to a jumble of houses west of the great mosque. After a long period, a smoke pot was lit on the roof of a house and both cars drove away.

Welch eased the plane down and flew parallel to a street directly downwind of the smoke. He had the smoke clearly visible in the periscope. The bomb aimer released two bombs a few seconds before they crossed the target. Welch flung the plane hard right as soon as the bombs had been dropped to avoid any blast damage to the Vimy.

Holmes swung round to look at the rear gunner. He was leaning over the coaming, then he gave a thumb's up. As he did so a series of holes appeared as if by magic in the left wings. Holmes saw them at the same time. *Hell, we're under fire*, he muttered to himself.

He nudged the pilot and pointed to the holes. They swung back over the town trying to locate the two armored cars. When they spotted them, they found both were under attack by riflemen on the roofs of nearby houses. The pilots alerted the gunners by pointing down and positioned the plane for a strafing run. Welch flew about five hundred feet above the rooftops and slowed down to seventy knots. Both gunners opened up on the Arabs attacking the armored cars, which had begun to evacuate the area.

Suddenly there was a bang and a jolt they all felt. A strut on the right wings disintegrated. Welch added power and climbed to a thousand feet. The cars were speeding down the road to the gate. The houses they bombed burned fiercely.

They waited until the cars cleared the wall and then flew low to flash a message by lamp, *Going Home.*

An hour later, they landed at Hinaidi and the ground crew surveyed the damage with amazement. They counted fifteen bullet holes in both wings altogether. The remains of the strut between the upper and lower wings on the right side had damaged both wings as they threshed in the airstream on the way home. It would take the airframe fitters a couple of days to get the plane serviceable again.

"Well, that was a bit of a codswallop," the C.O. said as they all walked towards the crew room.

Several hours later, the major showed up for a consultation with Welch. They both agreed the mission had not been a great success. An arms cache had been destroyed but at the cost of damage to the cars and the Vimy. One of the car drivers had been wounded. The Arabs had a machine gun set up somewhere near the cache, possibly a pair.

The other loser was Hamid Mustafa. The property in Najaf had belonged to him. He also got a stinging telegram in code from Herr Weiss demanding to know how on earth a fatwa was in the works aimed at neutralizing the forces they had been arming in the south.

Chadwick flew to Shaibah as a passenger in the transport version of the Vimy. It took three hours, and towards the end of the trip he could see the ziggurat in the west as they circled near Basra.

He flew on a routine patrol with Holmes as the first pilot. While they rested after the flight in the shade of the wings, Holmes told him about the raid on Najaf. The lack of communication between the plane and the armored cars, except by the Aldis lamp, was obviously a detriment in closely supported ground operations.

"I wonder if we could use wireless telegraphy?" Chadwick asked Holmes.

"Dunno," Holmes replied. "I read somewhere they used it during the war, but the apparatus was very large."

Chadwick determined to look into the current state of wireless communication.

The next day he was informed by the squadron clerk that he needed to be certified in first-line maintenance. He duly showed up on the flight line and Evans signed his logbook to certify that Chadwick was capable of changing a spark plug and filling the oil tank. Evans chuckled, as months earlier Chadwick had helped strip an Eagle engine for a five-hundred-hour overhaul. But bureaucracy had to be obeyed.

Chadwick was also required to change a wheel on the undercarriage. An aircraft fitter took him to a plane that was not flying that day. The Vimy had a pair of wheels on a short axle on each side of the undercarriage. "Chock the wheel on the other side, sir," the fitter told him, "then put a screw jack between wheels and lift up one side."

Chadwick knelt on the ground and jacked up the pair. The wheel was held by a large castellated nut. Before it could be removed the split pin had to be pulled out. The fitter handed him a pair of pliers. Chadwick bent the pin straight and tried to pull it out.

"It's usually a bit tricky," the fitter said, as Chadwick struggled.

The pin refused to move, then suddenly came out and Chadwick barked his knuckles on the rim of the wheel. He cursed and sucked the blood off the back of his hand. The fitter hid a sly grin.

"Next is the nut sir," he said, handing Chadwick a large spanner. "Anti-clockwise," he added.

The nut came off easily and Chadwick laid it on the ground.

"Excuse me, sir, you mustn't put the nut on the ground. Even one grain of sand in the thread could cause it to jam when you put it back."

Chadwick blew on the nut and put it in his pocket. He grasped the wheel and pulled it off the axle. By this time, he was sweating.

"Would you like to remove the other wheel?" the fitter asked innocently.

"No, I think I've learned enough to get the damned log signed."

"Oh, yes, definitely," said the fitter. "Could I have the nut back, please?"

Low cloud and rain moved into the area and flying was scrubbed. Chadwick asked the engineering officer if he had any publications on wireless telegraphy, but the officer drew a blank. The station library had nothing but some old newspapers and a few novels. Chadwick asked his flight commander, Lattimer, for permission to go into Basra and try the library there.

He changed out of his uniform and took a taxi from the base for the seven-mile ride to Basra. The weather was miserable when the taxi dropped him at the city library. A librarian spoke English. When Chadwick asked about guides to wireless telegraphy, she looked puzzled. She suggested looking at the magazine rack. Chadwick could have hugged her when he found an old copy of *Wireless World*. In it was an article about the successes of American amateur radio buffs transmitting on short wave.

He sat in a corner and devoured the information. The article gave details of the aerials, frequencies and range of several experimental transmitters. They used a relatively new invention, the thermionic valve. He was fascinated and quietly folded up the magazine and pushed it inside his shirt before leaving. *I'm stealing for the good of the Empire,* he told himself.

Chadwick knew the center of Basra quite well from his sojourn when he left the troopship. He had lunch and went to see what was playing at the cinema. It was *Wings*, and a Laurel and Hardy short. *Sounds good!* he thought. He paid nine pence in local currency and sat in the best seats. He had entered in the middle of the flying film. It was silent, but someone kept putting records on an old Victrola. He laughed heartily at the famous comedians and left when the main feature came around to the point where he had come in.

He took a taxi back to the base. He felt pleased with himself. Since his evening with Margaret he had experienced a burst of self-confidence. He felt he could do anything.

He reluctantly concluded a wireless transmission link in a Vimy was not too practical. The main problem was that the transmitters used by radio amateurs needed a high voltage power supply. He couldn't think of a way of providing that except by installing a special generator. He talked it over with Lattimer, who guessed the boffins at Farnborough were working on it.

Chapter Eighteen

Chadwick flew several times with different plane captains, but no further joint operations were carried out with the Armored Car Corps. On a routine flight, the left engine developed a problem when they were about seventy miles from Shaibah. The oil pressure stayed up, but the engine rpm dropped by five hundred revolutions. The plane could barely maintain height.

On their left they could see the great ziggurat at Ur, and the captain made a skillful landing on the desert near a complex of tents and a Bedouin encampment. After they landed, they could see no obvious cause for the engine failure and the captain and Chadwick walked towards the tents, leaving the gunners to guard the plane. Both had shed their flying suits and were dressed in shorts and a shirt.

As they approached, a European came to greet them. "Welcome to our archaeological excavation," the man said in accented English. "Professor Scharf."

The plane captain introduced the Englishmen and asked the professor if there was a phone nearby.

"Unfortunately not," was Scharf's reply. "The nearest phone is in Nasiriyah."

"Blast!" exploded the captain. "Is there some way of getting there?"

The professor said he would be only too pleased to have them taken in the expedition truck.

"It only needs one of us to go," said the captain. "Chadwick, you stay here. I'll call the base and see what they intend to do." He walked off with the professor.

To Chadwick's surprise, the professor came back after about fifteen minutes. "The driver is taking him into town," he explained. "Lieutenant Chadwick, would you like to see some of our work here?"

"I would be very interested, thank you," replied Chadwick.

They walked over to where the graduate students were sifting sand. The professor held up a pottery fragment. "This is piece of a large jar," he said. "We can date it by the patterns on the surface. This is probably three to four thousand years old." He walked with Chadwick to the shrine, saying, "And this is our *pièce de resistance*, a figure of a goddess from Babylonian times. We think she is called Ishtar."

Chadwick gazed at Ishtar. "She's wonderful! You found her here?"

"Yes, a few weeks ago. The funny thing is the Arabs think she's very powerful, although they are Muslims."

Chadwick knew his flight commander, Lattimer, would be very interested in seeing Ishtar. "I have a friend who would love to meet her. Could we come sometime for another visit?"

"Of course," replied the professor. "We'll probably close the dig for the season in a few weeks. Then we'll put Ishtar in the Baghdad museum where she'll be closely examined by experts. Would you like a drink?"

"Thank you, yes," replied Chadwick. "Also, I'd like to send some water and maybe a sandwich to the men guarding the plane."

"Come to the dining tent. All can be arranged there."

One of the Bedouin boys was sent with vittles for the two men at the plane and Chadwick enjoyed a conversation with the professor, while sipping on a glass of juice. Within thirty minutes the plane captain showed up, saying, "They're sending a Crossley with a couple of mechanics. They're pretty sure we have fouled plugs. Apparently, the petrol has got contaminated. With luck we'll be able to fly out later this afternoon."

"I've sent some food out the men at the plane, sir," Chadwick told him. "Professor Scharf has invited us to lunch."

After a pleasant meal, they saw an RAF Crossley cross the open desert and stop at the Vimy. They walked out to the plane and saw that the mechanics already had the nacelle removed from the left engine. Within half an hour, the senior mechanic reported to the plane captain that the engine was ready for a test.

"Would you like me to change all the plugs in both engines, sir? If the fuel is contaminated that would be the best thing," he said.

The captain looked at the sky. Perhaps they had two hours of daylight left. "We'll take a chance on it. It's only forty minutes to Shaibah. The engines can be overhauled there tomorrow."

On command, a mechanic swung the left propeller. The left engine started and seemed to be running perfectly, and the mechanics cleaned it up. The pilots donned their suits and thanked the professor. Chadwick told him he would try to get back with his friend for another look at Ishtar. The pilots climbed aboard, the mechanics swung the right propeller, the engine fired, and they took off heading south. After putting their tools away, the mechanics started the Crossley and drove to Nasiriyah for a couple of beers before heading back to the base.

Chadwick grabbed Lattimer as soon as they returned to the airfield, knowing he had strong interest in the history of Mesopotamia. Lattimer was intrigued to hear Chadwick's glowing account of the Ishtar plaque.

Chadwick went on, "The dig will be ending soon and then it will go to the Baghdad Museum, but it won't be on general view. We should go the Ur dig site soon if you want to see it."

"I certainly do! Leave it up to me."

True to his word, the next weekend when the squadron stood down, Lattimer wangled a Crossley out of the transportation pool and invited Chadwick to join him for a cross-desert ride. They arrived at the dig before lunch and, fortunately, the professor was still there. Chadwick performed the introductions and mentioned Lattimer's interest in early Sumerian history.

The professor took them to the shrine. The area was crowded, and some Arabs were on their knees. In front of the plaque was a pile of papers, some wrapped round a coin.

"It's curious," said Professor Scharf. "Their Imam told them Ishtar had a message for today, even though their religions are four thousand years apart."

"For today!" exclaimed Lattimer. "In what way?"

"*Enfin*," said the professor, who spoke better French than English. "He compared her to your great planes, although I see no resemblance, except for the wings. He sought protection for them."

"Did he now?"

They repaired to the dining tent for lunch, where the professor showed them many photographs they had taken of the plaque. Lattimer mentioned that the plaque lacked text of any kind and wondered why the professor attributed it to Ishtar? He was familiar with the Babylonian literature, especially *The Epic of Gilgamesh.*

"Could she be Erishkigal—the Sumerian queen of the underworld?" he asked.

Scharf was delighted to find such a knowledgeable visitor and expounded at length on the justification for the name he had assigned. When they made their goodbyes, he pressed each of them to take a glossy photograph of the plaque. "Come back anytime," he said. "You never know what we'll find next."

Driving back to the base, Lattimer said to Chadwick, "Damned interesting that the Imam decided to look after us. Usually we're not too popular with the wogs." Thinking of the squadron intelligence officer, he added, "I know someone who might be very interested in that." And then out of the blue, he said, "Allan, how's your French?"

"French? Not bad, I suppose, I took four years in school. Why?"

"There's a rumor the squadron may be paying a visit to Syria."

Chapter Nineteen

In early 1930 Herr Weiss was called to a meeting of senior officials in the German Foreign Ministry to explain why the coup against King Faisal had failed. Weiss told them that the Arab sheikhdoms the Germans supported had splintered.

"Feuds among Arabs last a long time," he said, "often for centuries." He did not mention the rise in support for the British triggered by the discoveries at Ur. The involvement of the intelligence department in the German dig was well hidden, and he prayed would stay that way.

A deputy minister rose to address the gathering. "We must not lose sight of our main interest in Iraq—the oil fields. I propose that the main obstacle to achieving control may not lie in Iraq, but in Germany. From time immemorial those lands have been battled over for their riches. We must allow for a somewhat longer-term plan and then take over by force of arms."

There was a hubbub of dissent. "Fight the British again?" someone cried.

The Deputy Minister held up his hand, "Yes eventually, but first we must re-arm."

"What about the Treaty?"

"We shall ignore it. There is no love for another war in France or Britain."

"Hindenburg would never agree," someone chipped in.

"True. That is why in the forthcoming elections in September, the right party must be elected."

"And which is that?" someone asked.

"The National Socialists," the Deputy Minister said. "I think their leader, Herr Hitler, is the right caliber for the job. General," he turned to Herr Weiss, "have you kept the party under observation?"

"Loosely," replied Herr Weiss. "Until recently the party was an unruly mob of mostly ex-Army dissolute thugs, but recently they've cleaned up and a number of powerful men and intellectuals have joined the party."

The Deputy Minister addressed the meeting. "Are we in support of a little interference in our next election?" Nobody objected. "General, please arrange some infiltration and surveillance of the National Socialists and Herr Hitler. Can we expect a progress report in, say, three months?"

The British Administration in Iraq was surprised to receive a letter from the French administrators in Syria suggesting a meeting of RAF squadron commanders with their opposite number in the French Air Force. The subject of the meeting would be a vaguely worded "Tactics."

Further communications cleared up the French request—in Iraq, the British had strived to install a puppet monarchy, King Faisal, and had early on suggested Faisal might well be the titular head of Syria and Iraq as well. This idea was firmly rejected. The French wanted a Syrian republic, just like France. Unfortunately, this was much harder to put in place, and for years the French mandate was rocked by uprisings as ambitious sheikhs tried to establish a dominant position as the majority party to rule the country. The civil unrest had mostly been dealt with by the French army, as much of the fighting occurred in urban areas. The French had looked east to the relatively calm conditions in Iraq and when they discovered the British had virtually no troops there, they thought a discussion of the RAF tactics might be profitable. The RAF commanders complained bitterly to the politicians that they had plenty to do without being diverted by joy rides to Syria. A compromise was reached: two planes from an operational squadron would be sent to Syria for a week as guests of a French squadron.

Back at Hinaidi airfield, 314 Squadron, after an uneventful posting at Shaibah, was selected to send two Vimys to Tartus on the Syrian coast. Squadron Leader Welch decided to head the little expedition himself with Lattimer as the captain of the other plane. Chadwick would fly with Welch and Holmes would fly with Lattimer. The gunner positions would all be filled by flight sergeants—one engine fitter, two airframe fitters and one airframe rigger. They carried a few engine spare parts and a spare wheel. The weather had been fairly mild that winter, so the C.O. waited for a good window for the four-hour flight to Tartus.

The two planes left together and stayed within sight of each other. The course was roughly northwest. The planes ascended slowly as they flew over the hills north of Baghdad and stayed at an altitude of five thousand feet, a safe height for crossing the Jebel el Ansariye mountain range. The bituminous tar lakes west of Baghdad were clearly visible, like two ink blots on the landscape. The desert gave way to some vegetation as they flew over the higher ground. Landmarks were few and far between as they crossed the border with Syria.

It was cold at the high altitude, and everyone wore thick flying suits. Chadwick desperately needed a landmark to give him navigational information on a north-south axis. He suspected the wind was southwesterly and was blowing them north of the desired track. They had left the Euphrates River, which wandered off to the north. It had been a very helpful guide for the first part of the leg. They crossed the railway line to Damascus, which meant they were about fifty miles from the coast, but Chadwick still lacked knowledge of their exact position. Ahead the mountains loomed, reaching nearly four thousand feet. The ground was wooded and looked pleasant.

Once they were over the mountain ridge, he could see the dark blue Mediterranean Sea stretching to the west. On the coast there were several small towns. To the south of their position there was a larger town with a jetty poking into the sea. Chadwick guessed it was Tartus. He nudged the C.O. and pointed to the left. The captain throttled back and turned to take a look. From two thousand feet, they spotted an airfield with several small planes parked near a hangar. It was about five miles from the town.

The Vimys made a leisurely circuit and prepared to land. A telephone call had been made to the French Air Force HQ on their departure, and so with luck they were expected. A green flare was fired from a small hut on the roof of the hangar and a minute later the great planes settled with a bang on Syrian soil. They taxied to the hangar and switched off. The engines creaked as they cooled. The crews climbed down stiffly to meet men running from the hangar.

"Welcome! Welcome! Royal Air Force," cried one of the Frenchmen in English. "I am Major Henri Joachim, 54 Pursuit Squadron."

Welch grabbed his hand and introduced the other crew members. The Englishmen clambered out of their flying suits, put on their service caps, and followed the major into the hangar. In a room built against the hangar wall was a table loaded with sandwiches, coffee pots and two bottles of wine. Several members of the French squadron were there to greet them. A hubbub of conversation broke out in French and English. The major spoke English and told Welch that there was no suitable accommodation on the base and so rooms had been booked for them in Tartus.

Later that afternoon, the English retrieved their gear from the planes, made sure the cockpits were covered and the wings tethered, and took a truck to Tartus. They sat on plank benches in the back, not very comfortable, but it was a short journey. Major Joachim left them in the hotel lobby, promising to meet them at 2000 hours and escort them to a nightclub and dinner.

Welch tried to make some kind of schedule for the next few days, but the major was casual. "No hurry," he said several times. "We can talk about it tomorrow."

The plane captains had a room to themselves. Chadwick and Holmes shared a room, and the flight sergeants divided themselves between two rooms. As usual on operational outings, differences in rank were largely ignored. The hotel was not large but was quite clean and pleasant. It was only a few yards from a wide boulevard that ran through the center of the town. Graceful palm trees shaded each side and a central median. There was no bar in the hotel, but several bars and restaurants were located on the boulevard within easy walking. The C.O. told them to meet in the lobby at 2000 hours, but otherwise the time was their own. Most chose to take a nap.

At 2000 hours, they all gathered in the hotel lobby dressed in the only civilian clothes they had brought with them. The major swept them up, using the same truck as before to drive them to a fancy-looking club on the coast. The club was about a hundred feet above sea level and had small terraces, with a few tables on each, which descended to a stage with an elaborate concrete arch. To one side of the stage was a bar counter. Along with the French hosts they numbered twelve. They put some tables together and occupied a terrace to themselves. Soft guitar music emanated from a couple of musicians on the stage.

Chadwick was enchanted by the view. The moon was nearly full and reflected off the calm sea. Fortunately, there was no wind, as the air temperature was barely warm enough to be eating al fresco. A few bottles of wine appeared, and the major assured them that the costs would be borne by a grateful French government. When they switched to a fish course, the musicians concluded and a slim, elegantly dressed woman walked onto the stage and leaned against a grand piano. The pianist was a Negro in tails. She sang a plaintive love story in a low, husky voice. The fish was replaced by a plate of nuts, fruit and cheese, along with hard, crusty French bread. Chadwick had knocked back quite a few glasses of wine by this time and was feeling on top of the world. *Now, this was living!*

When the singer finished, one of the Frenchmen leaned over and asked Chadwick and Holmes if they would like to meet her. They both accepted eagerly and made their way to the bar with the Frenchman. He introduced them with a big smile on his face. The singer spoke no English, so their French friend translated their congratulations on her singing. Chadwick tried a little of his schoolboy French and edged closer to the singer. He became aware of her very heavy make-up and when she lifted her glass, he saw her hands were quite large for the demoiselle she appeared to be. They said *au revoir* and climbed back to their table.

Once Chadwick sat down, he turned to the Frenchman and asked vehemently, "Was that a man or a woman?"

The Frenchman laughed. "It is a man who wishes to be a woman!"

"I've never heard of such a thing," exclaimed Chadwick.

"Oh, it's quite common. Many boys are bought up as girls in French Polynesia, although we're not in the Pacific. I think, *peut-etre*, it is spreading."

When they got back to the hotel Chadwick flung himself on his bed and decided he had some large gaps in his knowledge of the way the world worked.

Breakfast at the hotel was a simple affair. A waiter brought a covered trolley to each room. On it were croissants, butter, comfiture, fruit, juice and coffee. The English gathered in the hotel lobby and in due course a truck took them to the airfield. Welch and Lattimer went with the major for a private conversation. The rest returned to the planes and arranged to refuel them and carry out first-line servicing.

They met in the dining room of the French squadron. The lunch was quite elaborate and ran to four courses. It was decided they would inspect some of the French fighters in the afternoon. The weather was not conducive for flying, but several French pilots expressed a wish for a ride in a Vimy, and so they agreed that could be done on the next good day.

The French pilots gathered around a Vimy. They were interested in the range, armaments and the bomb sight. All of them climbed into the center cockpit, one after the other. Most expressed concern about the proximity of the propellers. The group then walked over to a French fighter, the Gourdo Leseurre GL-31. It was a fairly modern monoplane, designed for one pilot. The British said it would be no use for ground support and the French pilots agreed. It was a *chasseur*, designed for high altitude interception.

Chadwick climbed into the cockpit. He was impressed by the visibility; he had never been in a monoplane before. A French pilot said a chasseur was more concerned about a view of the rear. They broke up with a promise of an evening on the town.

In the evening, one of the French officers showed up at the hotel and suggested an exciting time was coming for those who wanted to tag along. The four flight sergeants, who were all family men, found a quiet corner in the hotel and played whist. Lattimer said he wanted to study a book he had on local archaeology. There was a castle built by the Crusaders in the vicinity and he was hoping to organize a visit before they left.

Welch looked at Holmes and Chadwick and said, "All right, lads, let's see what earthly delights the Frogs have in store for us." They left in a taxi with their French guide and stopped at a small restaurant on the outskirts of the native quarter, the Casbah.

During an excellent meal, the Frenchman told them that a few meters away was a "*maison de tolerance*," a very superior establishment, he claimed. "A couple of years ago we discovered the squadron was spending so much money there that we decided it would be cheaper to buy the place and own it outright. Now each squadron member owns a share. When he's posted, the new incoming officer buys his share. The residents are examined by the squadron doctor on a regular basis. There's a frequent turnover, facilitated by a subterranean network of similar establishments. All the *jeune filles* are French."

Holmes had been listening with a slightly puzzled look on his face, then the light dawned. "You mean, it's a cathouse!" he cried.

"*Oui*," said the Frenchman, "Naturally, as our guests the pleasures are all yours, gratis." They finished their drinks, gathered their hats and coats, and followed the Frenchman to an innocuous door a few steps away.

They entered a large, dimly lit room. The air was thick with smoke and the characteristic pungent smell of Gauloises cigarettes. There was a small bar in one corner tended by a beefy man who looked like he doubled as the bouncer. About a dozen well-dressed men in lounge suits chatted with a handful of young women, each in a dress displaying a ripe décolletage. There was a low murmur of conversation and from somewhere came the tinkling of a piano playing ragtime.

They hung their coats in a tiny alcove and their host took them over to an older woman sitting on a tall stool. A leather bag hung on a strap from her shoulder. He introduced them in French. "Madame Celeste," he said, "these gentlemen are English, guests of the squadron for tonight."

She nodded.

"Help yourself to a drink at the bar," he said. "While I'm here, there's an old friend I must say hello to. When you're tired, the madam will call you a taxi. *Bonne chance!*" He walked across the room and was soon talking to a dark brunette who smiled when she saw him.

Welch led the way to the bar and Chadwick ordered a beer. He saw their French friend disappear through a thickly beaded doorway with the brunette. They were not left to stand alone for long.

A young woman in a startling yellow dress stood next to him. "*T'aime moi?*" she said.

"*T'es tres belle,*" Chadwick replied, proud of his French.

"*Regarde,*" she said. The top of her bodice was made of stiff material rather like papier mache. A long zipper ran all the way down the front. She seized the zipper and ran it down to her navel. She had shapely breasts with pink nipples. Chadwick looked at her. Under the rouge and lipstick, she looked very young. He thought, illogically, she had attractive brown eyes. He was very embarrassed.

He gently zipped her up. "*Merci, mais non.*"

A look of anger flashed across her face for a second, then she smiled and turned away.

Chadwick leaned against the bar and sipped his beer. Nailed to the wall near the madam was a large notice board. Welch and Holmes were nowhere to be seen. He cursed himself for being an idiot. As he watched, a couple approached the madam, and the girl pointed to a line on the board. The man fumbled in his pocket and gave some money to Celeste, who dropped it in her satchel.

My God, Chadwick thought. *They actually post a price list!* He eased himself over to get a better view. "Coitus normal, 100F" read the top line. Below that, "Coitus au Fond, 300F." *I wonder what that means,* he pondered. He read on, fascinated, "Fellatio 100 F. Cunnilingus 100 F. Soixante-neuf 150

F." His eyes ran over the list, which listed common perversions he didn't comprehend. The bottom line read, "Ménage a Trois, 400 F."

He felt a little dizzy. He was out of his depth. He asked Celeste to get him a taxi, and he waited outside until it came.

Chapter Twenty

The next day was overcast with light drizzle, not suitable for flying. The truck appeared and they drove out to the airfield. The sergeants took some of their French opposite numbers to a Vimy and by miming, they managed to go over the engines and the armaments. They got permission to fire the Lewis guns, and a plane was pushed into position near the butts and the sergeants had a great time emptying a couple of ammunition pans.

Lattimer went to find Major Joachim. Welch had given him the afternoon off, along with as many of their party who wanted to visit an old castle. The major was able to find a taxi driver who could carry six, including the driver.

Welch sat down with Chadwick and Holmes and brought them up to date on discussions with the French. The first mystery was why they had been directed to land at Tartus. The squadron based there was equipped with fighters and had not been engaged in ground support. The major believed there had been a great deal of political maneuvering to extend the invitation in the first place and somewhere along the line, someone had managed to sabotage the initiative. The C.O. told the major that, in his experience, close ground support was impossible without wireless communication between the planes and the ground forces. The major was delighted. Suitably dressing up a report along those lines would sound like solid progress, without actually producing any change, as French planes were not equipped with wireless sets. Holmes and Chadwick listened to Welch's summary without making any comment.

Lattimer sounded out the party for anyone wishing to see the Crusader's castle. Two sergeants expressed an interest, Holmes and Chadwick signed on, but Welch declined. That meant five of them could just squeeze into the taxi.

They left after lunch for the castle. Lattimer had been boning up on the history of the place, which he regaled them with during the one-hour ride. "There's been a castle at this place since very early times," he told them, "because it occupies a very strategic spot in the Homs Gap. The gap is a way for armies to avoid the Jebel el Ansariye Mountains. The castle itself is on top of a prominent hill two thousand feet high. Much of what we'll see was built by the Moors in the eleventh century. It was given to the Knights Hospitaller in the twelfth century and they hung on to it for over a hundred years, during the Crusades. They greatly expanded it, adding a central keep, and they repaired earthquake damage. The Moors recaptured it in the late twelfth century, led by Sultan Baibar. It is now one of the most original medieval castles in the Middle East. It is called Krak des Chevaliers. I have a lot more information if anyone is interested."

No one was. The bouncing taxi, on top of a good lunch, suppressed all thoughts except getting to the castle as soon as possible. The driver drove as close as he could to the outer wall of the castle. At one point it had collapsed, and a stream of people scrambled over a pile of rocks heading in and out. They spilled out of the taxi and climbed over the jumbled rock to the space inside the outer wall. To their surprise they discovered many Arabs were living there in tents and lean-tos. Smoke from a dozen fires curled upwards, and small children played in the dirt. More people were living in the keep. The smoke from their fires clung to the walls and escaped through small windows, leaving black stains. The interior was in good shape. Many rooms were completely empty but smelt of poverty and human excrement. The chapel had been converted into a mosque but seemed to be unused.

Climbing the battlements towards the top of the highest tower, Chadwick found himself out of breath. The stone underfoot was surprisingly rough, although the steps themselves had been worn smooth by generations of soldiers. He asked Lattimer how many troops had been stationed at the castle.

"I believe a maximum of two thousand."

Standing on the highest point, Chadwick looked south towards the city of Homs, which he could not make out in the haze. Thinking of the route home, Chadwick thought a leg through the Homs Gap would save at least two thousand feet of height. He could see no serious obstacle south of the castle. He gripped the rough stone wall and tried to imagine the tribulations of building the place high on a hill in summer heat. Thousands must have died to erect this, he decided. Lattimer fished out a Brownie camera and took a photograph of the group at the summit of the keep.

They made their way back to the taxi and stopped at a small inn recommended by the taxi driver for refreshments. For supper they went to a restaurant near their hotel and had crepes. Chadwick proposed to Welch that they fly home via the Homs Gap, if the visibility was good.

"You're the navigator. Just don't fly us into any clouds with hard centers."

Major Joachim and Welch conferred about the program. The weather looked settled for the next two days. The next day would be taken up with flying the Vimys, followed by a farewell dinner. The following day, after the dinner, the British would fly back to Iraq. The major took Welch aside after the plan was announced. "Normally after a dinner the girls from our house in Tartus would put on a show. You know, dancing on the table and an American striptease. But half a dozen of our officers are married and their wives would like to meet *Les Anglaise*. If it's all the same to you, we'll invite the wives to the dinner and save the girls for another visit."

"Of course," Welch replied. "We've been wonderfully entertained. I look forward to meeting the ladies."

When word of this compromise reached some of the single French officers, they had an even better idea. When the dinner was over, they would run over to Tartus for an after-dinner show. Two of them owned a private car and taxis were always available.

The next day they all gathered in the crew room of the French squadron. Six French pilots asked for rides in a Vimy. It was decided to take them up, two at a time, in the front and rear cockpits. The trips would be listed in the Duty Log (Form700) as a demonstration of close ground support. Chadwick asked the French C.O. if he could fly a GL-31. Major Joachim considered this request for a second and said without hesitation, "Of course."

He assigned one of his pilots to go over crucial data with Chadwick such as landing speed, maximum engine rpm and lift-off speed, all in metric units. Chadwick asked if the engine was equipped for inverted flying, and the answer he got was "In theory, yes. But don't try it."

Chadwick was fitted out with a parachute and walked with his French mentor to a GL-31. They checked the exterior and went over the cockpit controls. He started the engine and tax-ied for takeoff. The tail came up nicely at 10 meters per second and he climbed away at 25 meters per second. The plane was light and easy to fly. At 2,000 meters, he throttled back and kept the nose up until it stalled, entering a vicious left-hand spin. He pushed the stick fully forward and applied opposite rudder. The plane was reluctant to stop spinning, but finally entered a steep dive that he was able to control. He brought the nose up gently and applied power—he had fallen to 650 meters. Climbing back to 2,000 meters, he tried a barrel roll and decided he had had enough.

He chopped the throttle and glided towards the airfield but forgot the fighter pilot's trick of warming the engine every 150 meters. As he approached the field, the engine quietly died due to icing. The airscrew continued to turn but he jiggled the throttle, mixture and ignition without the engine firing. Fortunately, he had height to spare, and he lined up into wind and side-slipped for a good dead-stick landing. He was sweating when the French ran to the plane and pushed it to the dispersal point.

As he climbed out Welch approached. "Showing off, are you, Chadwick?" he asked. "Good thing you didn't bend it!"

After lunch the Englishmen were driven to the hotel for a free afternoon of souvenir shopping and packing. They planned to fly home in the morning. In the evening, they donned their uniforms and were driven back to the Officer's Mess of 54 Pursuit Squadron. Cocktails were served before dinner. The British flyers were introduced to the wives of several officers, some of whom spoke English. Chadwick found himself talking to a well-dressed woman who asked him if he had enjoyed visiting Syria.

"It's been a wonderful experience," he said. "Yesterday we toured the Krak des Chevaliers. It's unique."

"And what about the house in town?" she asked, with a twinkle in her eye.

He reddened, not sure what to say. "It's very, very French," he mumbled. "I don't think there's a single squadron in the Royal Air Force that's so well—uh—organized."

"*Très diplomatique*," she said. "You should go far in the military."

Dinner was called and waiters served a delicious meal. There was plenty of wine between courses. Major Joachim cut the low hubbub of conversation by tapping his wine glass. He spoke mostly in French, thanking the British for being gracious guests and treating members of his squadron to a flight in an aircraft that had been the first to cross the Atlantic, non-stop. "Very *historique*," he said and slyly added, "I'm sure the squadron leader will join me in urging the British government to buy some new aeroplanes!"

Welch rose to thank everyone for the wonderful hospitality shown during their visit. He presented the major with a plaque bearing the 314 Squadron shield and a motto, *Accipe hoc*—Take this.

As the party broke up, Chadwick again found himself talking to the French wife he had met earlier.

"I hear some of our wilder members are going to introduce you again to our house in town," she said. "I think you may find that sometimes professionals are not as much fun as amateurs. I'm sorry you're leaving. My husband says you like to land a plane without using the engine."

Chadwick did something he had never done before; he kissed the back of her hand. "*Au revoir*," he stammered.

She smiled.

Chadwick and Holmes drove back to Tartus with one of the French flyers who owned an old Renault. The driver told them the treat of the evening was to be a special show.

"These are for men who do not, want to—er— touch flesh."

Several other Frenchmen were already there. After hanging up their coats and hats, they followed Madame Celeste to a door which led to a small balcony. A few feet below was a stage covered by a thick carpet with ornate cushions scattered about. Oriental recorded music came from a speaker. The lights came on and two young women came on stage dressed as they may have in a harem at the height of the Ottoman Empire. They wore gauzy pantaloons and tightly buttoned bodices.

The music faded and a voice intoned in French, "They are two of a hundred concubines in the sultan's harem. Very rarely are they told to share the sultan's bed. What do they do the rest of the time?"

At this the women looked at each other and joined arms in a close embrace, kissing full on the lips. Eventually their hands fell to their mons and they began to writhe in ecstasy. Their pantaloons were ripped off and one woman searched behind a cushion for a large dildo which she applied with some vigor to her companion. They frantically unbuttoned their bodices and kissed the breasts that spilled out. Then they found a rubber snake behind the cushions. After shrieking in pretended horror, they used both ends of the snake on each other.

Chadwick watched with fascination, disgust, repulsion and excitement, all at the same time. Later they dropped the toys and entwined their legs, moving against each other. Slowly they brought themselves to a climax and lay back on the cushions, breathing heavily.

"That is how they keep happy when the sultan forgets them," droned the voice from the speaker. "In the harem, they would have been beaten if a eunuch caught them. Please show your appreciation."

The men clapped and whistled and flung money onto the stage. One or two Frenchmen suggested moving back to the main room, but Chadwick was glad when his driver said he had had enough for one night and he dropped the Brits at their hotel. *It's been a long day*, Chadwick thought, as he climbed into bed.

The next day dawned fair with high overcast and a northerly wind. The French arranged to guide the Vimys to Homs. Three fighters were in the air when the Vimys lumbered into wind and took off. They flew south for a few minutes and then turned left into the Gap. The white castle stood out starkly on their left. The French fighters waggled their wings and climbed rapidly.

Chadwick aimed to intersect the Euphrates River and allowed fifteen degrees to the left to counteract the drift caused by the wind. The river did not show up when he expected it and he began to sweat a little. He decided the wind was stronger than he had allowed for, but then to his relief the front gunner pointed dead ahead.

Soon familiar landmarks began to appear and in due course the planes were safely on the ground at Hinaidi. It had been a trip that Chadwick would remember for a long time.

Chapter Twenty-One

In Berlin, Herr Weiss pondered the directive to engage the National Socialist Party and Herr Hitler. He reviewed all the files they had on Hitler and his immediate associates. It was almost beyond belief that a man who had been a corporal during the war had risen to control a party which was strong enough to enter the national election. In addition, Hitler had been jailed and had survived assassination attempts. The party had a paramilitary force of over a million men. The more he read, the more Herr Weiss became puzzled. Infiltrating the party at a high level would not be easy. These people were survivors and ruthless to boot.

He decided a direct approach might be best, a surreptitious attempt could result in violence if discovered. Obviously, a simple phone call was not going to work. He needed a contact. This he set up through the Krupps Armament AG. Normally Herr Weiss felt he was master of a situation, but when he finally met Hitler in his Munich office, he felt the power of the intense man behind the desk. He explained his position in the War Ministry. The hope was that a strong government would see the need to re-arm.

Hitler was contemptuous. "A few bureaucrats in Berlin are not going to help me get elected," he said. "When Germany does re-arm, it must be understood that the modern army, air force and navy run on oil. The British know this, and their empire provides it. Germany must acquire secure sources. What are you cloak and dagger men doing about that?"

Weiss was pleased to seize an opportunity to justify their operations in the Middle East. Hitler listened to his summary of the attempted coup.

"You cannot trust the Arabs. They're Semites, just like the Jews. When we take over the government I shall re-arm, you can count on that. You tell me how we can secure and protect reliable sources of oil."

He gave Herr Weiss the name of a trusted aide. "You can contact me through him," he said. "Our meeting is over. *Guten tag.*"

Weiss sat in a comfortable, first-class compartment, on an express train speeding north to Berlin. He turned the interview over in his mind. *That man is going to be president,* he thought, *unless he is killed first. And that is unlikely.* The security had been tight. He had been frisked twice before finally meeting Hitler. *The nearest sources of oil for a re-armed Germany were in the Ukraine and the Middle East. The Russians and the British would fight fiercely before losing them,* he reasoned. *Suppose the oil is simply denied the British due to sabotage. But then it would also be unavailable to Germany after conquest.* It was a taxing dilemma.

Back at the War Ministry, he reviewed the reports from Iraq and held confidential consultations with foreign affairs experts. He then wrote an appreciation of the situation for Hitler's eyes only. He believed a weakness in the British position was in northern Iraq, where the Turkish border divided lands that had been ruled by the Kurds for centuries. There was plenty of oil in the region, centered on the city of Kirkup. The Kurds were willing to fight the Turks and the Iraqi government for independence. If that could be achieved, Germany was in a strong position to gain control of the oil.

In the short term, every effort should be made to reduce British power in the region. He suggested more strife and sabotage in the south to draw British forces away from the north. In secret, he delivered the appreciation to Herr Hitler and received a quick reply, which was to begin the plan he had outlined.

Herr Weiss realized that, for better or for worse, he had tied his star to the National Socialist Party. *We had better make sure they win the next election,* he told himself.

Chapter Twenty-Two

Spring weather brought a renewal of digging at Ur. Ishtar was safely stored in the Baghdad Museum, but not on view to the general public. Professor Scharf returned to the dig-site and brought Frau Scharf, who was delighted by the acclaim heaped on her husband by the discovery of the plaque. Lieutenant Goelz, who was tired of his "civilian" assignment, petitioned Herr Weiss to be relieved, but was ordered to stay.

At first, further north at Hinaidi, 314 Squadron found that the number of retaliatory raids was decreasing, and so the squadron also spent a lot of time practicing gunnery and bombing. Pilot Officer Chadwick was promoted to Flying Officer, an automatic step, but he was not yet considered to qualify as a first pilot. And then air activity began to increase because of a long, coded telegram sent from Berlin to Hamid Mustafa.

The first sign of change was the derailment of a train to Basra from Baghdad. When inspectors examined the wreck, they found the fishplates had been unbolted from the rails. Security along the line was increased but most people knew Colonel T.E. Lawrence had played havoc with the Turks in Arabia using the same tactics during the war. It was a form of sabotage that was extremely difficult to detect without elaborate inspections.

A Shiite burial service was attacked near Najaf and several mourners killed. British Intelligence began to hear hints of German agents in the area—some had apparently worked in Persia and southern Iraq during the war.

Then came a shocking incident, a large explosion at the Abadan oil refinery, which killed over twenty workers and disrupted oil production for weeks. Although located in Persia, the refinery was under lease to the British and located only a short distance from the border with Iraq.

The increasing tension brought changes to the way RAF patrols were conducted. Routine patrols were increased in number, retaliatory raids became more common, and finally 314 Squadron was ordered back to Shaibah. The countryside in the area was much swampier than around Hinaidi in winter but dried out to some extent in summer. This complicated the construction of emergency forced landing fields. The Royal Navy established patrols along the coast as far as Abadan, and the sailors became a common sight at the waterfront bars in Basra. This too, led to eruptions of violence as local gangs targeted vulnerable sailors.

RAF personnel were not allowed into Basra on their free time. Chadwick came to think of his first year in Iraq and the trip to Syria as a Golden Age. His mind glossed over the forced landing and the discovery of Bill Smethurst's body. Unfortunately, the harsh reality of the increased German presence in Iraq was about to impact on his life.

Mustafa had imported several crates of "machine parts," which contained Mauser heavy caliber rifles with telescopic precision sights. Good Arab marksmen were trained in their use and then told go after the low-flying RAF bombers. It was felt these shooters would be far more difficult to detect than machine gunners.

The marksman had been camped in a small grove of trees for three days. Mustafa had chosen the spot based on his observation of RAF flights over a couple of weeks. The marksman's German tutor had emphasized the need to minimize the lead angle, which was large if a moving target was attacked from the side. If he was lucky, the next plane would fly almost directly over him. By firing as it approached, there was almost no lead angle to allow for, only gravity drop, which was dealt with by an adjustment of the sight.

Three hours after sunup, the marksman's patience was rewarded. The characteristic drone of the heavy Eagle engines alerted him to an approaching plane. When he estimated it was about five hundred meters away, he banged off two rapid shots. The plane continued unperturbedly on its way and he decided he had missed. He stripped the gun on a clean cloth, cleaned the barrel, and put the pieces away.

In fact, he had inflicted a mortal blow on the old Vimy. The bullet had entered the bottom of the main fuel tank, located between the center and rear cockpits. Undetected by the crew, fuel began to pour out, and vaporized immediately in the slip stream underneath the plane. Each engine on the Vimy was fed with fuel from a small service tank in the upper wing, each connected to the main tank. These tanks contained enough fuel for about twenty minutes of running. The main tank bled dry in about ten minutes. About thirty minutes after the attack, the left engine sputtered to a stop, although the propeller contained to turn.

The pilot, Holmes, immediately applied right rudder and increased power on the right engine. It ran for another minute and then died.

The second pilot, Chadwick, twisted in his seat to look at the sight glass on the fuel tank behind him. It showed empty. He yelled in disbelief into Holmes' ear, "We're out of fuel!"

Both pilots scanned the ground ahead. It was not very suitable for a forced landing. Small streams intersected swampy islands, interspersed with bushes and small trees. Holmes did the best he could. He signaled to the front gunner to get rid of the bombs which they routinely carried. The gunner jettisoned four bombs and they exploded behind them. The blast shook the plane.

Holmes eased the speed to just above stalling. "Brace yourselves," he shouted, and seconds later the plane struck the ground.

The noise was deafening. The nose of the plane suddenly dug down and the tail rose almost vertically. Chadwick was stunned. He came to his senses with the rear gunner shaking his shoulder, demanding, "Are you all right, sir?"

Chadwick looked right at Holmes. Blood was pouring down his face.

"See if you can help him," he said to the gunner, pointing.

The gunner dropped out of sight and then reappeared on the other side. He unclipped Holmes and tried to lift him out of the cockpit. The first pilot was still strapped to his parachute harness. It was impossible to move him.

Chadwick was still confused. He shook his head and tried to think straight. He pointed to the front cockpit. "Help him," he shouted to the gunner.

He began to unfasten his own straps. Somehow his hands didn't seem to be connected to his brain, but eventually he got the straps undone, climbed over the side and jumped down to the soft earth. He walked under the tail and pulled himself up to the center cockpit.

"Brian," he said, "Are you all right? Can you hear me?"

There was no reply. The gunner came back and stood behind him. "It's Grimes, sir. He's out cold, or dead!"

"Come up here, then," Chadwick said. "Let's lift Holmes down."

They managed to lift his body over the cockpit coaming and lay him on the ground under a wing.

"Grab the first aid kit," Chadwick said. He opened the box and mopped Holmes' face with cotton wool, then applied come iodine.

Holmes came to with a start. "That smarts!"

Chadwick grinned. "At least you're alive!"

Chadwick moved down the wing with difficulty, gradually reaching the front cockpit. The gunner, Grimes, was slumped over the front of the coaming. He pulled the gunner's shoulders back. The lower part of his body was a bloody mess. The force of the impact had driven the skid and its support through the floor of the cockpit. Grimes was indubitably dead. Chadwick climbed down and told Holmes the bad news.

Holmes decided their only option was to stay where they were and trust that squadron scouts would find them when they failed to return. They opened a parachute and laid out the circle of cloth, tying it to bushes so that wind would not disturb it. What to do with Grimes's body was a problem that would have to be solved soon—flies were already gathering round the front of the plane. The three of them managed to pull the body out of the front cockpit. They wrapped it in another parachute and securely tied it using the shrouds. They laid the body on top of a large bush so that it was clear of the ground.

Holmes reviewed their resources. They had an Aldis lamp, a Very pistol and flares, a Webley .45 revolver and ten cartridges, three canteens of water, the first-aid kit, which fortunately had scissors, and two Lewis machine guns, which they lifted down from the plane. They still had one unused parachute. The one in the forward cockpit was ruined and soaked in blood.

A noise made them turn around. Two tall Arabs had materialized behind them. They were very brown, dressed only in loin cloths with short capes and small cloth caps.

"They're Marsh Arabs," said Holmes. "Not usually belligerent."

He addressed the Arabs. "*Al salamu alaykum*. Peace be with you." This was his only painfully learned Arabic.

They responded with same phrase. He made several attempts at conversation speaking slowly in English, without success. Eventually the Arabs left them.

They opened the remaining parachute and made a shelter, although the sun was not oppressive.

Holmes said, "It's going to be near sunset when a scout shows up. I think we're stuck here for the night."

They had no food, and after another couple of hours they began to feel peckish. To their surprise, the Arabs reappeared. They laid some large, green leaves on the ground and lifted the top one. Underneath was row of small dried fish. They gestured to the fish and then to Englishmen and made a chewing movement with their jaws. They helped themselves. The fish were tasty and quite salty.

"We should give them something in return," Chadwick suggested to Holmes.

They had a large bundle of rope shrouds, cut off when they rigged the shelter. Holmes picked up a handful and walked to one of the Arabs, he pointed to the fish and then to the bundle, he made an offering gesture and handed it over. The Arab took the rope and nodded, then they left.

In due course they spotted a Vimy about two miles north of their position. They fired a red flare, and when there was no observable effect, they fired another. The plane turned towards them and they communicated by Aldis Lamp using Morse code.

Three alive, one dead, Holmes flashed.

Rescue tomorrow, was the reply.

While they waited and there was still some light, they examined the Vimy. With the tail poking almost straight up, the damage caused by the heavy caliber round was quite obvious. They tore away the doped fabric on the bottom of the fuselage, exposing the underside of the tank. The bullet had entered at a slanted angle, causing a hole about half an inch wide and two inches long.

"By God," cried Holmes, "We were shot down!"

They posted watches and endured a dreary, chilly night, beset by a million insects. A detachment of police found them by noon the next day. They had brought a stretcher for the body. They carried out the guns but left the wreckage for the Marsh Arabs to salvage. The rescuers had come by boat along the Euphrates River and then struck overland when they were close to the wreck. Holmes, Chadwick and the surviving gunner gratefully climbed aboard one of Hamid Mustafa's ferries after a two-hour hike though swampy land.

When Holmes told the intelligence officer, Becket, about the bullet hole in the fuel tank, he was very keen to go back to the wreck and take a look for himself. Also, the Engineering Officer wanted to retrieve some of the more valuable engines parts. The next day a party returned to wrecked Vimy. Half a dozen aircraftmen carried bulky rucksacks in which they stored the magnetos, carburetors and a few engine and flight instruments. Becket had brought a long, straight dowel he inserted into the bullet hole in the tank. It clearly indicated the shot had come from the front of the plane and slightly to one side.

Assuming the plane flew for about half-an-hour after the shot, we have a pretty good idea of where the shooter stood, Becket thought. *I wonder if it's worth taking a look about forty miles back?* He decided the chances of finding anything were slim. He asked the captain of the ferry if there were any settlements about forty miles down the river and was told many people lived on the banks of the river.

The activities of the rescue party and the questions from the intelligence officer were duly reported to Hamid Mustafa. This enabled Mustafa to identify the shooter and, on the orders of Herr Weiss, he rewarded him with a substantial bonus.

Chapter Twenty-Three

Now that the squadron was stationed at Shaibah, Lattimer was keen to re-establish contact with Professor Scharf at Ur. One afternoon when the squadron was stood down, he borrowed a Crossley and drove with Chadwick to the dig site.

The professor was pleased to see them and showed some of the artifacts they had stumbled upon recently. "Nothing like Ishtar," he said. "That was probably a once in a lifetime find." He glanced at his watch. "How about some tea? My wife is visiting today. We can meet her in the dining tent."

He walked with the two airmen to the camp and spotted his wife. "Ah, yes, she's brought a friend with her today. They're both staying in Basra at the moment."

He introduced the two women to Lattimer and Chadwick. "This is my wife, Frau Scharf, and her friend Frau Koepka."

They shook hands. "Call me Schuttzi," Maryana Koepka said.

They sat down together and sipped some tea. Chadwick looked at Frau Scharf. She looked vaguely familiar, but he couldn't place her.

Professor Scharf addressed his wife in German. "These gentlemen are British aviators. They fly those big planes we sometimes see overhead."

Schuttzi was interested. She said in fair English, "How fascinating! Where did you come from today? You didn't fly here did you?"

"No, we drove from Shaibah, near Basra," Lattimer said. He turned to Professor Scharf. "I wanted to tell you about a recent trip I made recently to Syria. I was able to visit the Krak des Chevaliers. Not as ancient as the period you are interested in, but fascinating, just the same."

"I've heard of it," said the professor. "Amazing that those medieval knights came from all over Europe to rescue Jerusalem from the heretics."

"They meant to stay," Lattimer said. "That castle was built to last."

Schuttzi glanced at him again. She wondered if he was married.

After more small talk, Lattimer and Chadwick rose to leave. Professor Scharf wished them a pleasant journey.

Schuttzi said, "It must be boring for you on that air force base. I sometimes have cocktail parties at my house in Basra. Please let me have your address. I'll be very happy to invite you to the next one."

Lattimer gave her his card, on which he wrote, *C/O Officer's Mess, RAF Shaibah.*

Chadwick and Lattimer drove back to Shaibah. By the time they arrived it was dark, and they found the base in a state of uproar. An hour earlier, a sentry had shot a man dead. In fact, when they parked the Crossley, there was the body of an Arab lying on a board between two trestles in the garage. He was dressed in a dark cape and keffiyeh and had an ugly wound in his chest. They both crossed over to get a look at the corpse.

Chadwick stared and said, "I've seen that fellow recently. He was crew on the boat that picked us up on the Euphrates after we walked out of the swamp."

Lattimer told him to mention the recognition to the intelligence officer, Becket. They both went looking for him, and when they found Becket, Chadwick told him where he had seen the dead Arab before. Lattimer asked what precisely had happened.

"The sentry was on guard duty at the line of squadron aircraft," the intelligence officer said. "He challenged him, and the fellow ducked down behind a wheel. Then he challenged him again and the chap started walking towards him. As there was no response, and apparently, he looked a bit ominous in the twilight, the guard pulled the trigger. He says he didn't mean to hit him. However, the trespasser was up to no good. He had bottle of petrol and in his pocket, there were two boxes of matches and a candle."

In the morning, Becket told an inspector of the Basra police of the incident and mentioned the tentative recognition. The inspector was Egyptian—the British had installed many Egyptians in the higher ranks of the police force, as they came without the baggage of family allegiances and feuds that plagued Iraqis. The inspector said he would pay a visit to the office of the Euphrates ferry company. He asked for a photograph of the dead man and several prints were sent over via dispatch rider.

Before the inspector arrived at the office, he sent one of his street undercover men to the waterfront with a photograph and got a positive recognition from the sailors who gathered there every day looking for work.

When the inspector quizzed the manager, he at first denied knowing the dead man. "Let me see your payments ledger," the inspector demanded. He thumbed to the day of the rescue of the downed flyers. There was a payment recorded to the dead man of eight shillings, six pence for six hours' work.

The inspector put his thumbnail on the line and said to the manager, "This is him."

"Ah, yes, Abdul," the manager said. "I scarcely remember him. Just casual labor."

The inspector thumbed through back pages. Abdul's name figured prominently on many crew musters. He put a finger on each entry, without saying a word. "I think I'd better have a word with the boss," he said. "Where is Mr. Mustafa?"

The manager made a telephone call. "Mr. Mustafa is at home," he told the inspector. "He will come here shortly. You can wait in his office." As he led the inspector to the office he asked, "Is Abdul in trouble?"

The inspector didn't reply. The manager left him sitting in a chair by a desk and went out, shutting the door. The inspector bounded up quickly and opened the door a crack. As he suspected, the manager was talking urgently on the phone.

Within a quarter-hour, Mustafa walked into his office and apologized to the inspector for keeping him waiting. The inspector introduced himself. "Inspector Adam, Basra police. I'm looking into an incident at the Royal Air Force base at Shaibah. Last night a man who was trespassing was shot dead by a sentry. It appears he frequently worked on your ferries."

Mustafa looked suitably shocked. The inspector pulled out a photograph and placed it on the desk. "Do you recognize him?"

Mustafa, of course, knew the man well, but said, "He does look familiar, but we use so many casual crew." He spread his hands down. "I am not personally involved in day-to-day operations of my boats. What was his name?"

"I believe he is Abdul al Salam," said the inspector. "Do you know any reason why he would be trespassing at Shaibah?"

"Of course not," said Mustafa. "His personal life was his own." In fact, he had a very strong suspicion about what Abdul was doing at the base, but he kept his mouth shut.

"Do you know if he had any family?" the inspector went on.

"I don't know," Mustafa told him. "Maybe my manager would know."

"Ask him in, please," the inspector said.

Mustafa opened the door and beckoned the manager. "Ahmed, we are trying to pin down details about this man Abdul al Salam, who you have hired occasionally."

The inspector watched them both keenly. He had been a policeman for many years, and the body language of the two men was revealing.

The manager looked at Mustafa before replying, "I know nothing about him."

Mustafa gave in imperceptible nod and asked, "Was he married?"

"I don't know," Ahmed replied.

The inspector suggested, "Perhaps some of the crew he worked with in the past may know more about him. Perhaps you could just pop down to the waterfront and ask."

While they waited, Mustafa arranged for some coffee to be bought in. The inspector was silent. Mustafa began to sweat a little. This was an unfortunate development, as it tied him indirectly to the incident at Shaibah. He guessed what had happened. He had told Abdul that Berlin had been so pleased that they authorized a large reward for the shooter. Abdul had obviously decided on a little private enterprise and gone after a Vimy for himself.

When the manager returned, he told them both that Abdul lived with his mother and was unmarried. The inspector asked them to get in touch with her and have her visit the police station to make arrangements to collect the body of her son. He bid them good day and thanked them for their time.

When he got back to the police station, the inspector called Becket, the intelligence officer. "I just spoke to the people at the ferry office," he said. "They claimed he was just casual labor and they knew almost nothing about him. I discovered he was unmarried and lived with his mother. I got the impression they were lying. Abdul had worked on the ferries for many days. His mother might be worth talking to."

Becket suggested moving the body to the Basra mortuary, getting the mother to make an identification and questioning her at the same time. He had a very practical reason for suggesting that the body be moved—there were no refrigerated facilities at the base. He told Inspector Adam of the objects found in the pockets of the victim, and explained Abdul planned a simple delayed action fire using the candle. Embedding a piece of woolen thread in the wax of the candle and dipping the other end in a pool of petrol gave the arsonist time to make his escape, providing he was very careful when he lit the candle. He also told the inspector that Hamid Mustafa was under suspicion of gun-running the previous year, but no action was taken.

The inspector asked why he had not been arrested. Becket told him that, on the advice of the intelligence department in Baghdad, Mustafa had been left in place but watched. The Germans would replace him with someone else if he was arrested.

Inspector Adam accompanied Abdul's mother when she made the formal identification. She was stoical and made no relevant addition to the facts known about Abdul.

When another Vimy was attacked by rifle fire in the north of Iraq, without bringing the plane down, it was decided to add armor plate to the underside of all the Vimys in service. Suitable steel plate was dispatched from Baghdad, and the planes were modified one at a time, a process that took two days. Several second pilots were drafted to removing the underside doped fabric before the plates were attached. This was done under the supervision of a rigger. The plate ran forward from underneath the rear cockpit to the front cockpit, covering the spaces occupied by the fuel tank and the center cockpit. After it was bolted in place, the fabric was replaced and doped. The bomb load was reduced by the extra weight, but the trim was hardly affected. Chadwick enjoyed seeing the space under the cockpits exposed—the elevator and rudder control cables ran through the area.

One day as Chadwick was returning to his room, grimy from working under a plane, Lattimer stopped him, saying, "I've had an invitation from Frau Koepka to attend a soirée at her place in Basra a week on Saturday. Would you like to come?"

Chadwick thanked him and said he would be delighted. On the appointed day, the two of them made their way to Basra by taxi.

"I hope you're going to enjoy this party, Allan. You'll probably be the youngest person there."

"I shall try to act maturely," replied Chadwick, with a grin. He had persuaded his batman to clean his best suit and starch a good shirt. He wore a Cranwell College tie.

When they arrived, they found the place was crowded. Most of the guests were European. Alcohol was flowing freely, and sweetmeats such as Turkish delight, stuffed dates, baklava and halva were arranged in profusion on a table against a wall. Maryana Koepka saw them arrive and detached herself to greet them. She introduced them to Dr. Rawlins and some archaeologists from the British dig at Ur.

"And of course, you know Frau Dr. Scharf and Professor Dr. Scharf." She introduced Chadwick and Lattimer according to German custom, in which the wife assumes the honorifics of her husband. They politely shook hands and exchanged pleasantries in English.

In a corner, an Arab with a large turban sat cross-legged, plucking with both hands at a large stringed instrument that lay on his lap. The music was barely audible over the babble of German, English and Arabic. Most of the men were smoking. It was very hot.

Lattimer and Chadwick both grabbed tumblers of scotch whiskey, which they diluted with a splash of soda water. Mrs. Koepka took Chadwick by the hand and pushed her way to a tall young man standing by himself.

"Felix," she said, "this is Allan Chadwick. He's English." To Chadwick she said, "Felix Goelz. He's German."

They shook hands. "I think we are the younger end of this crowd," Chadwick said.

"My English is not gut," Goelz replied.

They stood in silence for a minute or two. Chadwick stared at Frau Scharf across the room, and then it came to him. He had met her at a hotel bar when he arrived on the troopship at Basra. At the time he was still smarting a little about the success that army chap had had at Cairo by so easily picking up a woman in a hotel bar. He was hoping then that he might emulate him at Basra. It was all a long time ago, but fortunately Margaret in Baghdad had taken in hand that part of his education.

He now looked at Frau Scharf with what he thought was the eye of an experienced man of the world. *She was getting on. She must be in her thirties*, he thought. *Still, she has kept her figure.*

Frau Scharf did look smart in a slim frock with a short jacket. She wore string of pearls above the modest décolleté of her dress.

Goelz saw Chadwick starring at Frau Scharf across the room. "You like?" he asked, nodding in the direction of the professor's wife.

Chadwick smiled, a little embarrassed at being so obvious.

"I think she may be, tch, *verfugbar*—" he searched for the English word, "—available, for a young mensch like you."

Chadwick lifted his eyebrows.

"I work mit Professor Scharf. He is very busy at Ur. I think she is, tch, *einsam, ach*—lonely." He patted Chadwick on the arm and went to get another drink.

Chadwick decided it might be fun to remind Mrs. Scharf that they had met a year earlier in Basra. He refilled his own glass and wandered through the party, keeping a discreet eye on Mrs. Scharf. He found Lattimer describing at length his visit to Krak des Chevalier to Dr. Rawlins.

Later on, as the party began to wind down, he noticed that Mrs. Scharf was alone for a few minutes. He walked over to her and said, "Lisa, so we meet again!"

She was surprised by his use of her first name, "Ja," she said. "We met at dig a few days past."

"No," said Chadwick. "I mean the time we first met in Basra in 1928. We met at the hotel bar. I bought you a drink."

Frau Scharf looked puzzled, then her face cleared. "Ja, ja," she said slowly. "I think you— forward, you were trying to—." Here her English collapsed.

Chadwick knew what she was trying to say. "I wish I had. Perhaps it's not too late."

Frau Scharf gave his hand a surreptitious squeeze. She was definitely interested. Then she withdrew her hand, saying, "Not private here. We could meet at a hotel sometime. Give me your address at Shaibah."

Chadwick jotted it down on one of his visiting cards, with the message, *Send telephone number.*

Soon after he left her side, Chadwick was accosted by Lattimer, who said, "Time for good-byes." They thanked Mrs. Koepka and went outside where taxis were waiting.

Hamid Mustafa had been watching carefully. He noticed Frau Scharf drop Chadwick's hand and look around quickly. Her thoughts were easy to read. He crossed over to her and said quietly to her in German, "Nice young man. Perhaps you would like to see him again?"

Frau Scharf was surprised but she said nothing. Mustafa began to scheme. A liaison between Frau Scharf and the young English officer might give him a little leverage over someone who was at the center of activities at Shaibah airfield. It might be useful someday.

He said to Frau Scharf, "I seem to spend most of my time in Baghdad these days. My house here is unoccupied while I am away."

Frau Scharf didn't know what to say.

"If you wish, you can borrow it if you need a little privacy."

She remained silent.

"I will leave an envelope with a key at my office here in Basra. Call and they will let you know if I am away and send the envelope to your pension."

"You're very kind," Frau Scharf said. "If I get bored with the same scenery here, I will let you know."

Chapter Twenty-Four

When Chadwick next read the duty roster, he saw he was due for a check flight with the squadron commander. As they walked out to the plane, Welch explained to him, "I see you have nearly five hundred hours of flying time. Within a year you should qualify as first pilot. I just want to make sure you're not developing any bad habits. Five hundred hours can be a critical time. You've learned to fly, got self-confidence and feel you can do anything. Over-confidence can lead to careless-ness."

They inspected a Vimy, climbed on board and Chadwick started the pre-flight checks. They were flying without crew. Chadwick pointed to the left engine and spoke to the airman standing by.

"Switches off."

The airman swung the propeller through a full turn.

"Switches on, contact."

The airman swung the propeller and the engine started and settled into a steady roar. Chadwick repeated the proce-dure with the right engine. When it was running well, he ran both engines to full rpm and tested the magnetos, one at a time. Then he throttled back and waved away the chocks. He began to taxi towards the take-off point. He checked carefully to make sure no planes were on approach to the landing area and opened up both engines. The great machine lumbered over the grass and reluctantly left the ground.

Welch pointed to the north and Chadwick eased the plane to the right. Welch pointed to the altimeter and signaled four with his fingers. They climbed to four thousand feet. Chad-wick trimmed the throttles and slightly leaned the mixture. The plane was running smoothly. Some distance on the right

Chadwick could see the massive ziggurat. He was expecting the C.O. to simulate engine failure by chopping back a throttle. When he did, he quickly made the corrective actions and pointed to a suitable forced landing area. The C.O. nodded and signaled he could open up the idling engine.

They flew along and then the C.O. passed him a message, *What is the azimuth of the moon?*

He thought quickly. He couldn't see the moon. He guessed it was in its first quarter, and wrote down, *160° true.*

The C.O. covered the compass with a cloth and wrote, *Take us home.*

Chadwick swung the plane onto a southerly heading, using the sun. He was pleased to see the quarter moon was on the nose. The ziggurat was a good landmark, and before long Chadwick had the airfield in sight. He half-expected the C.O. to throttle back an engine again but nothing happened. He flew downwind, made a wide turn and landed without difficulty.

They walked back to the crew room, dropped off their flying gear and parachutes, and the C.O. asked him into his office. "You're a competent pilot, Chadwick," he began, "and I don't think you're over-confident. If I have any criticism at all it may sound strange, but you're a little too brainy. The best pilots are at one with their machine. A sudden emergency, which is common in times of war, and the pilot acts completely from instinct and does the right thing. Right now, you're still thinking a bit like an engineer, working things out. There's nothing wrong with that, but I think with a little more experience, you and the plane will be a single unit. You'll be the perfect pilot. Thank you for a smooth ride. I think I can safely predict that our next trip will be your check-out as first pilot."

Chadwick went for lunch feeling pleased with himself. He knew that some day he would have to start working on examinations so that he could qualify for the next level of seniority, Flight Lieutenant. But that could wait.

Later in the week, his flight commander mentioned that the check flight went well, and then said to Chadwick, "How would you like a couple of days at Hinaidi? I have to take a Vimy up for some technical stuff. You can come as second pilot if you like." Chadwick agreed.

When they got back to Baghdad, he phoned the hospital and eventually managed to speak to Margaret. They agreed to meet in the hospital lobby the next day. He talked to the engineer at Hinaidi and discovered the plane was to be fitted with an experimental "Turn and Slip" indicator. Naturally, he was intrigued, and wanted to know what turned the gyro. The engineer said it ran off a vacuum, at seven thousand revolutions a minute.

"Where does the vacuum come from?" was his next question.

"Normally," the engineer replied patiently, "a vacuum pump would be fitted, as it is believed aircraft will carry several gyroscopically controlled instruments in the future. In this case, just for a test, we're tapping the inlet manifold of the port engine."

Chadwick looked quizzical.

"I know your next question," said the engineer before Chadwick could say anything. "The case is evacuated, and the incoming air spins the gyro. The flow is kept constant by a venturi."

"Sounds dashed clever," said Chadwick. "I'll be really interested to see how it performs."

In the afternoon of his second day he took a bus and walked into the hospital lobby. Margaret was waiting for him, dressed in a nurse's uniform.

"I only have a couple of hours," she said. "I had to swap some time just to get this much."

"You look very smart in your uniform," he said.

"So do you," she replied.

There was a hotel a few blocks away. Chadwick suggested a drink at the bar before the two hours evaporated. When they were comfortably seated with Pilsners in front of them, she wanted to know what he had been up to. Naturally, as his one-time and only partner in romance, he was eager to tell her about the French brothel.

"The French squadron have this maison de tolerance, that's a—," he began, but she interrupted him.

"I know enough French to work out what that is. Did you dip your pecker?"

"Of course not," he indignantly replied. Then he told her about the price list kept by the madam, and the number of variations.

"What was the cost of a fuck?" she wanted to know.

"A hundred francs," he told her.

"What's that in our money?" she asked.

"About a pound," he replied.

"Then you owe me a quid, Allan," she said.

He looked at her, not sure if she was joking or not. Then she burst out laughing.

Chadwick and Lattimer flew back to Shaibah the next day. They were both fascinated by the new instrument, but without a stopwatch they couldn't test its accuracy. Chadwick remembered spinning in the French plane and thought the instrument would be useful in a situation like that, although neither pilot had the slightest intention of ever spinning a Vimy. When they landed, they turned over the paperwork on the turn and slip indicator to the squadron engineering officer. Chadwick half hoped there would be a message from Lisa Scharf waiting for him but there was nothing

Lisa Scharf was having serious reservations about her behavior at Schuttzi's party. *I must have been mildly drunk, or perhaps it was the heat. Then that creepy Iraqi, Mustafa, sidled up and as good as told me I could use his house for an assignation if I wanted. The last thing I would ever do is put myself in his clutches. Then there was that nice English boy. He had come on a bit strong, but of course, young men of that age rarely thought of much except sex. And I mildly encouraged him. I must be going mad.*

Nevertheless, thinking about what she might get up to with Allan produced a warm glow.

Lisa Scharf had lunch with Mrs. Koepka once a week at her house. At lunch Maryana said, "Lisa, I think we'll skip lunch next week. My cook is planning to visit her mother in some remote village for a week. I'll take the chance to spend a few days in Baghdad."

Lisa surprised herself when she asked, "Could I borrow your house for a few days? It would be a great favor to me."

Maryana looked at her sharply. "What's the matter? Are you getting cabin fever?"

"Well, to tell the truth, there is someone. I would like to meet him in a private place. I'm too well known in Basra."

"Oh, it sounds too thrilling! Of course, you're welcome, but I want all the gory details afterwards."

Frau Scharf posted a letter to Allan Chadwick and asked him to call her at the pension. When they got in touch, she suggested a drink at a small hotel in the al-Ashar district, not popular with archaeologists. They arranged a rendezvous in the evening, a day ahead.

Chadwick showed up early and ordered a scotch at the bar. When she arrived, Chadwick looked at her carefully. She really wasn't as old as he had first thought. Their conversation was stilted until she asked Chadwick if he spoke French.

"Yes," he said. "I was just in Syria, and I practiced my French."

"Bon," she said. "My French is fair. I worked in Alsace Lorraine for a couple of years."

They sipped their drinks. She asked why he wanted to meet her.

"I think you're very attractive," he said, "and, perhaps a little—." Here his French faltered. "—alone," he said in English.

"We must be very careful." she said. "This is a very small town, so far as Europeans are concerned. You know Frau Koepka? She has lent me her house for a week, starting Saturday. Do you remember where it's located?"

"Yes, I remember. About five hundred meters from the square."

They sat for a while. "How old are you, Allan?" she asked.

"I'm twenty-three," he replied.

"I'm thirty-five," Lisa lied, without being asked. "When can you get off the base?"

"This Saturday I can leave after lunch, and I can get away most evenings."

"Take a taxi to the square, and walk from there," Lisa demanded.

Chadwick spent Friday in a fever-pitch of excitement, although he tried to keep a calm demeanor. He signed off the base as soon as he could on Saturday and took a taxi. Five minutes after stepping into the old square he was knocking on Frau Koepke's front door. Nobody seemed to have paid him any attention.

Lisa opened the door slightly right away. She let him squeeze into the house, then shut and locked the door. The curtains had all been drawn and the interior was quite dark. She put her arms round Allan and gave him a kiss. As she did so she ran her hand down the front of his trousers. "I see you have come ready," she said. She led the way into a bedroom.

"I've been ready since Thursday," Allan said.

Lisa slipped out of her gown and Allan had his clothes off in an instant. They fell on the bed and kissed again.

"I need warming up," Lisa said.

"Yes," Allan murmured. "Yes, you need your engine starting."

"What?" said Lisa.

"Nothing," said Allan. "Just an old Air Force joke."

She opened her legs and Allan's fingers soon had her moist. Lisa was a noisy lover and she moaned loudly as he entered. He plunged on, and she felt delicious to him, but in a minute, Lisa said, "Slowly, slowly, *Liebchen*, we have all day."

He held back as long as he could, but soon the anticipation was unbearable. Lisa screamed as he came, and he felt her internal convulsions. They were both covered in sweat. He lay by her side. "That was wonderful," he said.

They lay silently for a while and then Allan asked, "Should we be taking precautions?"

"Ach. Kurt and I tried for years to have a child when we were first married. The doctor said there was something wrong with my tubes. I have periods but something is wrong. So, bang away, lover, and have fun."

Allan didn't need a second invitation. Tumescence had returned and they frolicked the afternoon away. They had a shower together and Allan told her he had to return to the base, as he had signed out only for the afternoon.

"I should go down to my room, as well," said Lisa. "What about tomorrow afternoon?"

"There should be no problem," Allan told her.

They left the house one at a time. Chadwick strode briskly to the main square and caught a taxi. Frau Scharf walked slowly to her pension, where the landlady greeted her. "I have a message from your husband," she said. "He's coming to Basra for the weekend. I think he should be here soon."

Damn, thought Lisa. *That's going to complicate things.* There was no easy way to get a message back to Allan Chadwick. They had agreed that telephone messages should be kept to a minimum.

Kurt Scharf arrived at the pension an hour later. He apologized for his lateness and blamed the rail service from Nasiriyah. They went out for dinner and returned to the pension for a nightcap. Kurt was unusually attentive. Perhaps the pheromones had lingered, and when they went to bed, he made violent love to her. Lisa smiled to herself. *After the drought comes the flood.*

Chadwick made the trip to Mrs. Koepka's house on Sunday afternoon but, of course, there was nobody at home. So, he walked to the Shams al-Basra Hotel for a drink. There were a couple of British archaeologists at the bar. They told him heat conditions at the dig were intolerable and the British and German digs had closed down for the weekend. Chadwick put two and two together and concluded Lisa would be tied up for a day or two.

It was Thursday before they could make arrangements to use the house again. Mrs. Koepka was returning on Friday. When they met at the house, Lisa and Allan embraced in a way that showed real affection. Allan remembered her injunction, "Slowly." He resorted to solving arithmetic—what is thirty-seven times nineteen? — and kept his mind off the writhing, passionate woman lying beneath him. It worked for perhaps a minute before he surrendered to his lust.

When they were recovering from his first orgasm Lisa said, "What's next? What do you want to try now?"

It reminded him of the Madam's list, which he described to Lisa.

"Lucky Frenchmen," was her comment.

"Which one first?"

"I think the first line is a good place to start. I can think of a nice variation," she said. "Are you ready for action? Yes, I see you are."

She sat on his pelvis and impaled herself. She began to jog up and down, simultaneously contracting her womb.

"Oh, God! You're killing me, Lisa, you are killing me." Allan whispered.

"You are dying for a good cause. I like this position," Lisa groaned, "I can adjust the movement just so."

The sensations he was experiencing and the sight of her breasts bobbing in front of his eyes soon brought on a second orgasm.

Afterwards, Allan lay exhausted for a while. "Lisa," he said, "What are we going to do when Frau Koepka returns?"

"I don't know, but love finds a way," she said.

They finished the evening with a joint shower and a tentative exploration of cunnilingus, which Lisa said would be nicer at the beginning. She promised to write to him.

When Mrs. Koepka returned, the first thing she did was to invite Lisa Scharf over for coffee. Lisa Scharf knew she was in for a grilling. When she arrived, she apologized for the soiled sheets.

"Oh, don't worry about it. The Dhobi wallah will take care of it." She was agog to learn the details of Lisa Scharf's tryst.

"Schuttzi, I confess I met a man here, but I was insane, mad, unthinking. I'm a married woman, and my husband is highly respected. I must ask you to say nothing. It could destroy my marriage. I'm going to sever all contact with the man involved." Lisa Scharf looked desperate.

Mrs. Koepka was very disappointed. Very rarely did such juicy gossip come her way. But Lisa was her friend, and she didn't have that many in Basra.

"Of course, dear Lisa, I'll be as quiet as the grave."

When Mrs. Scharf returned to her room, she wrote a short, poignant letter in French to Allan Chadwick. Then she sent a letter to her husband. She claimed the heat was killing her, and she was fed up with living in a small room, alone mostly, and it would be better to return to Germany.

When Allan Chadwick received her letter, he was thunderstruck. But he could see it her way. She had everything to lose. If the facts came out, he would just be considered a rake.

At the base, Chadwick flung himself into work. He asked the squadron adjutant for the requirements of the Flight Lieutenant's examination. He bothered the engineering officer for all the details of the new turn and slip indicator. He found a magazine article which predicted that the introduction of gyroscopically controlled instruments would enable pilots to fly "blind," in cloud or bad weather. He nagged the patient engineering officer to get these instruments for evaluation. The one thing he did not do was think about Lisa Scharf.

Chapter Twenty-Five

The air activity at Shaibah base got busier and busier. Sometimes 314 Squadron had six bombers in the air or being refueled. Roaming gangs targeted Europeans in Basra. Public meeting places like the cinema were closed. There were frequent attacks of arson.

Eventually, Welch sought out the squadron intelligence officer, Becket. "Bob," he asked, "What's going on? What do you hear from HQ in Baghdad?"

"Frankly, sir, I think they're as confused as we are. They're bringing down another squadron from Mosul. That should ease the load on 314."

"Listen, Bob, this isn't just the Bedouins stealing a few sheep or robbing a convoy. It's an insurrection, and it's getting worse. Somebody's running it. It smells like an organized plan."

"You might well be right, sir. But for what purpose? The only strategic assets are the port, the refinery and the oil wells. Maybe you could include the railway. If those were threatened in any way, HQ would bring in troops from India. So far, the raids have been cut and run, with no salient objective."

"What about that Arab you mentioned a while ago, Mustafa? Is he up to his thick neck in all this?"

"If he is, he's been very careful. I believe he's under watch, but that sort of thing is handled by HQ. I only know the crumbs that filter down to me. My job is to liaise with the squadron, the Armored Car Corps and HQ. Very low-level stuff."

Becket had noted an item in a two-week-old British newspaper that finally had arrived in Baghdad. It reported the unexpected success of the National Socialist Party in the German elections. He wondered if this was connected with events in Iraq.

151

Herr Weiss received a summons to party headquarters in Munich. He was met by a senior aide to Herr Hitler. "Herr Hitler is pleased with way the situation is developing in Iraq. I have a message for your ears only," the aide said. "An incursion will be made into northern Iraq in December. Every effort should be made to delay British forces being transferred to the north. That is all."

Weiss thanked him and made his way to the Hauptbahnhof. He thought as he settled down in the carriage, *This was a game Hamid Mustafa has played before.* He composed a long telegram in his mind as the train thundered north.

Frau Scharf arrived in Hamburg the same week. Her husband had congratulated her on her perspicacity in leaving Basra, in view of the unstable atmosphere that had developed in Iraq. He told her that he, too, would be returning home soon. She travelled to Bonn to open their house a little earlier than planned. As the train click-clacked its way east, she thought about the tumultuous events a thousand miles south that had resulted in her being on that train. *Ah, Kurt, it's a good thing you don't know the whole story,* she thought.

The revolution came a few weeks later when thousands of Kurds attacked oil wells near Mosul. They were joined by thousands more who crossed the border from Turkey. The British garrison in Mosul hunkered down, and reinforcements were dispatched from Baghdad. A Vimy was shot down by a fighter, believed to be Turkish, but no markings were observed. The crew was killed. If the fighter was indeed Turkish, this represented a serious escalation in Iraq. Discreet diplomatic questions were made in Ankara. All Turkish involvement was denied.

In Germany, the Nazi Party quickly seized the reins of power. The Reichstag was burned to the ground by an arsonist, ostensibly a communist, but more likely it was a Nazi false flag operation. Emergency powers were granted to deal with the alleged coup.

Then President Hindenburg died. Whether or not he received a push into Valhalla would never be known. Hitler refused an autopsy, stating it was sacrilegious to mutilate such a fine soldier after death. Hitler assumed all leadership roles and declared himself the Fuhrer.

All of this passed way over the head of Frau Scharf, who went to see her doctor because she had missed a period. To the doctor's surprise, he discovered she was about two months pregnant. When she told her husband, who had returned from Iraq, she reminded him of their night at the pension in Basra. He was overjoyed.

The consequences of the Nazi victory in Germany were serious for the British in Iraq. German foreign policy was to create a separate Kurdish state in northern Iraq which included the oil fields. Although this did not come to pass, at least for the time being, there was almost continuous warfare in the north.

314 Squadron was moved back to Hinaidi airfield, although the fighting had not moved that far south. Most flights were

routine patrols and reconnaissance. Sabotage of the railway to Basra was common. The line was now included in the patrols, but most of the damage to the line occurred at night.

Much of the north-south traffic was carried by boat to Baghdad or Mosul on the Tigris River, to the satisfaction of Hamid Mustafa, but he was now facing competition from a large company based in Baghdad. He explained the situation to Herr Weiss in a coded telegram. Shortly afterwards his competition began to suffer from mysterious sinkings, usually at anchor.

Chadwick was kept busy, with five or six patrols a week. When he wasn't flying, he pursued the idea of operating an aircraft entirely by instrument readings. He believed the tactical advantage of air power was greatly diminished by the inability to fly at night or in heavy weather.

With difficulty, he managed to get a hold of Margaret and set up a date at the hotel bar near the hospital. He arrived late but she had sat it out. She said, "Allan, before you say anything, I want to show you something."

He looked at her quizzically, "Yes?"

She opened her left hand, and on the third finger was a small ring. It took a while for the import to sink in. "You're engaged!" he blurted out.

"Yes, to a doctor at the hospital. I'm sorry. We had a jolly good fling, but a girl has to think of her future."

"He makes a lot of money, I suppose," Allan started.

"A lot more than a pilot officer."

"I'm a flying officer now," Allan said. "Got promoted."

"Allan, let's not quarrel. In a few years he could be a consultant. That's good pay!"

"Well, I can only wish you good luck," he said sullenly.

Margaret said, "This is the last time we'll meet, probably, unless there's another Hospital Hop. The hospital is a rumor mill running on full steam. That's why I wanted to meet you here, away from the prying eyes."

Chapter Twenty-Six

Welch had encouraged Chadwick to keep interested in the problem of flying an aircraft purely by reference to instruments and asked for a list of the instruments that would be needed. Chadwick sat in the C.O.'s office to explain what he had discovered so far.

"The Americans are really pushing this, sir," he told Welch. "You would need five basic instruments plus a compass. Two would be gyroscopic, so we're looking at an expensive installation."

Welch thanked him for the list. When he had a moment to spare, he called in the squadron adjutant, asking, "Remember that letter about our bombsight we got from Farnborough, a year or two ago? Can you find it?"

"Certainly, sir."

When he had it in hand, Welch composed a letter to the corresponding officer explaining the interest in the squadron in instrument flying. He asked if it would be possible to obtain a set of instruments for field evaluation. When it arrived, the letter caused a stir at Farnborough. Sending equipment directly to an operational unit was not normal procedure. However, the head of the group investigating "blind" flying was a civilian scientist and he took on his own responsibility to send a carefully packed box of instruments to 314 Squadron, along with a vacuum pump.

When it arrived, Welch created a small group to install them in a Vimy. The group consisted of the engineering officer, Ashurst, two flight sergeants and Chadwick. When they decided on an appropriate layout, the flight sergeants organized construction of a panel to hold the instruments, which was mounted on springs. The vacuum pump was adapted to run off an engine, and a light was placed at the top of the panel to illuminate the instruments.

After a dry run on the ground, Welch and Chadwick took the plane into the air with great anticipation. At first, the results were disappointing. They found that without some way to blot out their view of the horizon outside the plane, it was impossible to concentrate entirely on the instruments. They also found it was extremely difficult to ignore their normal flying instincts when these were contrary to the information on the instruments. The C.O. concluded it was going to take a lot of training before pilots could safely fly just on instruments.

Chadwick loved the challenge and flew many hours in the instrumented Vimy with different first pilots. He designed a visor that obscured his view outside the plane if he kept his head still, rather like the blinkers used on horses. Chadwick soon found that using the traditional magnetic compass, which was mounted on the inside of the cockpit wall, was very inconvenient. The natural motion for the pilot was to scan the instruments one at a time in a rotary pattern. Deflecting his gaze to the side and down disrupted the rhythm.

One day Chadwick had a "eureka" moment. All gyros worked on the same principle—the gyro remained fixed in space if it was mounted on suitable gimbals while the outside world moved. If a gyro was initially aligned with north, it would remain that way even if the plane turned. It behaved exactly like a compass needle. That way it could join the other instruments on the panel.

He talked to the engineering officer about his idea. The officer, in a slightly condescending way, said, "They've been using gyrocompasses on ships for years, at least since the war."

"Well, why don't they use them on planes?" Chadwick asked.

"I don't know," he replied. "Perhaps they're too big."

Chadwick asked Welch to contact the scientist at Farnborough who had originally sent the instruments to see if gyrocompasses for planes were being developed.

The military situation in the north suddenly turned worse. Large numbers of Kurdish tribesmen began gathering on the Turkish side of the border. The weather in early 1931, with plenty of low cloud and rain, was not good for flying. The British moved Assyrian mercenaries into the area, but they began to attack their traditional foes, the local Kurds, instead of remaining as a cohesive force.

314 Squadron was suddenly assigned to an airfield near Kirkup. It was not a permanent base; accommodation was in tents. Six bombers made the one-hundred-and-fifty-mile journey from Hinaidi. Chadwick made the trip by truck, along with about half the squadron's pilots and all the ground staff. The British had spies on the Turkish side of the border. They reported a large attack on Kirkup was likely. Kirkup was an important town, as it controlled passes into the mountains to the north and housed oil pumping stations.

Morale in the squadron sank as the weather prevented flying, day after day. Welch planned a reconnaissance into the Turkish border. He proposed to take the instrumented Vimy and asked Chadwick to fly as second pilot. They took off in marginal conditions and flew north. They flew just below the cloud cover, but the occasional low cloud forced them to refer more and more to the instruments. Chadwick handled the controls while the C.O. kept a watch on ground activity. Cold and slashing rain was blown into the cockpit. The rivers below them were swollen.

They flew along the main road that led to the border. On the Turkish side, the road passed over a substantial stone bridge that was being battered by the rushing river, which carried a large assortment of branches and small trees. They pressed on into Turkish air space. A mile beyond was a large assembly of tents, vehicles and camel enclosures. Suddenly Welch punched Chadwick's shoulder and pointed. Almost spectral as it flew in and out of wispy cloud was the outline of a small monoplane on their right. It was flying a parallel course and slowly drew ahead.

They were now flying a little more than five hundred feet above the ground. Visibility was poor. Chadwick concentrated on the instruments, particularly the artificial horizon and the vertical speed indicator. Every thirty seconds he snatched a quick glance at the compass. He was sweating, despite the cold. Welch nudged him and pointed south. Chadwick started a rate one turn to the left. He had learned that as soon as the wings lost lift due to the bank angle, he would have to pull the nose up a touch and to keep a sharp eye on the vertical speed. He straightened out on a reciprocal course and flew steadily for twenty minutes. If anything, the cloud base was lowering, and they were flying blind most of the time.

Then Welch spotted the airfield. The ground crew had laid out smudge pots to mark the wind direction. He took control, made a graceful landing and then made a beeline for the intelligence officer, Becket.

"Bob, the first thing is that they have an air patrol on the border. The second thing is that there is a large concentration of men a mile or two north of the bridge. The bridge should be attacked as soon as possible."

"How can they have an air patrol? The Turkish Air Force is primitive."

"Someone is doing it for them," guessed Welch. He turned to Chadwick, "You did very well. Your instrument flying practice is paying off."

A bombing raid on the bridge was approved by HQ in Baghdad. It only remained to find a good weather window. Obviously, time was of the essence, as the bridge needed to be destroyed before any insurgency began.

Welch called a meeting of all the bomber crews and told them he had made the decision for the strike for the next day. He told them the weather would not be ideal, but he hoped they would be able to bomb from seven hundred to a thousand feet above the ground. This would provide a reasonable chance of not being struck by flying debris. Each plane would carry two two-hundred-pound high explosive bombs. They would bomb in turn, considering the narrow target, flying parallel to the road. After release, the plane would have to make a sharp turn to avoid flying over the encampment, which would certainly attract a lot of small arms fire. A Flight would be followed by B Flight, each plane separated by about half a mile.

Welch mentioned the possibility of fighter interference, which drew some gasps of surprise. To provide some protection, he told them, the earlier flight would fly a second circuit shadowing B Flight as the planes made their run. After the second flight has unloaded, they would head for home. Welch would lead A Flight, with Chadwick as his second pilot. Lattimer would lead B Flight.

The next day dawned gloomy, as expected, with a cloud ceiling of a thousand feet. It was cold and damp. Welch navigated. He had carefully noted landmarks on the previous reconnaissance flight. As they flew north towards the Turkish border, the cloud base slowly lowered. When they had the bridge in sight, the clouds were only five hundred to seven hundred feet above the ground. Welch dispersed the formation with an arm-waving gesture.

He flew south a for minute and then turned and commenced the bombing run. Chadwick kept a close eye on the periscope, which he centered on the road. They felt the sudden lift as the aimer released both bombs, and then Welch flung the plane left. When Chadwick looked back at the bridge, it appeared undamaged. He watched the second bomber make a run and drop its load. One bomb exploded on the road, but the second landed on the bridge itself, which still stood as the smoke settled. The third bomber dropped a little early and both bombs landed on the road. Then they saw the plane stagger, a large piece of masonry thrown up by explosion had hit the tail plane, but it continued to fly.

Now B Flight was running in. That was when Chadwick saw the fighter. It was approaching Lattimer's plane from ahead on the right. Muzzle flashes showed it had opened fire. Welch saw the fighter at the same time and he immediately pulled their craft into the clouds. In a split second, they were depending on the instruments. It was black and dark in the heavy cloud. After about ten seconds, Welch put the nose down, and they popped out into daylight just as the fighter flashed under them. The front gunner put a long burst into the fighter. The pilot slumped in the cockpit, but the plane flew on.

Things were happening too fast for Chadwick to comprehend everything. Lattimer had positioned his bombs nicely and both landed on the bridge, which began to collapse. As the rest of B Flight lined up for a bombing run, Welch was torn. He wanted to observe the bombing results, but he also wanted to follow the disabled fighter which was flying steadily in a southwest direction and slowly losing height. He decided to follow the fighter. It crossed the border and finally struck the ground at a shallow angle. It did not splinter the way most planes did when it crashed. It appeared to be in fairly good shape. Smoke rose from the engine.

To Chadwick's surprise, Welch put the Vimy into a shallow turn and began to lose height. The ground was level, and he realized Welch intended to land near the wreck. He made a masterly landing and taxied towards the smoking fighter. He ordered the front gunner and Chadwick to run to the wreck and try to save the pilot. As Chadwick approached, he saw the plane was metal, which explained why it had not shattered in crashing. It was painted green, without markings of any kind. Flames were beginning to lick around the engine cowling. He and the gunner stood on the broken undercarriage and reached into the cockpit. The pilot was inert, and dark red blood soaked his flying suit. They managed to haul him out before the cockpit was engulfed.

As they laid the pilot on the ground, Chadwick saw that he was not young. He opened his eyes and stared intensely at Chadwick and uttered one word, "*Mutti.*"

Chadwick's heart felt like bursting with compassion. He wiped his eyes. He sensed Welch standing over him. The Vimy stood a hundred yards away, the engines idling. Just below the clouds the squadron circled overhead.

"Is he dead?" Welch asked.

"I think so," Chadwick replied.

Welch stared into the face of the dead pilot, trying to discover his nationality.

"I think he's German," Chadwick said.

Welch had no scruples. He unbuttoned the bloody flying suit and looked inside for papers. He found none. "There's a border post not far from here. We'll fly over and drop them a note to retrieve the body and search the wreck, if anything is left."

They took off, made the detour and flew back to the airfield. Lattimer told him the bridge had been destroyed. Welch briefed the intelligence officer on the downing of the fighter and told him where he could find the body of the pilot.

That night they had a big party in the tent that served as the mess bar, but Chadwick couldn't get over the pilot's eyes as he died. He wondered if he would die like that. He went to bed early but found it difficult to fall asleep.

HQ in Baghdad were very pleased at the success of the raid by 314 Squadron, though no public recognition was made because the border war officially did not exist. Intelligence came out with an assessment of the fighter that had attacked the squadron. The plane was originally French, probably shipped to Turkey in crates and assembled at a secret airfield near the border. It was an all-metal construction using mainly duralumin, probably built by the Wibault company. The pilots and most ground crew were thought to be German veterans of the war. The intelligence department in Baghdad believed the raid had considerably delayed, if not postponed, a planned attack on Kirkup.

Chadwick was standing in front of a mirror, shaving, on a quiet Sunday morning after the raid. He was debating whether to attend Sunday Service. The Chaplin was a friend, a quiet man in his late forties, who had lost all his faith in the trenches during the war. When the Royal Air Force was formed in 1918, he transferred from the Army. He felt the death rate was bound to be lower, but he was wrong. He conscientiously attended to those who still believed and prayed for his own retirement.

Chadwick found him an introspective, mature person to talk to. As these thoughts flashed through his mind, he was suddenly brought down to earth by the loud roar of engines and then the staccato ripple of machine gun fire. He dashed out of his tent in time to see two green monoplanes disappearing over the airfield boundary. As he stood, indecisive, three more planes, no more than a hundred feet above the ground, zoomed in from the north. Their machine guns chattered as they as they aimed at the rows of tents. Chadwick flung himself to the ground. The noise soon passed. He wiped his face, put on a jacket and dashed to the encampment. Airmen were already carrying wounded from the shattered tents.

He stopped a sergeant. "Did they get the Vimys?"

"The first two did, sir," the sergeant replied.

Chadwick ran towards the flight line. Miraculously, there was no sign of fire. Men were unhitching Vickers guns from the Scarff rings in the Vimys. They did not elevate enough when mounted to provide effective anti-aircraft fire. Other men were bringing ammunition pans. The C.O. was directing this activity. He clearly expected a return attack.

"What can I do to help, sir?" Chadwick shouted above the racket.

"Get over to the tents and help with triage," Welch told him.

The squadron doctor and two nursing orderlies were busy near the tents. Wounded men were lying on stretchers. He approached the doctor, who glanced up and said, "We've run out of stretchers. Organize a party to bring tables from the dining tents."

Chadwick sped off. The sky remained quiet and the attackers did not return.

Ten men were badly wounded; one died during the night. The squadron received a reprimand from Baghdad HQ over its lack of anti-aircraft defenses, but of course, no one had expected an attack from the air. As a mild punishment, almost the whole squadron manpower was set to work filling sandbags, and revetments were built to protect each parked aircraft. Four aircraft had been damaged, but within ten days the squadron could muster six serviceable Vimys.

After a month at the forward airfield, 314 Squadron was ordered back to Hinaidi, much to everyone's relief. Back at Baghdad, Chadwick was pleased to find that Farnborough had sent them an experimental gyro compass. It had vertical numerals on the edge of a disc attached to a gyro. The case was the same size as the instruments received earlier. They ran it on a bench, and it performed admirably. An accompanying letter warned them that the gyro would slowly lose accuracy as it precessed over time and the compass would have to be re-aligned with the master magnetic compass now and again.

When they got the time, the flight sergeants willingly fabricated another panel so that the compass could be added to the earlier instruments. Welch and Chadwick, as pilots, gave their opinion on the best layout. Everyone agreed the artificial horizon should be in the center. On the left, they placed instruments showing horizontal motion, airspeed and direction, one above the other. On the right, they placed indicators of vertical motion—altimeter and vertical speed. The turn and slip indicator was placed under the artificial horizon.

Chadwick flew with several qualified first pilots, and some adapted easily to the strange way of flying without looking at the outside horizon, while others had difficulty ignoring their instincts. Lattimer took a photograph of the instrument panel they had made with his Kodak Brownie, and Welch included it in his letter of thanks to the scientist at Farnborough. He also mentioned in his letter that a recent successful operation was greatly aided by the instrumented Vimy and added that, in his opinion, a good deal of training would be necessary before pilots were qualified to fly blind, which might require special two-seater trainer aircraft with one pilot on look-out while the other was practicing blind flying.

Chapter Twenty-Seven

At lunch the adjutant asked Chadwick to stop by his office. "You've got ten days of leave coming up," the adjutant said. "I can get you on a service flight from here to Cairo, if you like. Shepheard's Hotel gives a discount to serving officers."

Chadwick suddenly realized that the thought of leave was wonderful. To get away from rigid hours and flying in cold planes was just what he craved. "Yes," he said. "Please set it up."

Two weeks later he found himself at Heliopolis Airfield at Cairo, disembarking from an RAF Vernon transport. After searching for his suitcase, he caught a bus into Cairo and checked into Shepheard's Hotel. It was very expensive, even with the service discount, but Chadwick reasoned he had spent virtually nothing in the past two years. A little luxury for a few days would do him good

A grand avenue ran past the hotel. He settled into a comfortable wicker easy chair on the terrace, with a beer in hand, and watched the traffic, the camels, carts and pedestrians. He was very tired. After a light meal he went to bed early.

The next morning, he was served a typically English breakfast of eggs and bacon, even though the day promised to be hot. He decided the Cairo Museum would be the first stop on his agenda. The museum was dedicated to the funeral practices of the Old Kingdom. He found after a few hours that he could probably spend his whole leave there—the treasures heaped in room after room were fascinating. The mummies with black, wizened skin were slightly frightening. He could not believe the standard of workmanship achieved by artisans more than four thousand years ago.

He left in the middle of the afternoon, having seen a small percentage of the displays, and walked back to the hotel, past crowded alleys with small stalls selling spices, cloth, copper pots, and every variety of goods imaginable. Old men sat cross-legged smoking hookahs. In the hotel lobby, he bought a six-day-old British newspaper. There was no news of Iraq, but the financial crisis in the U.S. and much of Europe dominated the headlines.

He went to the American Bar, known familiarly as the Long Bar, not because of its size, but because of the time it took to get a drink. He was able to get a beer promptly and moved to a small table by himself. Most of the men at the bar seemed to be servicemen in mufti, civilian clothes. There was a sprinkling of well-dressed women, and his mind flashed back to the bar he visited when he got off the troopship in Port Said. It seemed like ages ago, and certainly a lot had happened to him since then.

Naturally, his thoughts then turned to women, and he looked at the ones sitting at the bar. All seemed to be in animated conversations with men nearby. He was thinking fondly of Margaret when his thoughts were interrupted by a gruff voice with a Midland accent asking if he minded sharing his table. The place had filled up and he hurriedly said. "No, no, of course not, sit down."

A burly man plonked down next to him, held out his hand and said, "Douglas."

Chadwick shook his hand and replied. "Allan."

"Army?"

"Air Force."

"Really? Not many of your fellows in Cairo."

"I'm on leave, just arrived couple of days ago from Baghdad."

"Is that so? How are things in Iraq? Plenty of action?"

"Oh, we keep pretty busy." Chadwick nodded towards the bar. "How's the action here?"

Douglas shrugged. "I drop in from time to time, but things are much the same. Those broads are mostly Americans, looking for a little exotic adventure in mysterious Egypt."

They sat in silence for a few minutes, and then Douglas said, "I'm billeted here, been here for years. If you like, I could show you a few spots. What did you do today?"

"I spent the day at the Cairo Museum," Allan replied.

"Ah, an intellectual. That's good."

"Not really," Allan responded. "I know next to nothing of Egyptian history, but I know craftsmanship when I see it."

"Look, my name is Larson. I'm a captain in the military police. I get around a fair amount. I have a friend who is doing some digging here, an archaeologist. Normally they won't let you anywhere near the Pyramids, but he has some pull. Would you like a conducted tour?"

"That would be terrific!" Allan replied. "My name is Chadwick, Flying Officer Allan Chadwick. I fly Vimy bombers when they want to scare someone."

"Much of my work here involves the Crown property," Larson offered. "Did you know the Army has over a hundred thousand acres of fuel dumps, ammunition storage, not to mention food, armaments, you name it, between here and Port Said? For a poor country like this one, that's a terrible temptation. I'm kept pretty busy. Next time I tour a site, would you like to come along?"

"Yes," replied Chadwick. "If you have time."

"A pleasure. Tell you what, meet here at lunch time tomorrow. I'm off to inspect some food warehouses. Give you a chance to see a bit of the countryside."

The following day, Chadwick enjoyed a leisurely breakfast and a stroll in the area near the hotel. He met Douglas Larson as planned and got into his Austin 7, which was parked in front of the hotel. They drove through the suburbs of Cairo, which mostly consisted of tents and ramshackle wooden huts sheltered by palm trees. After a spell of open countryside, they arrived at a large military depot. Sturdy wire fences protected the perimeter, and the buildings inside were single-story galvanized iron huts.

Larson explained he was there because of a break-in. Thieves had tunneled under the wire and broken the door of a hut containing wooden chests of tea.

He spoke to the sergeant in charge of the guard. "Sergeant McSlie, I think? Captain Larson."

"Aye, sir. I do remember ye," replied the sergeant, with a strong Scottish accent. He saluted, which Larson returned.

"What patrols did you have posted?" Larson questioned.

"Two men inside the perimeter. They circled the depot every two hours. It was very dark. Nobody noticed the hole until daylight."

"How much did they take?" asked Captain Larson.

"They smashed in four cases and pretty well scooped all the tea out. They must have used bags to get the tea back under the fence."

"We're talking about four hundred pounds. Let's go and have a look at the hole," said Larson.

They all climbed in the diminutive Austin and drove along the fence. Chadwick tagged along. He had not been introduced to the sergeant.

"Stop here," said the sergeant.

"Please stay clear of the loose dirt," commanded Captain Larson. He went forward himself, peering for footprints. "Quite a number of men, I guess. No sign of camel prints." He continued examining the dirt. "Yes, you can see the marks left when they dragged the bags under the fence. I would say half dozen were needed to pull off this job."

They drove back to the entrance gate and walked inside the fence to the hole. Larson again made them stand back while he examined the pile of loose earth. "Some of this hole was made by digging downwards, not upwards," he said.

"Maybe they widened it to get the bags out," the sergeant suggested.

Larson grunted. "Let's have a look inside."

Hundreds of tea chests were stacked in the hut. The shattered lids from four chests were propped against a stack. Four chests lay on their side, the tinfoil inside shining dully. Dried tea leaves were scattered all over the concrete floor.

"The bags were no more than eighteen inches wide," Larson said, "judging by the marks they left. So, they needed at least a dozen, if not more, to carry this much tea. Those bags must have been carried in. They knew what they were going for."

He turned to the sergeant, and asked, "Do the wogs often get in here?"

"If there's an inventory change, yes sir, wogs do the laboring."

"Let me know when this hut was last opened to add or remove chests."

They went back to the car, and Larson reminded McSlie to send him the information he had requested. As they drove back to Cairo, Larson said, "There was some inside help there. The thieves knew what they wanted and where to find it. Who helped them is not clear, but we have our little ways. We'll find out. McSlie hates the wogs. A few months ago, he caught one inside the perimeter, forced him to the ground and knelt on his chest with his knees on his upper arms, to disable him. Then he gouged out an eye with his thumb. He grew up in a tough part of Glasgow, the Gorbals. Sorry I didn't introduce you. Your presence will keep McSlie guessing, that's a good thing."

They drove in silence back to the hotel. As he dropped off Chadwick, Larson said, "I'll leave a message at the desk for you concerning the Pyramids. If we go, wear old clothes, it's dirty inside. Cheerio."

Chadwick had a drink at the bar without talking to anyone. None of the women scattered along its length showed the slightest interest in him. After a light but expensive dinner at the hotel, he went to bed and read.

There was no message for him at the desk in the morning. He took a tram down a street parallel to the Nile and enjoyed browsing the myriad small shops and stalls. The smell was unique— a mixture of exhaust fumes, camel dung, spices and incense.

When he returned to the hotel, Douglas Larson had left a message. They were to meet at nine a.m. the next morning outside the hotel. He made his way to the now familiar bar. It was less crowded than it had been. He wasn't sure what he wanted to happen, but he squeezed in next to a middle-aged woman and ordered a beer. He noticed her glass was empty.

"Good afternoon," he said politely. "Can I get you a drink?"

The woman swung round. "That's very kind. Gin." She looked at him appraisingly while he signaled the bartender.

When her drink came, he tipped his glass and said, "Cheers."

"Cheers," she said. "From what I hear about what the Brits pay you Guardians of the Empire, I should buy *you* a drink."

"We serve out of sheer patriotism," he replied in the same vein.

"That's a wonderful accent you've got," she said. "Where're you from?"

"I'm from Liverpool," he said. "The accent is pure north of England."

"Well, I think it's wonderful. My name's Mavis. I'm from Schenectady, Nooo York."

"Allan," Chadwick relied. "Pleasure to meet you, Mavis." He paused, "Are you enjoying Cairo?"

"It's dirty, and it smells, but this joint isn't so bad," she replied.

"Have you tried the Cairo Museum?" he asked.

"Oh, yeah, all those mummies. It's spooky!"

"What about the Pyramids and the Sphinx?" he persisted.

"Well, they're pretty impressive, but you can't go inside—unless you're dead." She laughed at her own joke. She looked at a man who was signaling from the other side of the room.

"There's my husband. Gotta go. Thanks for the drink." She slid off the barstool and made her way across the room. Chadwick watched her go with mixed emotions. He hadn't seriously thought of trying to pick her up, but she seemed like a nice, breezy person with a sense of humor. He would have liked to have talked to her some more.

In the morning he spotted Douglas's car waiting outside the hotel. He climbed in and they drove west through streets crowded with cars, streetcars, donkeys and a vast number of pedestrians, dressed in all manner of clothing, from western suits with Trilbys, to fully cloaked Arabs wearing keffiyehs.

Soon the great Pyramid dominated the view. In front was the battered remains of the sphinx. Larson drew up to a low modern building and they went inside. He introduced Chadwick to a tall, aesthetic-looking man.

"Earl, this is my friend Allan Chadwick. Allan, this is the distinguished archaeologist Dr. Earl Newby." They shook hands as Douglas continued. "Earl, I'm very obliged to you for taking a few minutes off your work. Allan has travelled a long way to be here, and I just felt it would be great if he could see inside the Great Pyramid."

"I'll be very happy to show you a little," said Dr. Newby with a strong Midwestern American accent. As they walked towards the great heap of limestone blocks, Dr. Newby began talking. "It was built about forty-five hundred years ago as a tomb for the Pharaoh Khufu. It's believed to have been constructed in only about twenty years, an astonishing feat requiring hundreds of thousands of laborers."

"Were they slaves?" asked Chadwick.

"It used to be thought so," replied the archaeologist, "but modern opinion is swinging away from that notion. The blocks are cut so accurately it's believed the work was mostly done by skilled artisans. There are three chambers inside the pyramid. The upper one, almost in the center of that great mass, is the King's chamber, although a mummy has never been found. Below that is the Queen's Chamber. Again, no body has ever been found. The pyramid was looted in antiquity. They're both reached by long passages originally blocked by massive granite slabs. The looters tunneled round all of them."

As they approached the Pyramid, he continued. "It will take too long today to get to those upper chambers. I'll take you to the lower chamber, which is unique because it's chiseled out of the bedrock on which the Pyramid stands. It's basically the basement. We'll use the original entrance. After the king was buried, the entrance was hidden by alabaster casing stones, which looked like the rest of the Pyramid. Now, all the casing stones are gone and what you see today is the underlying structure."

They reached the entrance on the north side, and workers helped them scramble up the blocks to the massive portal. They greeted the doctor enthusiastically, "Morning Doc! What are you looking for today?"

He grinned and ushered the visitors inside. A narrow, dark tunnel sloped downward, illuminated by dim electric bulbs strung from wires. They slowly and cautiously descended in the corridor until the floor levelled off and they entered a huge cavernous space. In the low yellow light, Chadwick could see that two walls had been chiseled smooth, but the rest of the space was lumpy rock. The ceiling was flat and as he stared at it, Dr. Newby said, "We're standing underneath a few million tons of rock. That the whole thing has survived for over four thousand years, including earthquakes, is a miracle."

Chadwick could almost sense the immense pressure bearing down on where he stood. There was not a sound, only absolute stillness. Then the lights went out and they were plunged into Stygian darkness.

"Damn," said Newby. "This happens all the time."

Deprived of vision, Chadwick felt completely disoriented.

"Don't move," the archaeologist said. "The floor is uneven. You'll trip and fall."

Chadwick had never experienced in his whole life such darkness. It was palpable. "What happens now?" he asked.

"Oh, someone will change a fuse in a minute or two," Newby replied. The silence was broken by the sound of a match scraping on sandpaper when Dr. Newby lit a match. After a few minutes the lights flickered into life, and he continued. "We don't know what this space was used for. Possibly it was going to be the king's burial chamber, and then they changed their minds and it was never finished."

"What is your particular interest in the pyramid, Doctor Newby?" Chadwick asked.

"Oh, a number of things. I'm interested in the looting that occurred after the pharaoh was entombed. There are many suggestive clues. For example, when the robbers broke in, they tunneled through the interior limestone at just the right angle to avoid the granite blocks, suggesting an intimate knowledge of the interior. So, the break-in occurred within a generation of the king dying. Quite a few in the palace must have been in on it. I'm looking to written evidence in the hieroglyphics of the period."

They began to move back up the narrow passage and eventually reached the entrance, where the bright sunshine hurt their eyes. Going back to the car, Chadwick thanked Doctor Newby and Douglas Larson for the mind-boggling experience. They pushed their way back to the car through the throng of touts that had begun to gather.

"I can't thank you enough," Chadwick said as they drove back to the hotel.

"Look, old chap, I'm afraid I shall be very busy the next few days. When are you leaving?"

"Wednesday," Chadwick told him.

"Right, we'll have a drink before you go." When he parked at the hotel, Larson jotted a few things down and gave a scrap of paper to Chadwick. "Here's a few suggestions to keep you busy. I'll call before Wednesday."

Chadwick followed up on most of Captain Larson's suggestions. He enjoyed a sumptuous presentation of "Aida" at the Khedivial Opera House and was delighted to learn it was first performed in Cairo in 1871 to celebrate the opening of that very same theatre. He balanced his cultural level by roaring with laughter at a burlesque, which also featured a few girls from the Folies Bergère. He saw his first talking movie at the Diana Cinema, "Anna Christie," with Greta Garbo. He was very impressed by the technology of talkies and determined to know more about how it was accomplished. He felt he was living in an age of technical miracles. During the days he toured the bazaars and Nile waterfront. Most afternoons he drank a coffee on the terrace at Shepheard's Hotel and made casual contact with several long-term residents, who also gave him advice on how to spend time in Cairo.

Captain Larson met him at the Long Bar on the day before he left. He was pleased Chadwick's visit had gone so well. Chadwick asked him if he had solved the tea robbery case.

"Ah, yes, that case. One of the guards had been bribed. Open and shut."

"Does most of your work involve theft of Crown property?" Chadwick asked.

"Lord, no," Larson replied. "Just a small percentage. The military police deal with desertions, any crime involving servicemen—assaults, gun-running, smuggling, manslaughter, even murder. We work closely with the Egyptian authorities and, unlike police work in England, we have close ties with military intelligence."

"Really?" exclaimed Chadwick. "Are there many spies here?"

"You'd be surprised," Larson said. "Since that fellow took over in Germany, Hitler, the Germans have been very active. They would just love to see Great Britain lose India, the Canal and, of course, there's all that lovely oil where you're stationed."

"Funny you should mention that," said Chadwick. "Just a few weeks ago we shot down a fighter operating out of Turkey and the pilot was German."

"That's interesting," said Larson. "There's no doubt the Germans have big plans for the Middle East."

Somehow the British presence in Egypt, Iraq and India seemed so permanent and unchanging that Chadwick couldn't conceive of it ever changing. "Do you think it could ever come to a shooting war?" he asked.

"Well, not right now. Germany is limited by the Armistice to a small army and air force. But if they ever break those terms, watch out!"

"Are you going to spend much more time in Egypt?" Chadwick asked.

"I still have a couple of years to go," Larson replied. "Then I think I'll resign my commission and go back to Blighty. I could walk into any job in a large police department in England, thanks to my experience here."

They parted good friends and promised to stay in touch.

Chapter Twenty-Eight

Within a few days of re-joining the squadron at Hinaidi, Chadwick was approached by Welch. "I think it's time for your check ride, Chadwick. I've reserved the instrumented Vimy for 1300 hours this afternoon."

They both carried their parachutes to the plane and after a thorough external inspection Chadwick climbed aboard. Naturally, as this was a check ride, he somewhat over played the inspection and the preflight drill.

At two thousand feet, Welch indicated he should level off. Then he gestured to the blind flying visor and wrote, *Fly 2000 ft, 245 degrees, make a rate one turn left after 15 minutes onto 065 degrees.* Chadwick donned the visor and concentrated on flying the great plane as accurately as he could.

After ten minutes, Welch eased the left engine to idle rpm and the plane skidded to the left. Chadwick saw the movement of the slip indicator and applied full right rudder. As the plane began to sink, he increased rpm on the right engine and watched the artificial horizon to get the plane in a stable attitude. They passed 1800 feet with the plane under control. Welch pointed at the left engine throttle and Chadwick slowly gained a few feet by added power to the left engine.

Then he glanced at his watch. Fifteen minutes was coming up. On the dot, he eased some pressure on the rudder bar, gently added bank, and carefully watched the turn indicator needle to settle into a rate one turn. He added a little power to the right engine and, as the gyro compass swung around, he again levelled off. The heading was 070 degrees. He adjusted the course to the left, but the plane had climbed to 2,150 feet. He eased off power on the right engine. He was perspiring copiously.

Welch tapped the visor. Chadwick removed it to see the airfield ahead, and Welch wrote, *Make a short landing*. He flew down wind, turned into the wind, and made a slow approach. As the wheels touched, he gently let the skid brush the ground for few yards and then pulled the stick back into his stomach. The ground crew helped taxi the plane to the dispersal and he shut down the engines. His palms were damp with sweat. The gyros still whirred noisily as their speed dropped off. The C.O. told Chadwick to follow him to the crew room, adding. "Bring your logbook."

He returned with a blue book and Welch said, "Congratulations," and wrote in the book *Qualified as rated first pilot, RAF Vimy*, and dated it.

The next day Welch called a meeting of all the squadron officers, commissioned and non-commissioned. He started by saying, "Yesterday I carried out a check ride with Flying Officer Chadwick and rated him qualified to fly the Vimy as first pilot."

There was a murmur of congratulations.

"But let me say this, almost the entire trip was carried out flying on instruments, including a simulated engine failure."

There were a few "wows" from the pilots.

Welch continued, "This is the way we'll fly in the future, not restricted to daylight and nice weather. All our planes will have a full instrument panel, enclosed cockpits and wireless sets for communication with ground stations as well as other aircraft. Flying blind on instruments is not easy. You have to learn it and unlearn some conventional flying habits. Our Vimys won't all be instrumented but before long the British Government will re-arm with modern aircraft and it's those we'll be flying in a few years. But I want all squadron pilots to have a nodding acquaintance with instrument flying. Those of you who haven't tried it yet will fly with Flying Officer Chadwick, who's worked hard to become proficient in this new art."

A few of the older pilots did not look very happy at this announcement, but he went on. "At the moment Britain is sleeping. The horror of the last war is still vivid for many of our citizens and politicians. But world events, over which we have little control, will bring re-armament and probably another war."

There was a collective gasp from his audience.

"I want you to hear about a recent assessment of the world situation from our intelligence officer, Bob Becket." He gestured to the officer sitting at the front.

Bob Becket rose. "I was recently given a briefing by officers in the intelligence HQ in Baghdad. Not long ago a politician in Germany effected a coup that left him in sole charge of the German government. His name is Adolph Hitler. He's been quite open about his vision for Germany and has even written a book describing his plans. He'll re-arm Germany in violation of the armistice accords and will seek more land for the Germans, either by diplomacy or force of arms. The politicians on our side will be slow to react because they've been burned by the terrible suffering in the war, and the loss of millions of soldiers by Britain and France. Switching to the local situation, it's believed Germany will encourage Turkey to infiltrate the northern part of Iraq and try to seize the oil wells and pipelines. Germany will probably aid the Turks as surreptitiously as possible. The actions will get diplomatic cover as siding with Kurds for a national land of their own. We can expect to be busy."

"One last word of caution," Beckett added. "The Turks are staunch fighters with good generals. We tend to underestimate them. We were put here to control the desert Arabs, support King Faisal and keep the oil flowing. Dealing with large troop movements will be another game. Our strategy will have to be revised. In the last war, dealing with troop concentrations was a job for gas bombs. But these have been outlawed for several years now."

Several hands shot up. "What *will* we use to deal with troop concentrations?"

"We'll have to wait and see what instructions we get from HQ."

In the days that followed, Chadwick made introductory flights with all the pilots who had not until then flown the instrumented Vimy. The instructions were simple—fly straight and level on instruments, maintaining a constant altitude, plus or minus one hundred feet, and a constant heading, plus or minus ten degrees. The younger pilots seemed to adapt more quickly than the experienced ones. In fact, one of the most experienced pilots on the squadron, Flight Lieutenant Pearson, who had accumulated more than four thousand hours in the air, had enough difficulty that Chadwick had to take over the controls on several occasions in the one-hour flight.

After landing, when they climbed down from the plane, Pearson was angry with himself, and to some extent with Chadwick. Trying to control his anger, he said thickly, "You know, Chadwick, I was flying in the war when you were still in short pants."

"It does take some getting used to, sir," replied Chadwick diplomatically. "I'll be happy to fly with you again if you would like more practice."

"We'll see," snapped Pearson.

Chadwick also flew several routine patrols in the next weeks as first pilot. One afternoon he was ordered to take a pilot, newly posted to the squadron but a little older than Chadwick, for a familiarization flight. Chadwick asked him where his last posting had been.

"Singapore," he replied.

"Gosh," said Chadwick, "Iraq must seem a bit drab."

"I think my last C.O. had that in mind. He thought I was too fond of the Chinese ladies."

As summer faded and the changeable weather of autumn became more prevalent, the squadron was ordered to Mosul. They were told this would be a fairly permanent posting. The British were reinforcing their presence in the north of Iraq, and an army regiment was drafted in from India and stationed at Mosul.

One day Lattimer suggested to Chadwick, whom he regarded as his co-conspirator in archaeological matters, that they pay a visit to the digging at Nineveh before they ended for the season. It wasn't far from the airfield.

They first visited the museum in Mosul. Although much smaller than the museum in Baghdad, the exhibits were fascinating. Mosul had been a site for human habitation since Neolithic times. Four thousand years ago the Assyrian Empire rose to prominence at Nineveh on the same site. Chadwick noticed several artifacts credited to Professor Scharf and drew these to Lattimer's attention. "Remember him? We met him at Ur. He discovered the plaque of Ishtar."

They talked to the museum director and mentioned that they had met the professor at the diggings at Ur and asked if it would be possible to visit the dig at Nineveh. The director said he would be honored to write them a letter of introduction to the head of the British expedition at Nineveh. "You might even meet Professor Scharf," he added.

They were both surprised. "I thought he worked at the German dig at Ur," said Lattimer.

"He returned to Germany a while ago," the director told them, "but before he worked at Ur he dug here. Now a squabble has arisen among the experts about the dates he assigned to some artifacts. He's made a quick visit to Iraq and stopped here before he proceeds to Ur. He may still be staying in Mosul."

A few days later they took a horse-drawn carriage to the dig and introduced themselves to the archaeologist in charge. They mentioned that they had met Professor Scharf at Ur, just after he discovered the plaque of Ishtar.

"If it is indeed Ishtar," said the archaeologist. "Dates and attributions are tricky in this profession. I'll show you some of the dig and perhaps you can catch him when he comes to tea."

Later in the afternoon they ran into the professor in the dining tent. He said he remembered them when they visited the dig at Ur, but Chadwick had the impression he was being polite. He couldn't help asking the professor, "And how is your wife, Frau Scharf? Did she come with you to Iraq this time?"

"Oh, no. She's far too busy," he said. "Four months ago, she became the mother of a beautiful baby boy." And he beamed.

Lattimer uttered a perfunctory, "Congratulations."

Chadwick was astonished, but he kept his face straight. He could clearly recall Lisa's words in French—*The doctor said there is something wrong with my tubes, so bang away.* He did the arithmetic and felt quite dizzy at the implication. He sat silently at the table, toying with a biscuit. He glanced at the professor, who seemed quite happy. *Lisa kept her mouth shut,* he thought, *and her legs open.* He smiled ruefully to himself at his own crude joke.

He could hardly remember the trip back to the base. His mind kept turning over the realization of what he had learned. He was apparently a father, but without any of the responsibilities—or joys— of fatherhood.

Chapter Twenty-Nine

Mosul lay about fifty miles from the Turkish border. Routine patrols covered the border area, including the wells and pipeline. The terrain was hillier than the plateau at Baghdad. On clear days, which were few, patrols could see a few miles inside the Turkey border. Unusual troop movements were carefully noted.

The Tigris River marked a point where the borders of Turkey, Syria and Iraq joined. No flying was allowed over either Turkey or Syria.

Intelligence Officer Becket had a conversation with Welch. "Intelligence HQ have reports of troop movements on the border, but they're surprised our reconnaissance hasn't confirmed it."

"We don't penetrate into Turkey," Welch responded. "On clear days we can see a few miles into the country, perhaps as much as five miles. But the visibility is usually limited. Perhaps they're camouflaged by day and move at night."

"That's possible. Could we lay on a night patrol?"

"Let me think about it."

When Becket left, Welch pored over the maps in his office. The obvious route for an invading army aiming for Mosul was to take the road from Cukurea in Turkey to the small town of Amadiyah in Iraq. The railway line passing through Zakho was another route through difficult terrain. Probably both would be used by a large-scale invasion. He gave orders for pilots flying routine patrols to supplement the maps of the area between Amadiyah and the railway. He checked the calendar. The next moonless night would be in ten days.

Then he sent for Chadwick. "Allan, I'm contemplating a night patrol into Turkey. Do you think your blind flying could successfully traverse a hundred miles in total darkness, perhaps as much as an hour?"

Chadwick thought about it. "I think the bigger problem is navigation."

Welch showed Chadwick the map. "If we stay at four thousand feet, we should clear all obstacles if we head generally north. A southerly wind could push us into the higher mountains, but they're rare. I expect the wind to be sou'west to nor'west."

"When do you plan this flight, sir?"

"In about ten days."

"I'll get the instrumented Vimy's compass swung again."

The waning moon slowly disappeared from the sky. The weather on the night of the planned trip was fair, with a light westerly breeze. Welch and Chadwick boarded the Vimy at sunset. Chadwick took the right-hand seat. Navigation was to be the responsibility of Welch, who sat on the left. They carried no gunners.

They flew slightly west of north on a carefully calculated leg that should take them over Zakho, flying at four thousand feet with the engine rpm cut down a little below normal cruising in order to minimize noise. The dim lights of the town appeared on schedule. Chadwick was finding the flying fairly easy, as the air was not turbulent.

Welch passed him a note. *Now over Turkey, chng co to 045.*

They droned on through the inky darkness. Welch passed another note—*090*—and then suddenly nudged Chadwick and pointed ahead. A myriad small flashes of yellow light had sprung up on the land under them. The headlights of vehicles delineated a road. Welch knew that the terrain was rising under them although he had no way of judging the elevation of the lights they were flying over. A fear gripped his stomach. If they pushed too far east, they would run into the high mountains in Kurdistan. He passed another note to Chadwick—*120*. They droned on. For all Welch knew, the angry fangs of the mountains were reaching for their belly. He marked their dead reckoning position on the map and decided it was safe to head north again, hoping to sight the lights of Cukurea.

The lights of the town gave him renewed confidence in their navigation, and he ordered Chadwick to head over the valley that lay to the north of the town. It was a blaze of activity, with campfires and the lights of traffic clearly visible. Welch passed a note, *180,* and Chadwick guided the plane right and settled on a southerly course. The lights faded behind them and Welch decided to head for home.

Suddenly they were startled by a rending crash and the plane shuddered. A blast of cold air funneled into the cockpit from underneath. Chadwick instinctively pulled the stick back and pushed both throttles to the limit. He had no idea what had happened, but the plane continued to fly, and both engines were running normally. He turned to look at Welch, who caught his glance and lifted up both hands in supplication. They levelled off at five thousand feet and the C.O. laid off a course for Mosul. He passed a note to Chadwick, who adjusted their course, and thirty minutes later the lights of Mosul were visible. Kerosene lights had been laid down at the airfield to indicate a landing strip.

Welch passed a note—*The undercarriage may be damaged.* Chadwick spiraled down and slowly approached the upwind end of the landing strip. They touched down gently and ran unevenly across the ground, swerving viciously to the right. When they came to a stop, the plane was tilted. Both jumped down quickly and inspected the undercarriage in the faint light. Two wheels on one side were bent and had lost their tires. A tree branch was entwined with the axle. The fuselage fabric was torn away, exposing the steel plate installed a few months earlier.

Welch made his report to the intelligence officer and then joined Chadwick at the bar. He raised a glass to Chadwick. "Here's to being born lucky!"

In more ways than one, Allan said to himself, thinking of Frau Scharf.

The engineering officer and most of the pilots came to examine the Vimy in the morning. All were of the opinion that if they had been flying a few feet lower the flight would have ended in disaster. The engineering officer pointed out to Welch that the steel plate installed to thwart sniper's bullets also saved their lives. Without it the tree branches would have almost certainly damaged the control cables that ran under the cockpit.

The intelligence gathered was greatly appreciated in Baghdad and tactical dispositions were made with the new army regiments to frustrate a Kurdish thrust though Amadiyah into Iraq. Mine fields were laid on either side of the railway right of way leading from Zakho.

Fierce fighting broke out when the invasion started three week later. Bombers of 314 Squadron were sent to attack Kurdish forces, although they achieved little. Their major role was reconnaissance. This was a classic ground war reminiscent of the Great War, with barbed wire and machine gun nests defining a front. Without clear communication with the ground, bomber crews could not easily identify enemy and friendly forces. Bridges over small rivers that might be useful to the enemy were bombed. German staff officers observed the performance of the Kurdish soldiers. It was this battle that convinced them that lightning strikes by mechanized armor were essential if the stalemate of trench warfare was to be avoided.

On the third day of the invasion, enemy fighters put in an appearance. They were the same green monoplanes seen earlier. Chadwick was flying a standard Vimy as part of A Flight when they were attacked. Bullets smashed into the cockpit, and the instrument panel was suddenly shredded. He felt a numbing blow to his right shoulder. Blood was pouring down his right arm, but he felt no pain. Strangely, he found he couldn't move his right hand. His second pilot took over and they headed back to the airfield. When they landed, he discovered the rear gunner had also been wounded. They were both carried by stretcher to the base hospital. The bones in his shoulder had been broken, but the gunner was in more serious trouble. Two bullets had penetrated his lower abdomen and he died from infection a week later. Chadwick, his arm in a sling, attended his funeral, along with those of the squadron who could be spared from essential duties.

As he was temporarily removed from flying, Chadwick was asked to prepare an assessment of the reconnaissance flight they had made almost entirely using blind flying instruments at night. He dictated his statement to a clerk who typed it after he had corrected it. He stated he had about thirty hours of blind flying practice before the flight. As conditions were not turbulent, he had little difficulty flying for an hour or so entirely on instruments. They were nearly killed when the plane grazed a tree. In his opinion, blind flying of itself would only be a limited asset unless it was combined with a means of bringing down a plane to the ground safely if unsure of its position or flying in thick cloud. Also, some means of indicating the height of a plane above the ground, rather than above sea level, would be extremely valuable. Welch was impressed by his logical approach, endorsed his report and sent it off to his contact at Farnborough.

His non-flying status left Allan Chadwick with time on his hands. Wearing civilian clothes and keeping one hand in a

pocket instead of wearing a sling he walked on several occasions into Mosul. The ancient city was crowded with every
race that had ever lived in the Middle East—Jews, Arabs, Kurds,
Assyrians, Turks, Circassians, Armenians, and Persians jostled in
the narrow alleys and twisting by-ways. They were all trying to
make a living. Some set up desks on the street offering letter
writing. Water sellers threaded their way through the throngs
of humanity and animals. Although fierce fighting was in progress less than forty miles away there was no sense of tension
or hostility in the crowd. Apart from the tangle of electrical
wires that hung from every building, Chadwick imagined the
scene would be little different if he could magically go back a
thousand or even two thousand years.

Peering into the dim recesses of small shops he could see
hookah smokers and coffee drinkers. Chadwick tried a cup
of coffee, which was small, strong and bitter. He lost all sense
of direction in the dark labyrinth of the Bab al-Toub, but suddenly glimpsed a tall tower with a clock through the dingy
awnings of the small shops. Aiming for that he found himself
on a broad thoroughfare thronged with people, carts, cars and
buses. Properly oriented, he made his way again to the archaeological museum, which was a quiet haven from the bedlam
of the street.

Chadwick was examining a wonderfully elaborate stone
carving of a winged bull when he saw the museum director
striding across the exhibition hall. He crossed over to inter-
cept him. "Hello, sir," he said, "I'm Allan Chadwick. We met a
few weeks ago when you gave my friend Frank Lattimer and
me an introduction to the head of the dig at Nineveh."

"Ah. Yes," the director replied, "My name is Dr. Mulla Barzani.
Did you find Nineveh of interest?" He put out his right hand.
Chadwick shook his hand using his left hand and gestured to
his right arm, shaking his head. "You've been in the wars?" said
Dr. Barzani.

"I'm afraid so."

"Look, I'm just on my way to lunch. Why don't you join me?"

"You're very kind. I would be delighted."

They walked two blocks from the museum to a blank, unremarkable door in a nondescript building. Barzani gave two taps. It opened almost immediately, and they entered a cool quiet room with a thick carpet. Men sat at widely dispersed tables attended by liveried servants.

"It's a small, private club a few of the local businesspeople support to get away from the masses," Barzani explained with a smile.

A servant approached. Chadwick ordered a beer and Barzani asked for a Cinzano. "You know," Dr. Barzani said, "I am ethnically a Kurd. We've lived in these mountains to the north for over four thousand years. Archaeology gives one a wonderfully detached view of the tide of time and waves of conquering armies that have swept over our land. Sumerians, Assyrians, Macedonians, Greeks, Persians, Romans, Arabs, Turks and now the British. We will always be here, but we are not very good at forming a government of our own."

Chadwick was slightly embarrassed and mumbled that he thought the long-term goal of the British was an independent Iraq. He changed the subject and mentioned how impressed he had been with the plaque found by Professor Scharf.

"Professor Scharf," mused Dr. Barzani. "You know, we archaeologists have our own intelligence network. Everyone gossips to everyone else. Did you know Professor Scharf's expedition at Ur is funded by the German Army?"

Chadwick was flabbergasted. "What's the point of that?" he asked.

"Oh, it forms a useful nucleus for their interests in the southern part of Iraq." Dr. Barzani seemed like a highly cultivated, sophisticated person, but Chadwick began to wonder if he was going mad. The idea that Professor Scharf was leading a German Army expedition seemed ludicrous.

After a simple meal they parted company. Chadwick decided not to return to the museum but to get back to the base as soon as possible and tell Becket about Dr. Barzani's assertion. When he tracked down the intelligence officer and repeated his story, Becket burst into peals of laughter and told him to stick to flying.

Chapter Thirty

The fighting north of Mosul degenerated into a stalemate. The Turks threw in limited forces, which the British were able to contain with reinforcements brought in from India. The 314 Squadron carried out reconnaissance flights whenever the weather was suitable. Fighter planes from the Turkish side did not venture south of the border. Welch always flew the instrumented Vimy. As he became more proficient and gained confidence, he pushed the limits. Normal practice was to always fly below the cloud level. Now he began to ascend into cloud and fly straight and level for longer and longer periods. Before entering cloud, he checked the terrain ahead so that a safe descent could be made. His crew became very nervous about flying blind in thick cloud.

One particular day had started off well, with about five miles' visibility and a cloud base of fifteen hundred feet. Unknown to Welch, a low-pressure cell traveling along the front was bringing wet, rainy conditions and a cloud base that became lower and lower. After about an hour of patrolling the area over the front lines, Welch made a one-eighty degree turn and began to slowly climb into the murk. He entered the clouds at twelve hundred feet, and wispy tendrils permitted a fleeting glimpse of the ground until they reached fifteen hundred feet when they flew with zero visibility. The plane slowly climbed to two thousand feet. It was wet and dark in the cloud. The gunners and second pilot strained to lean over the cockpits and stare down, but there was nothing to be seen except the driving rain.

Then the clouds began to thin. It got lighter and the plane climbed into clear air. A bright sun shone on the dimpled cloud tops beneath them which stretched all the way to the horizon. The cloud blanket glowed like an opalescent pearl. Although it was a scene of great beauty, it was also one of great peril; there was no break to enable the crew to see the ground. Welch made a slow turn onto a reciprocal heading and after ten minutes he eased back on the throttles and began a slow descent.

Ice began to form on the wings and suddenly the fuselage was bombarded by lumps of ice flung off the propellers. The pilots were distracted by the noise as the engines began to backfire with thunderous explosions and sudden yellow glares from the exhausts reflected off the raindrops. The crew were crouched for cover below the padded rims of the cockpits and prayed for Welch to get the plane into clear air. They passed a thousand feet with no sight of land beneath them. At seven hundred feet above the ground, the pilot began to sweat. The cloud base had descended, and he couldn't look ahead for a break in the enveloping murk and at the same time concentrate of the flight instruments.

The engines had settled down as the warmer air cleared the ice from the carburetors. The second pilot suddenly pummeled Welch's shoulder and pointed ahead. There, a fleeting vision of dark green and then a stone wall flashed by. They were only a few feet above the ground. Using all the skill he had accumulated, the pilot gunned the engines and climbed. At two thousand feet in thick cloud he levelled off, and after fifteen minutes began to cautiously descend. At a thousand feet they began to see flashes of the ground through the wisps of cloud and at eight hundred feet they were flying in gloomy, clear air. After a few minutes they were able to pick up a familiar landmark and return to base.

When they taxied in, Welch switched off the engines and addressed the crew. "I hope that didn't scare you too much," he said lightly. He didn't admit he had been as scared as they were, and he vowed to himself never to get caught in cloud again without a clear space ahead.

Chadwick was cleared for flying again after his shoulder had healed. On his first flight in the instrumented Vimy, he found his flying skills were rusty. He made several reconnaissance flights over the fighting area and followed the oil pipeline. He noticed that when Welch made a flight, he always flew the Vimy with full blind flying instruments.

One day, the squadron leader called him into his office. "Allan," Welch said, "Your tour on this squadron will be coming to an end soon. Normally, your next posting would be decided by the personnel people, but I'll be required to write a summary of your time here, and it may influence the next job. Do you have any preference?"

"Well, I always fancied fighters, but I have to admit there's a lot to learn flying bombers."

"I've been impressed by your interest in blind flying," Welch went on. "That's the future of flying, but a lot more development is needed. What would you say if I recommended a posting to Farnborough?"

Chadwick was thunderstruck. The thought had never crossed his mind.

"It may be a career dead-end. Most promotions are given for doing your time on operational flying."

"Can I think about it, sir?" Chadwick stammered.

"Of course, see me in a couple of days."

Chadwick stopped by Welch's office the next day. "If you're kind enough to recommend me, I would be very happy for a posting to Farnborough."

"Consider it done."

Chapter Thirty-One

The fighting on the frontier began to wind down as a result of some high-level diplomatic negotiations. King Faisal was given more power and a considerable increase in the size of the Iraqi army. The Kurds were given some autonomy. At the squadron level the effect of these changes was not what the brass had anticipated. Because of the fighting in the north, a good many modern weapons had infiltrated into the desert regions. Attacks on buses to outlying towns and the convoys between Cairo and Baghdad became bolder. The squadron moved back to Hinaidi and was very busy in cooperation with the Armored Car Corps suppressing desert tribes. Now return fire from the ground was common, using machine guns up to half-inch bore. Fortunately, the tribesmen loved to blaze off a whole magazine of ammunition and accurate aim was considered of secondary importance. The gun barrels frequently over-heated and accuracy suffered.

The paperwork began to flow from the adjutant's office to start the transfer of Flying Officer Chadwick. Welch wrote a nicely worded letter praising the effort made by Chadwick to improve bombing accuracy and to investigate the problems of blind flying using gyroscopically controlled instruments. He was of the opinion that a pilot with several year's operational experience would be of immense value to teams developing future blind flying and navigational systems so that they would be optimized for actual operational conditions. He pointed out that Chadwick had been rated first pilot on Vimys and thus had considerable experience with both single-engine and multi-engine machines. The letter disappeared into the paperwork maw of Baghdad HQ without any immediate effect.

The squadron was very busy, mostly flying retaliatory raids in conjunction with armored cars on the ground. At times Chadwick flew two sorties a day, although he rarely flew the instrumented Vimy, as Welch wanted as many squadron pilots as possible to get some practice with blind flying. He issued a direct order—Do not enter cloud!—as he still had very fresh memories of his own narrow escape. In view of the heavy machine guns now acquired by many of the tribes, the bombing raids were carried out from two thousand feet above the ground. Accuracy was poor and Chadwick thought that they rarely achieved the intended effect of dissuading tribes from violence. At a meeting of pilots with the intelligence officer, the question was raised of just how much good they were doing. It was decided to get an opinion from some of the armored car commanders, who concurred with the majority of the pilots. A salutary financial blow to the tribes could only be achieved from a few hundred feet altitude by killing livestock. In raids with this objective, Squadron Leader Welch authorized low-level attacks. The word came back from the Armored Car Corp that this was effective.

Welch was leading a raid on a large tribe that had attacked a road convoy heading to Baghdad from Najaf. As he flew past a wooded eminence parallel to the strafing run, a half-inch machine gun opened up and raked the plane from stem to stern. The Vimy crashed and burst into flames. None of the crew survived.

The attack was witnessed by an armored car crew located to the north of the wood, which had been there to monitor the attack on the Arab village. They heard the stutter of a heavy machine gun come from somewhere in the woods. The commander realized there was nothing he could do to help the crew of the Vimy. He raced the car to the east of the wood and arrived just in time to see three Arabs break from the trees carrying a machine gun, a tripod mount and boxes of ammunition, heading for some tethered camels. The gunner fired a shot from the light two-pounder they carried. The Arabs rapidly assembled the gun on the mount. At first, they didn't allow enough elevation and bullets tore into the ground ahead of the car, raising a small dust storm. As the car burst through the cloud, the Arabs adjusted the barrel elevation and heavy slugs tore into the armor, which was not designed to withstand bullets of that caliber at short range. The driver screamed and dropped his hands from the wheel as blood poured from his face. The car slewed sideways and stopped.

The commander quickly sighted through an observation port and opened fire with the Lewis machine gun. The Arabs crumpled over their gun and all firing stopped. After a minute the commander cautiously stepped down and walked over to the group of Arabs, a Webley in his hand. Two were clearly dead, the third was covered with blood and writhed with pain, screaming in Arabic. The commander coolly sighted down the barrel of his revolver and blew the man's brains out with a forty-five bullet. The red mist that envelopes many in combat began to clear and, with a shaking hand, he put the Webley in its holster and walked back to the armored car.

The third crew member called to him as he approached the car. "Corporal Spofford is dead, sir."

"Go and collect that machine gun and ammo, then we'll go and see what we can do for the wrecked plane," he ordered as he leaned against the cold armor plate. He moved the dead driver and wiped down the seat. He then started the engine and drove to his crew man, who was disassembling the machine gun. They drove back around the wood to the site of the crashed Vimy, but almost nothing was left. The engine blocks stood out amid a pile of charred wreckage. He averted his eyes from the things in the shattered cockpit. A few Arabs had gathered to look at the wreck, but they didn't appear to be armed. Soon another Vimy flew by and the commander gave them a quick appraisal of the situation by Aldis lamp.

When Chadwick landed his plane, he heard the rumors that a Vimy had gone down. Soon enough it was confirmed that

Welch and all his crew had been killed. Chadwick was shattered. It just seemed that the burly, hearty man who had been such an exemplary squadron leader, such an exceptional pilot, couldn't possibly be gone. To some extent, Welch had been a father figure for him. Flying together and dealing with the intricacies and occasional panics of blind flying had strengthened a bond between them.

The four crew were buried in the small cemetery at the base, along with the driver of the armored car. Chadwick stood in front of the squadron leader's grave. As he gazed at the coffin lying on the bottom, he realized he had lost a dear friend. His heart felt heavy and a tear crept down his cheek. He saluted and threw a handful of sand onto the coffin, though it seemed a futile gesture.

There was concern at HQ that squadron morale was bound to suffer with the loss of the commanding officer. Lattimore was temporarily made C.O. and given orders to move the squadron to the south, to Shaibah. New personnel were drafted in and Chadwick was quietly informed by the adjutant that his posting would be postponed for a while as the new men fitted in.

Chapter Thirty-Two

A replacement Vimy bomber was not available for immediate delivery to the squadron. Instead the acting commanding officer, Lattimer, was informed a machine would have to
be assembled from components shipped previously in crates
from England to Cairo. The engineering officer, Ashurst, flew
to Cairo to supervise the assembly. After a week he informed
Lattimer that the small RAF unit at Cairo airport required help
and that when the plane was ready it would require a qualified
first pilot to test it and then fly it to Shaibah in Iraq. Two flight
sergeants and Chadwick were promptly ordered by Lattimer
to take an RAF Vernon from Baghdad to Cairo and to get the
replacement plane back to Iraq as soon as possible. Unlike his
previous visit to Cairo when he was on leave, Allan Chadwick
was not resident at Shepheard's Hotel this time, but instead at
the spartan headquarters of the small RAF detachment at the
Heliopolis Airport at Cairo.

When Chadwick was informed that he was returning to
Cairo for an indefinite period, probably a few weeks, he sent
a letter to his friend Doug Larson to let him know he was returning and would telephone on arrival. When the group from
314 Squadron arrived, they found that the engineering officer had spent most of the first week simply getting the crates
containing the aircraft parts moved from the warehouse to
the airport. They set up an assembly area in a hangar with a
smooth concrete floor. The wings and tail had to be aligned
very accurately with the fuselage to ensure the plane would
fly without excessive forces on the stick. A number of airmen
permanently stationed at the base were assigned to help with
the manual labor of jockeying the major parts into position.

It was several days before Chadwick found time to telephone Doug Larson. They arranged to meet at the Long Bar
one evening. When they met, Chadwick thought that Larson

was looking older. He seemed subdued, compared to the confident policeman he had known earlier.

Chadwick filled in the policeman on the reason for his stay in Cairo. "We're assembling a new plane. One of our bombers was shot down and the C.O. killed."

"One of your bombers shot down, eh? That's rather serious. Ties in with the way things are going in Egypt though."

Chadwick asked for details.

"This new man in Germany has really stirred things up. You know, until a few months ago, secret service ops here were rather gentlemanly. We knew who they were, and they knew who we were. There was an unwritten code. We didn't kill their chaps and they didn't kill ours. Most of the German activity was run by their navy, but that seems to have ended. German intelligence ops have been coalesced under one command, known as the SD—the Sicherheist Dienst, the security and intelligence branch of the SS. Very tough customers indeed."

Larson waited for this to sink in, and then continued. "We picked up the body of one of our men this morning, an Egyptian. He was involved with ship movement scheduling in the Canal. A very useful chap, an Anglophile. He slipped us a lot of useful stuff. He left the office as usual yesterday afternoon and was apparently kidnapped by the SD shortly afterwards. He endured very rough interrogation using rubber truncheons. The doctor who examined the body said he would never have walked again, had he lived. His knees were pulverized, as it was. He was shot in the back of the head, so we assumed in the end he talked."

Chadwick was sickened. He was reminded of the claim by Dr. Barzani that the German dig at Ur was a front for the German Army. He recounted Dr. Barzani's story to Larson, who was immediately interested. He had a contact at British Intelligence HQ in Baghdad and resolved to call him to get the details. Chadwick had the impression that the squadron intelligence officer had dismissed the idea and said so to Larson. Larson suspected that the intelligence officer would have some inkling of German secret service involvement at the Ur dig if it existed but was too prudent to confide with Chadwick. He told Chadwick that many of the British intelligence team in Egypt felt they must fight fire with fire and the level of violence was rising.

Larson himself was under observation by an operative working for the Germans, and his long conversation with Chadwick was duly noted. Consequently, Chadwick, who was dressed in mufti for the meeting, was followed back to the RAF base. Inquiries with the local staff soon revealed he was involved with the assembly of a new bomber and the German station chief decided it should be sabotaged, if possible.

Larson talked to his contact in Baghdad and learned that Hamid Mustafa and Felix Goelz were under loose observation and their activities were well monitored. It was felt that Dr. Scharf was not directly involved in any espionage activities. Larson brought his Baghdad counterpart up to date with the rising violence in Egypt between British and German intelligence operations. He guessed that the same thing would happen in Iraq if the German station chief was replaced by someone with allegiance to the SD.

Under the direction of Ashurst, the 314 Squadron team carefully bolted the wings and tail plane to the fuselage. Control cables were strung from the stick in the center cockpit. These were adjusted by means of turnbuckles and would require final trimming when the plane was test flown. There was some debate about the armor plate that was installed by the squadron the year before. It was decided to omit it for the present and install it after arrival back in Iraq. The hangar in which they were working was also occupied by other users, and most days there was an audience gathered to watch progress of the aircraft assembly.

The SD sent a man to check up and estimate when they would be ready for a test flight. The information was relayed to the head of German Intelligence in Egypt, who had replaced the old head a few months earlier, as the SD in Berlin made sweeping changes to the German security and intelligence apparatus.

Heinrich Murken was typical of the many ex-army men who joined the National Socialist Party in the early 1920s. He was of average intelligence but very street-smart. A burly man, his face was pock-marked by shrapnel in the war. He had nearly lost an eye; it had been saved but he was left with a permanent squint. He kept his thick, black hair cropped short. He had a brutal nature which had once alarmed some of his comrades in the trenches when he went on a murderous rampage and bayonetted several French prisoners who were awaiting an escort to the rear. In the street fighting that characterized the early years of the Nazi Party, his brutality bordered on sadism and he came to the attention of senior party leaders when the SS was created.

Murken slowly rose in the SD, the security and intelligence branch of the SS, and his appointment to the Egyptian post was a significant promotion he intended to make the best of. He supervised the interrogation of the Egyptian working for the British and shot him once he decided he was squeezed dry. When Murken was established in Cairo he tracked down the high-class bordellos that specialized in rough sex and bondage, and soon got a reputation as a man to be avoided among the unfortunate women he hired.

Murken decided the RAF bomber should never get back to Iraq and was smart enough to realize he did not have the technical knowledge to arrange for the plane to crash after it left Egypt. To destroy the plane in Cairo before it even left would have been comparatively simple, but that would not have had the propaganda value of a crash en route when fully crewed. After several coded interchanges with Berlin he was put in touch with a former German army pilot who now flew to Cairo on a regular basis as a Luft Hansa pilot.

He arranged to meet the Luft Hansa pilot at a quiet bar the next time he flew into Cairo. His instincts told him not to ask the former army pilot for a way to bring down an aircraft once it was airborne. Pilots have a bond, regardless of nationality, and sabotaging a fellow pilot's plane would be seen to be a violation of that bond. Instead he told the pilot that he was a low-ranking member of the German intelligence community and he had been told to investigate the downing of a German plane which had crashed mysteriously in the Sudan while surreptitiously taking air-to-ground photos. The wreckage had been examined by an expert who said it was not destroyed by a bomb, Murken told the German pilot. Both engines had quit, although there had been plenty of fuel on board, which had caught fire when the plane crashed, destroying much of the evidence. The pilots and crew were killed.

The Luft Hansa pilot swallowed this lie at face value. Murken asked him to suggest what could have brought the plane down after an hour into the flight. The pilot pondered for a while and then said, "I've heard of similar incidents in South America. Rival airlines were fighting to become established on lucrative routes and were not above knocking the competition from the sky."

"How did they do it?" Murken asked eagerly.

"It was very simple," the Luft Hansa man replied. "A mechanic simply peed into the oil tanks of the engines on the plane they wished to sabotage."

Murken was astounded. "That seems impossible! How could a little water have such an effect, even though it was a trifle contaminated?" he added with a snigger.

"Normally such a small amount of water would not have such a devastating effect," said the pilot. "If it was in the fuel, for example. it would have been filtered out. But in the oil its presence is very dangerous. After running for an hour an engine reaches a stable operating temperature. For the oil, this is about one hundred and fifty degrees centigrade, well above the boiling point of water. The water boils, steam fills the oil tank and blows out the oil. The engine quits because of lubrication failure."

Murken could hardly believe his ears. Things could hardly be simpler—infiltrate the ground staff, add water and wait for the crash, conveniently much later. He thanked the pilot, cautioned him to keep their conversation to himself, paid for the drinks and left the bar in high spirits.

Murken decided his efforts merited some reward. On the way to the secret SD headquarters he detoured to a brothel he had found to be amenable to his unusual tastes. When the madam saw him, her face fell.

"The woman you had last time required the attention of a doctor. That is expensive, and so the price will be higher this time," she told him in German.

"That is acceptable," he said, as he had access to discretionary funds and didn't care. "I want the same room." The room was equipped with whips and bracelets and was soundproof. It also had several push-button switches which allowed a woman to signal for help, if she could reach one.

The madam escorted him upstairs and he sat on a bed waiting for his victim. He was already aroused when she entered, a strongly built Eurasian woman dressed in a flimsy negligee. She put her arms above her head and pivoted on one foot. He approved of her heavy breasts and prominent buttocks, which displayed six scarlet weals. She had tastes not unlike his own, but complementary, and she had already been working that day. Her body was completely shaved, in the Muslim tradition. It was late when he eventually got to the office, exhausted, a little sore—but gratified.

Chadwick worked hard on the assembly of the new plane. He wore a pair of borrowed overalls and wormed his way into almost inaccessible parts of the plane while he hooked up flight and engine instruments. To his disappointment, it proved impossible to get gyroscopic flight instruments, so the trip to Iraq would have to be flown in clear weather. Within two weeks they were ready to try the engines. Both were brand-new, shipped in crates from Rolls Royce and covered in protective grease, which had to be carefully wiped off. Lubricating oil was added via open spark plug orifices and the engine turned through several revolutions. A small amount of fuel was added to the header tanks in the wings. The oil tanks were filled, and the propellers turned by hand, first with magnetos off and then with the ignition on. One after the other, the engines fired up immediately.

The assembled crew were elated, as it was a significant milestone. After a few minutes of running, the engines were shut down and a small sample of lube oil collected from each. The samples were examined by the engineering officer using a strong light and a powerful magnifying glass. He had wide experience in running engines and knew what typical steel dust could be expected from a new engine. He was satisfied but opted to run the engines for an hour and then change the lubricating oil. It was decided on the next clear day to have a test flight.

Two days later Chadwick made a short test run, with Ashurst as a passenger. After taxiing trials, they took off. The right engine sounded a bit rough at full power. With the stick centralized, the plane slowly climbed and banked left. These faults could be corrected by adjustment of the control cables. The instruments seemed to work properly. The engineering officer made a note of the work still needed and they landed.

Chadwick phoned Larson and arranged to meet him at the Long Bar that evening. When they met, Chadwick thought the policeman looked tired. However, he greeted Chadwick cheerfully and asked, "So you've nearly finished. Did you dip your wick while in Cairo?"

It took Chadwick a few moments to decipher Larson's slang. Then he replied, "The first time I came to Egypt, in '28, an old squadron leader warned us off native women. He said they were poxed up to the eyebrows, and it was a court martial offence if you got a dose."

"Probably true. Even worse, more than ninety percent have been clipped, and you won't find the ones that haven't in a cathouse."

"What do mean, 'clipped'?"

"Where have you been living? In a monastery?"

"Well, the RAF is a bit like that," Chadwick joked. "Clipped?"

Larson explained, "In Egypt, the Sudan, and parts of Africa, young girls undergo a religious ritual. It's a tradition. The lips of the cunt and the sweet spot, the clitoris, are cut off or stitched up."

Chadwick was horrified. "What's the point of that?"

"Well, I'm not sure," said Larson, "but their religion is anti-feminine anyway, so maybe it's to deprive women of sexual pleasure."

They were silent for a minute.

"I'm told the whores are not much good in bed anyway," Larson went on. "There are plenty of European and American ladies in Cairo. A handsome pilot could score easily."

"I had a couple of flings in Iraq," Chadwick told him. "To be honest, I'm not so keen on one-nighters." He was still troubled by the affair with Frau Scharf. He felt guilty about the fact that he had most likely fathered a child, and uneasy about the fact that he might never see it.

"Ah, the romantic type," Larson chided cynically. "You want to find the perfect woman to keep for yourself, forever. Someone once said, 'Show me a beautiful woman, and I'll show you a chap who is fed up of fucking her.' Nothing lasts forever, Allan. So, enjoy yourself!" He paused to see the effect this had on his companion. "Listen, on a more serious subject, what kind of security do you have out at the airfield?"

"Virtually non-existent," Chadwick told him. "We share the hangar with other users and the field is civilian anyway. Why?"

"I just get a whiff the Germans are interested in your plane. They've been asking questions."

Herr Murken had asked his local agents to sound out Egyptians working at the airfield. They found a cleaner who for a fee was prepared to sabotage the British plane. Murken briefed him using an interpreter. "Can you climb on the British plane at night without being seen?"

"Yes, effendi, after ten p.m. everyone goes home. That is when we do the cleaning."

"Next question, do you know where the oil tanks are for each engine?"

The Egyptian looked baffled. Murken turned to one of his assistants. "Tomorrow find a plane well away from the hangar and have a mechanic show him how to open an oil tank." He then said to the interpreter, "Tell him he must pour something in each oil tank." He handed a bottle of German white wine, Liebfraumilch, to the cleaner. "Tell him to drink this two hours before he enters the hangar, and then use his own equipment." He patted the cleaner's crotch. The interpreter told him to drink the wine and then pee into the oil tanks, and they both laughed.

Before the next flight Chadwick voiced Larson's concern to Ashurst, the engineering officer. They decided the most likely form of sabotage would be to hide a bomb somewhere in the plane. After a thorough search, they both strapped in and took the plane for a short flight. The control cable tensions had been adjusted and the plane flew straight and level with little force on the stick at cruising power. They landed and made preparations to leave as soon as possible. Ashurst drew flying gear from the stores for the four crew who would fly back in the Vimy. Chadwick discussed the route with the senior navigator on the base staff. It was decided to fly back along the coast as far as Jerusalem and refuel before crossing the desert on the way to Iraq. This would allow them to get an up-to-date weather forecast before leaving on the long leg across the desert.

They decided to break the journey by making Hinaidi the first destination. This would keep them over well-travelled ground routes, an important consideration, should they be forced down for any reason. Discussing the possibility that someone might hide a bomb on the plane Chadwick suggested that they leave the engine cowlings off until ready for take-off. This would remove a few dark corners that might be used to hide a bomb.

Ironically, it made the task of the Egyptian cleaner much easier when he climbed on the wings the night before their departure. As a Muslim, the cleaner was unused to alcohol, and so now he was mildly drunk. With difficulty, he lit a small lantern and unfastened the cap of the oil tank on the right engine and pulled down his pantaloons. He dangled his penis over the tank opening, but he was unsteady. Much of the liquid ran down the outside of the tank until he adjusted his aim. It was difficult to stop the flow when he judged he had added enough. Then he noticed the tip of his penis was covered with black oil from contact with the rim of the opening. That was enough. He cursed the Germans, replaced the cap on the tank, and jumped down to the hangar floor. Outside the hangar, he leaned on the wall and vomited.

The following morning the Vimy crew carefully examined the plane, loaded their gear and installed the engine cowlings. Chadwick stopped by the RAF HQ and arranged for a phone call to be made to the RAF base near Jerusalem, at a small town called Lod. They took off in still air and banked over the still-sleeping city. The Pyramids and the Sphinx cast long shadows as they settled down on a northeast course at two thousand feet. The Suez Canal and Port Said were in view when suddenly the right engine gave a mighty cough, and Chadwick, who was sitting within four feet, felt hot oil droplets on his face. He stared at the engine cowling; it was stained with oil which was whipped away by the slipstream. The engine continued to run but he throttled back and began to search for the landing field at Port Suez. The flight sergeant in the forward cockpit spotted the field and pointed excitedly to the right. The plane began a slow descent, using mainly power on the left engine. Chadwick made perfect landing and cut the magneto switches.

"No point in running the engines a minute longer than necessary," Chadwick said to Ashurst, "until we know what's wrong."

Men came running to the plane and pushed it to the dispersal area. Ashurst and the two mechanics began to take off the engine cowlings. Chadwick reported to the station commander the reason for their unexpected arrival. When he returned to the plane, Ashurst gave him the news on the examination— the left engine seemed to be in perfect order with oil well up the dipstick. The cap on the oil tank of the right engine had disappeared and the oil tank was nearly empty. Why the tank had lost its cap was a mystery until Ashurst had a thought. He fastened a small rag with string to the end of a piece of stiff wire and pushed it to the bottom of the right oil tank. When he fished it out, the rag had absorbed a little water below the level of the oil stain. "That's the problem," said Ashurst, "water in the oil. When the oil got hot enough, the water boiled and blew off the cap, along with most of the oil contents."

Chadwick digested this news. "Do you think it was deliberate?"

"Almost certainly," replied Ashurst. "But why sabotage only one tank?"

"Perhaps he got interrupted," suggested Chadwick.

Ashurst went to the engineering section and came back with some clean rags, alcohol and a new container of oil. The rim of the filler opening had been bent. They carefully reshaped it and fitted a spare cap the mechanics had been able to find in the engineering section. They cleaned the tank and washed it with alcohol. When it had evaporated, they refilled the tank. They started the engine; the oil pressure was good. There were no obvious leaks, and so Ashurst pronounced it fit to fly. They took off immediately for Lod.

The watchers at the airfield reported to Murken when the Vimy left Heliopolis. He called on agents stationed to the east, warning them to watch out for news that an RAF bomber had crashed. The only report he got was the sighting of a bomber that landed apparently normally at Port Said. After waiting for half a day, he reluctantly concluded his plan had failed. He asked an agent to bring in the Egyptian cleaner. The man protested that he done exactly as ordered, but Murken sensed some hesitation in his answers and after a ferocious grilling the man confessed to only sabotaging one engine. A blind fury swept over Herr Murken. He hit the cleaner so hard with a truncheon that his skull was fractured.

"Throw the bastard in the Nile," he ordered the scared agent. "And next time I want better help. This man was a halfwit."

Chapter Thirty-Three

The flight to the RAF base at Lod took a little over an hour. By lunchtime they had the plane refueled and secured for the night. Chadwick decided not to spend time in the dreary barracks at Lod and took a bus into Jerusalem. Inside the walled city he visited two sites which claimed to be the location of Jesus's tomb. He discovered nobody really knew where Calvary was and the location of the three crosses. All races and nationalities mingled in the Souk, and it smelled rather exotic.

When he returned to the base, he checked the forecast for the leg of more than four hundred miles to Baghdad. The plane was not equipped with gyroscopic flight instruments and so flying in cloud was out of the question. To safely cross the mountains, he would have to maintain a height of at least five thousand feet above sea level. Six would be better. Once east of Amman and over the Syrian Desert, he could descend to three thousand feet. The cloud base at Jerusalem was forecast to be only a thousand feet above the ground and he reluctantly postponed a departure on the next day.

The next morning, Chadwick spent an hour with the senior meteorological officer. It looked like a high-pressure cell was moving in. He was optimistic that they could depart the next day. After lunch he changed into mufti and took the same bus ride into Jerusalem. Near the east gate he found a cinema that was showing the latest American film, *Frankenstein*. It was a talkie and he decided to watch it as much for the sound as the picture. The film had started when he settled in his seat, but he was soon able to put the plot together—a scientist had created a human being from the parts of dead bodies. He had come into the theater just as lightning brought the creature to life. When the mob set fire to the building he was hiding in, Chadwick felt sorry for the monster. When the movie ended, he sat through a tedious travelogue about vacationing in the

Canadian Rockies and when the feature film came around to the part where he had originally come in, Chadwick left, momentarily blinded by the sunlight outside the cinema. What he wanted was a nice pint of beer.

He found a restaurant a few yards down the street. In the back was a cool bar formed of huge stones from some ancient building. He was the only customer. He ordered a beer, which came deliciously cool from a barrel in the old basement. He had taken a few sips when a tall man walked up to the bar and sat on a barstool next to him.

"Hi," the man said, "Hiram P. Leadbetter. Pleased to meet-cha." He had an educated American accent. Addressing the bartender, he said, "I'll have a Coca Cola."

"No Coca Cola," the bartender told him.

"Okay, make it an orange juice."

As the bartender fumbled with an orange and the machine to squeeze it, Leadbetter turned to Chadwick and held out his right hand. Chadwick shook his hand, which was limp and sweaty. "Allan Chadwick," he mumbled.

"Say," went on the American, "Isn't this some place? History just oozes out of every brick."

"You mean Jerusalem," said Chadwick, "Yes, it's very old."

"I mean the whole country, the Middle East, this is where it all began."

"What did? "asked Chadwick.

"Why, Western Civilization," Leadbetter said.

"I haven't really thought about it," Chadwick said.

"I'm a student of history," the American said. "It's all come about so quickly. Ten thousand years ago the human race, throughout the world, lived in the stone age, just like animals. Then, powee! Palaces, castles, metal, it all began here. The civilization we take for granted now all began in the Middle East."

"Are you a history professor?" Chadwick asked.

"Why, no. I'm just an amateur. But I've travelled, I talk to history professors, anybody actually. I like talking to scientists. My father patented some special eye drops and I have an income sufficient to let me indulge in a useless life." He laughed. "What do you do, Allan?" he asked.

"I'm in the Royal Air Force. I'm just visiting. Probably be gone tomorrow."

"Ah, the military. The British run this part of the world, don't they? For the moment. Things change in history so quickly," he added.

Chadwick wasn't sure what to make of the voluble American. He felt he ought to mention something historical.

"I've been to the Krak des Chevaliers in Syria," he told Leadbetter, "and to archaeological digs at Nineveh and Ur."

"Terrific," said Leadbetter. "To understand today you must understand yesterday. The people were the same then as now." He changed the subject. "I'm fascinated by recent scientific discoveries. What do you know of quantum physics, Allan?"

"Nothing," said Chadwick curtly.

"It defies intuition. We are all made up of billions of particles. Atoms, if you like. Lumped together, the world behaves as we expect. But get the particles alone, which scientists can do, the individual particles behave very strangely, and not in a predictable way. German scientists seem to be ahead in this field. I've spent a lot of time talking to them and I begin to see parallels with human behavior."

Chadwick had finished his beer. He signaled to the bartender for another and gestured to Leadbetter's glass. "Another?"

"Thank you," said the American. "I hope I'm not boring you. It's such a pleasure to have a conversation with someone in English."

Chadwick smiled to himself. The American had done most of the talking. "You were saying—?"

"Ah, yes, in quantum physics you can't be sure of anything. You can only assign a probability that such an event will happen."

Chadwick looked confused. "Why do you say it has parallels with human behavior?" he asked.

"Sometimes momentous events occur because two unlikely conditions appear at once."

"Can you give me an example?"

"Yes, think of the conquest of Mexico. Cortes arrived just at the time the Aztec Emperor, Montezuma, had received a prophecy that the God they worshiped as the creator of all life would arrive. Thus, the probability that the forecast was made coincided with the probability that Cortes made his voyage to Mexico on the same date. Two probability distributions overlapped, and the conquest of South America had begun."

Chadwick excused himself and made his way to the toilet for a pee. The smell was awful. The toilet was a hole in the ground, surrounded by flies. Back at the bar he said to Hiram Leadbetter, "You certainly have a fascinating view of world history." He felt he ought to make a contribution to the conversation. "You know, I've often wondered what someone who lived, say, two hundred years ago, would think if they could miraculously come back and see the world today—steam engines, aeroplanes, moving pictures that talk, all the wonders of modern life."

"They would dismiss such things as incomprehensible magic. But I will tell you what would have a big impact—flush toilets."

Chadwick gasped.

"For millennia, humans have struggled to deal with excreta—shit, if you'll pardon the word." Leadbetter continued. "A thing that sweeps the stuff away, never to be seen again, now *that* would be seen as real miracle. Do you know English kings had several palaces, so they could move from one to the other when the smell got to be too much, I suspect that the hunter-gatherers moved on because of the smell, not because they had impoverished the current location."

Chadwick was not sure what a hunter-gatherer was. "Hunter-gatherers?"

"You know, stone age people, who moved around in tribes for tens of thousands of years."

Chadwick glanced at the clock over the bar. "I'd better get moving," he said. "Got a few things to do before tomorrow, and there is only an hourly bus service."

"Where's your base?"

"At Lod, about fifteen miles from here."

"I'll give you a ride in my car. It's just outside the gate."

"That's very decent of you. If it's not too much trouble."

"Give me a chance to see the historic countryside."

They finished their drinks, Hiram insisted on paying, and they walked in the evening twilight to the car, a fairly new French Renault. Hiram slipped a coin to an Arab who had been sitting on the running board, and they climbed in. Hiram started the engine and Chadwick directed him onto the road to Lod. The engine was noisy, and it was difficult to talk, but as they approached the field, Leadbetter pointed to the Vimy, which was silhouetted against the glowing western sky.

"Look at that antique plane," he cried. "Is there a museum here?"

Chadwick climbed down at the base entrance, thanked him, saying, "I'm going to fly that antique relic to Iraq tomorrow." He turned and walked into the base before Leadbetter could respond.

The weather was fair the next day, with a cloud level six thousand feet above the ground. Chadwick assembled the crew, they had an early breakfast, ran a last-minute weather forecast past the met office, and took off without difficulty. In forty minutes, they were over Amman, where numerous Roman remains were visible from the air. It had been an important outpost of the Roman Empire. They soon picked up the main road to Baghdad and flew steadily, two thousand feet above ground level. The desert was monotonous, livened by occasional emergency landing strips, camel trains and the rare vehicle. After passing Rutbah, the clouds thickened and the base lowered. They were slowly forced down to stay in clear air. Chadwick estimated they were flying only about eight hundred feet above the ground; he sorely missed the gyroscopic instruments he had become used to.

Three hours after leaving Amman behind they flew over Lake Habbaniyah and soon picked up local landmarks which led them to Hinaidi. The plane landed smoothly, and they all climbed out at the dispersal area, stiff after four hours in the cramped seats. Although it was only lunch-time, Chadwick felt they should stay for the night and make the last leg to Shaibah when the weather improved. Ashurst said he would call Lattimer at 314 Squadron and bring him up to date. When he returned, he told Chadwick that the C.O. had ordered him back to Shaibah. He would take a train to Basra in the morning. Chadwick and the two flight sergeants were to fly back to Shaibah when the weather permitted.

In the Officers Mess that evening Chadwick ran into several friends made during his postings to Hinaidi. They told him the old airfield was to be abandoned and a new one built further west. He enjoyed exchanging service gossip and told them about the apparent attempt to sabotage the Vimy before it left Cairo.

It was two days before the clouds lifted and the 314 Squadron crew could make the two-hour flight to Shaibah. On arrival Chadwick went to brief Lattimer about the flight. Ashurst had already made him aware of the attempted sabotage. The adjutant told him his posting had come through and mentioned he had about four weeks of accumulated leave and would be allowed three weeks of travel time. He saved the best for last: Chadwick's new posting was RAF Farnborough. Welch had virtually reached from the grave and directed his career into an entirely new path. The adjutant said he could travel back to England on a troopship that would make a stopover at Port Said in about a month or, at his own expense, he could make his own way to home.

Chadwick retired to the bar in the Officers Mess to think over the momentous news. He decided to take the leisurely way back to England. He would stay in Egypt for a week and then cross the Mediterranean to the Balkans or Italy and make his way across Europe. He had always wanted to see the battlefields of the Great War and this was his chance.

One night the squadron threw a wild party for him in the mess. He packed much of his gear, including his uniforms, in a large tin trunk, along with plenty of camphor, and dropped it off at the quartermaster. The air force would deliver it to RAF Farnborough. A day later, Lattimer flew Chadwick to Hinaidi in a Vimy on a routine patrol and he caught the RAF flight to Heliopolis, carrying a medium-sized suitcase, which he hoped held enough to get him all the way to England. In a money belt he had a hundred pounds in British currency. He caught a bus to Cairo and checked into Shepheard's Hotel. He felt he was beginning a great adventure.

Chapter Thirty-Four

As soon as Allan Chadwick was settled into the hotel, he called Doug Larson, and felt lucky to catch him at his office.

"Doug, there was an attempt to sabotage the plane after we left. I want to bring you up to date. I'm staying at Shepheards."

Larson was very interested but cautioned that things had changed since Chadwick returned to Iraq. "We must be discreet," he warned. "What's your room number? I'll meet you there."

"I'm in room 218. When's a good time to meet?"

They agreed on 6 p.m. and Chadwick had two cold beers ready when there was a knock on the door. They shook hands and Larson asked what Chadwick was doing back In Cairo.

"I'm on my way to England," Chadwick told him. "My tour is over. But I want to tell you what happened when we left Heliopolis with the Vimy we had assembled."

"What date was that?" Larson jotted it down in a notebook.

"We left early, before 8 a.m. We thoroughly inspected the plane first, and there was no sign it had been tampered with or that there was a hidden bomb. Half an hour into the flight the right engine suddenly erupted and most of the lubricating oil was ejected. I was able to land at Port Said without any problems. The left engine performed flawlessly. The squadron engineering officer was flying with me as a passenger. He examined the engine at Port Said and found traces of water. He decided the engine had probably been sabotaged by adding water to the oil tank. He felt it would take about half a liter to blow most of the oil out of the tank when the water boiled."

Larson was intrigued that such a simple operation could disable an engine. "I'll get some inquires going at the airfield," he said. "How are you getting to England from here?"

"I have the option of catching a troopship at Port Said, although I'm tempted to cross the Med to Europe and take a train."

"Don't forget it's winter," Larson reminded him. "The Med can be rough. Every year a few ships are lost."

Chadwick dismissed his concern. "I'll catch a big ship, not a fishing boat."

They chatted for a while and then Larson left. Chadwick walked downstairs to the dining room, and after a light dinner he went to bed early.

The next day was overcast and mild, Chadwick checked with the concierge and was directed to a travel agency within walking distance. He found it without difficulty and asked about ferries leaving Alexandria for Europe. There were several leaving for ports in Greece and Italy. Cost was a factor, as he was paying his own way. The agent strongly recommended an Italian line. They discussed possible destinations and eventually Chadwick settled on Brindisi at the heel of Italy. The ferry made a stopover in Crete and the voyage took about a week. There were only two classes—first and steerage. He paid a deposit on a first-class ticket, based on sharing a cabin with another man. Departure was set for four days hence, subject to weather conditions.

On the way back to the hotel Chadwick chanced across a wonderful used book shop, where about half the stock was in English. He conversed with the owner, an Indian, whose grandfather had started the shop when many Indians moved to Egypt as de Lesseps was building the Suez Canal. He wanted some reading matter for the upcoming voyage and chose an interesting-looking book by a former British Army Colonel, "A Brief Outline of the Campaign in Mesopotamia, 1914-18," which he felt would complement his own experiences. For fiction he found a book by a woman, Dorothy Sayers, that featured an aristocratic detective.

There was no message for him from Doug Larson when he got back to the hotel. After lunch he had a nap and idled the afternoon away reading old British newspapers on the verandah, a cold beer at hand. Just as his eyes slowly closed, he was startled by a gruff voice.

"Wake up, lazybones." Doug Larson was standing by his chaise longue, with two cold beers.

"Doug—? I must have dropped off."

"I thought I'd find you here. I have some good news. I've put a competent detective sergeant on your case. An Egyptian. My own Arabic is functional at best, so I decided we needed local who can sense the nuances in the atrocious Egyptian dialect. He'll be working at the airport tonight, so hopefully he'll pick up something unusual about the night before you departed for Iraq."

Chadwick told him he had booked a passage in four days to Italy from Alexandria.

"Be it on your own head," was Larson's comment, and then he sighed. "I don't know how wise it is to tell you about intelligence ops in Egypt. The game has changed. Knowing too much can get you in a lot of trouble."

"I'm leaving soon. Bring me up to date."

"After I talked to you when you were assembling the Vimy, I realized I was being shadowed, probably by operatives working for the Germans. We needed to know who was directing things on their side. So, we carefully shadowed the shadower. After a couple of days, it was clear he was working out of an old office building on the port waterfront, right on the Nile. We have photographs taken with telescopic lenses. The faces are being studied by the local police and we're comparing Europeans with passport data. We should know a lot more in a couple of days."

"Sounds exciting," said Chadwick. "Can I do anything?"

"Absolutely not. As I said, these fellows can be rough. Meet me tomorrow, in your room after dinner, say 9 p.m."

Chadwick whiled away the next day at the Cairo museum. As on his previous visit he was amazed at the high standard of workmanship in the many artifacts recovered from tombs. He waited eagerly in his room after dinner. A quiet knock came soon after nine and he opened the door for Larson. To his complete surprise, he saw an Egyptian man, who was pushed roughly into the room by Larson, who was holding a small automatic.

"This chap followed me to the hotel and up to your floor. I was able to double back in the corridor and invite him into your room, with a little persuasion." He waved the gun.

The Egyptian looked at Chadwick with wild, staring eyes. Chadwick was flustered. Violence to him was something that occurred yards apart, plane to plane. Violence at the personal level, man to man, was distasteful. He said nothing.

The Egyptian smelt of fear—it was probably pee—and his face was bathed with sweat. Larson suddenly reversed his gun and gave the prisoner a smart rap on his skull with the butt. He went down like a sack of wet cement.

"What on earth is going on?" Chadwick managed to stammer.

"This fellow works for the opposition. I recognized him from the photos we took when he followed me into the lobby. I don't usually carry the standard issue sidearm—a Webley, too bulky. But recently I've been wearing this fellow, a neat American thirty-two."

"What're we going to do with him?"

"Oh, I think when he comes to, he may be able to answer a few questions. Let's tie him up."

Using the strap from Chadwick's suitcase, they tied the prisoner's hands firmly behind his back. His ankles were fastened to a leg of the bed using the cord from Allan's pajamas. Chadwick was literally trembling with a mixture of excitement and fear. Larson was very cool, calm and collected.

"We've discovered that a cleaner disappeared the night your plane was nobbled. Probably he was the man. This fellow may be able to confirm it." He gave the prostrate figure a gentle kick. "It seems like the Germans have brought in a new man into Cairo to run their intelligence. Maybe this chappie knows something about that too. I think he's coming around."

Larson filled a tumbler with water from the sink and splashed it in the man's face. His eyes opened and he looked at the two Englishmen fearfully. Larson spoke to him in rapid Arabic.

"I've told him that if he answers a couple of simple questions truthfully, we'll let him go, uninjured."

He spoke to the man again, and in reply the Egyptian wailed piteously. Larson told him to be quiet.

"He says he's going to get killed if he tells us anything. I told him he's going to get killed if he doesn't tell us everything."

He pulled back the hammer on the automatic with an ominous click. The prisoner started talking quickly and Larson listened attentively.

"He says the German chief killed a man, one of their own, and the body was dumped in the Nile. I think my detective sergeant can work with that."

He spoke again to the frightened Egyptian. "I've told him we'll let him go and if he has any sense, he'll not tell the Germans what happened tonight.

Chadwick untied the Egyptian's feet and hands. Larson waved the prisoner to his feet with the gun and told Chadwick to open the bedroom door. When he did, the Egyptian bolted. Larson collapsed on the bed, laughing. Chadwick felt emotionally drained.

Larson looked at him. "A little too personal, eh? Close quarters, us coppers are used to it. There is one thing, though. He may talk or be persuaded to talk. You can't stay here. In the morning you'll have to check out. Don't leave a proper forwarding address."

"I'll just go to Alex, and wait for my ship," Chadwick said.

"I have one suggestion. When you're in Alexandria, buy an automatic like mine and a dozen rounds."

"Are you serious?"

"Deadly serious. The world's becoming a violent place, especially where you're going." He rose to leave. "I don't suppose we'll meet again. Give me a phone call before you leave Alexandria."

Chadwick grasped his hand. "It's been a pleasure knowing you, Doug. I hope we do meet again someday."

Chadwick took Larson at his word and checked out after an early breakfast. He took a taxi to the bus depot and an express bus to Alexandria, a two-hour trip. When he arrived, he found a taxi driver with some command of English and asked him to find a moderately-priced hotel. Once settled he found the shipping company of the ferry he had booked. He was told he could board the next day, although the departure date was not definite.

He went to look for a gunsmith. The price of a new automatic was outside the price range he could afford. The gunsmith suggested a second-hand gun. Finally, he chose a Belgian gun, with a shoulder holster and a dozen rounds. He haggled the price down to seven pounds. For another few shillings the gunsmith threw in twelve more rounds and a practice shoot in the basement of his shop. Chadwick had never fired an automatic before. At a range of twenty meters, his grouping on the target was within ten inches. Not so good but sufficient to deter most assailants, he decided.

Afterwards, he decided to kill his remaining time by exploring Alexandria, which he decided was rather dismal. The huge port area dominated the city, but the miles of warehouses had no architectural appeal. He did not even bother looking for a museum, his usual haven. Walking in the harbor area he chanced upon the Cecil Hotel, which looked quite elegant, and decided it was time for a beer. The bar was not crowded, and there were no attractive, unaccompanied women. After a few minutes a well-dressed Englishman sauntered up to him.

"Good evening, sir. The name is Culpepper."

"How do you do," Chadwick replied. "Chadwick."

"Are you expecting trouble, Mr. Chadwick?"

"What on earth do you mean? I just came for a quiet drink."

"Oh, no offense. Actually, I'm the house detective. I like to meet clients who arrive armed."

Chadwick was embarrassed. "You must have x-ray eyes. Is it that obvious? I just bought the gun in preparation for a journey to Europe. I was strongly urged to arm myself by a policeman friend in Cairo."

"Who was that? I probably know him."

"Doug Larson. I think he's a captain in the military police."

"Yes, I know him well. I'm surprised he recommended that you carry a gun."

"It's a bit complicated. Last night I got into a bit of a fracas with him, involving an Egyptian working for the Germans."

"Was this an intelligence matter?" Culpepper asked sharply.

"Yes. He suggested I move to Alex as soon as possible, board my ship for Italy and buy a gun."

Culpepper was silent for a few moments. "Alexandria is crawling with German agents. If they have a lead on you it's not safe. Why are they interested in you? Can you tell me?"

"I was the pilot of an RAF plane they tried to sabotage in Cairo a week ago. Their little plot failed. Doug is trying to track down the villains."

"Sounds tricky. Are you staying here?"

"No, I checked into the Metropole."

"I'll give you a ride back to your hotel."

"I was thinking of having dinner first."

"That's fine. I'll keep an eye on you."

"By the way, how did you know I was carrying a weapon?"

"Besides buying a gun, you should've seen a tailor. Wearing a shoulder holster needs the jacket to be let out a bit." Culpepper turned to go. "I'll join you for coffee when you've finished your meal. Cheerio."

Chadwick slowly finished his drink and walked into the dining room. It was a little early for a large meal, so he ordered Welsh Rarebit, and then ordered another beer. When it was half gone, he was joined by Culpepper.

"Just had a word with your friend Larson. He sends his regards."

"Thank you."

"He asked me to pass on a message. Call him at the office tomorrow about 9 a.m."

Chadwick finished his beer. "I'm ready."

Culpepper led him to a rear door of the hotel and pointed to a car parked on the street. Chadwick climbed into the passenger side. Culpepper started the engine and engaged the gear. The car lurched into motion. "It's an old Morris," Culpepper explained. "Clutch needs work."

"What's Alexandria like?" asked Chadwick, trying to start a conversation.

"Oh, it's not bad. Hellish hot in summer. Where are you based?"

"Iraq, but my tour is up. I'm on my way back to Blighty."

"Surprised his majesty is not running you back on a ship."

"I had the option, but I had some leave coming and I thought I would see a little of Europe. I'm sailing to Brindisi."

"Be careful in Italy. The Fascists run it now. Keep your gun out of sight. Germany is going the same way. We're getting a lot of Russian refugees here. Difficult to guess where it's all going to finish up. Here we are."

The car pulled up to Chadwick's hotel. "Nice to meet you, and don't wander the streets at night. Bon voyage."

Chadwick thanked him and watched him drive away.

After an early breakfast Chadwick called Doug Larson on a phone in the hotel lobby. Larson told him that an unidentified corpse fished out of the Nile had been identified as the missing cleaner. It was likely he was the person who tried to sabotage the Vimy, Larson said, but this would be difficult to prove. He had been killed by a vicious blow to the head. It was probably a murder and the case had been turned over to the Egyptian police. He wished Chadwick a pleasant voyage and hung up.

Chadwick went to his room and strapped on the shoulder holster and gun. He found a tailor near the ship he was going to board later in the day. The tailor said it would be twenty-four hours before the jacket was ready. By paying him ahead the tailor promised to deliver the jacket the next day to the ship.

Chadwick realized he was putting a lot of trust in the tailor's word but considering the time pressure he had little choice. The tailor wrapped the holster and gun in brown paper and Chadwick carried the neat parcel back to the hotel. He packed his suitcase, checked out of the hotel and took a taxi to the wharf where his ship was moored. He entered the dock area through a dingy customs office. His passport was stamped, and he was told he was free to board.

Chadwick walked down the long wharf to his ship. He stopped and looked at the stern. The hull was streaked with rust and clearly the vessel had sailed many sea-miles. Underneath the name painted on the stern he could just make out some letters welded to the steel plates, OSLO. He concluded the ship had started life in Norway and was now ending its days steaming for an Italian company. He mounted the gangplank and was directed by a seaman to the purser's office. The purser spoke a little English as he took the receipt from the shipping company and entered Chadwick's details in a ledger. He told Chadwick the ship was carrying a mixed cargo, much of it destined for Crete. There were six passengers. He led him through a number of confusing corridors, which smelt of steam and sulfurous smoke, to a small cabin with two bunks, one above the other. There was a wash basin and a locker for clothes. As he was the first arrival, Chadwick chose the lower bunk and put his suitcase on it.

The purser turned to leave and told him the toilet was two doors down the corridor and lunch was being served in the lounge. Chadwick found his hands were gritty and he washed them in the sink. After a few diversions he located the lounge. Two tables were set with cutlery, and a steward asked him if he would like some soup. He was the only person sitting at the table. Two ship's officers sat in easy chairs talking quietly to each other. They glanced at him when he entered but then resumed their conversation. When he had finished the soup, the steward returned with a plate holding some boiled potatoes, and unidentifiable piece of meat and some gelatinous peas. None of it had much taste and he turned down the offer of custard for dessert. The steward poured him some coffee and he moved over to a vacant easy chair to drink it.

One of the officers left and the other came over to introduce himself. "Chief Engineer Graziosi," he said slowly with a strong accent.

Chadwick took his hand and introduced himself. "Do you speak English?" he asked.

"No, no. *Mi dispiace*," he apologized in Italian. "Capitano Di Palma, good Engleesh."

During the afternoon the other passengers boarded. They were all Italian and none spoke a word of English. Chadwick's cabin companion introduced himself as "Stefano" and that was the extent of their conversation. He started to read the book he had bought about the war in Mesopotamia. He was concerned that his jacket would not be returned before the ship sailed the next day, and now he had cleared customs there was no convenient way of contacting the tailor on shore.

At dinner he sat with the Italian passengers. Several officers sat at the other table. When coffee was served one of them rose and talked to the passengers. Chadwick understood not a word. But then he crossed over and grasped Chadwick's hand.

"How do you do? I'm Captain Di Palma. Welcome aboard."

The captain spoke English with a strong American accent. He was of stocky build and radiated an aura of competence and authority.

"I was just telling our Italian passengers that we're expecting bad weather in a day or so. With luck we'll be under the lee of Crete. I worked for an American line for fifteen years. I wasn't always the captain of a dago slop bucket. Anything you want, just see me."

Chadwick introduced himself and thanked him for the invitation. "When we're underway, I'd like to visit the bridge."

"No problem. Just come up when you want. My cabin is aft of the wheelhouse."

Chadwick read for a while and then went to his cabin, where Stefano was already tucked up in the upper bunk and snoring gently. In the morning he shaved at the small sink and headed to the lounge. Breakfast consisted of juice and coffee with fresh bread, cheese and cold cuts. He was delighted when the steward came to him after breakfast and handed over a parcel containing his jacket. Back in the cabin he locked the door and then retrieved the gun and holster from his suitcase. The jacket fitted perfectly. He put the gun back and locked his suitcase.

The day was overcast, but he took a walk along the deck. The crew were putting the finishing touches to storing the cargo by hammering wedges into the hatches to secure the canvas cover. He stood at the bow and peered into the water, which was filthy. Flotsam and jetsam mixed with an oily scum washed against the hull. Several seamen approached him and indicated by signs that he must go below. He retreated to the lounge. After an hour there was a long hoot from the steam whistle and the ship began to vibrate. They were underway.

He watched through the window as the docks at Alexandria slid by. There were dozens of moored ships attended by gyrating cranes. In the outer harbor they passed many freighters at anchor, most flying the British red ensign at the stern. The engine rpm increased, along with the vibration, and the ship began to roll as she met the open sea.

All the passengers sat at the table in the lounge for lunch, though most of them just toyed with the food. At dinner time only three passengers, including Chadwick, appeared for the meal. It was a tasty paella of rice with fish, seasoned with fried onions. Chadwick chose blancmange for dessert, but he was the only one to taste the full menu. At breakfast the next day Chadwick sat alone for the meal, which was the same as the day before. The ship seemed to be making good progress. A swell on the starboard side from the northerly wind caused her to roll about ten degrees every fifteen seconds. At the extremes of the rolling motion the engine vibration increased noticeably.

In mid-morning, after a cup of coffee and a French chocolate biscuit, he decided to visit the bridge. He climbed up the exposed steel steps and entered the wheelhouse. A quartermaster constantly adjusted the spokes as he stared at a gyrocompass, which emitted a loud tick every few seconds. A large binnacle stood on his right. On the left was the telegraph to the engine room. It was set to "Full Ahead." The captain was standing by a table at the rear, lifting a brass sextant from a mahogany case.

"Ah, good morning, Mr. Chadwick. I'm just about to check our progress with a sight on the sun."

"Please, call me Allan. Can I do anything?"

"Yes, you can hold this stopwatch. When I call 'mark,' push the knob to stop the hand."

They walked out on the bridge. The sun was well above the horizon, intermittently visible between scudding grey clouds. The captain sighted through the telescope on the sextant as he lifted his arms up and down to match the motion of the ship. "Ready, ready," he called, then "Mark."

Allan clamped down on the large knob on the watch and they both went into the wheelhouse. Captain Di Palma noted the sextant angle by peering through a small lens over the scale, and asked Allan for the stopwatch reading. He jotted down the numbers in a large notebook.

"I'll go next door to work out this stuff. I should get a line of position that will confirm our progress after leaving port. It will take me about an hour."

Chadwick was intrigued, as he had no knowledge of celestial navigation. He followed the captain into the navigation shack and asked if he had any book in English that explained what he was doing. The captain reached up and passed him a thick tome off a crowded shelf, "American Practical Navigator," Bowditch, 1920.

"Read that and you'll know everything I know," said Di Palma with a laugh. "I think this weather's going to thicken. That's probably my last sight for a while."

Chadwick sat with two of the ship's officers for lunch and in the afternoon buried himself in Bowditch. Over two hundred pages described the tools and practice of conventional surface navigation, with which he was familiar. Then he got to the section on celestial navigation, which he found to be heavy going. He sat in an easy chair, buried in the book. Several times the steward brought him a cup of coffee.

The captain joined Chadwick and the same two officers for dinner. He chatted to Chadwick in English and with his officers in Italian.

"The wind has picked up," he observed, "and it's got colder. We're in for the 'Misery,' I think. That's what we call this wind in Italy. Further west the French call it the 'Mistral.' It will back further west, I think."

Chadwick asked him to explain a point he didn't understand about celestial navigation. Captain Di Palma showed he had a wide knowledge of the subject.

"Why, ol' Cap'n Sumner thought up that nearly a hundert years ago, an American," he explained putting on his idea of a folksy American accent. "He was just an ol' sea-dog, but he figured out something the astronomers and scientists had missed."

Chadwick didn't quite understand his comment but realized Di Palma was proud that a real ship's captain had made a useful contribution to the art of celestial navigation. He went to his bunk, satisfied he was passing the time usefully.

By morning the weather was markedly worse. The ship was rolling violently. The engine vibration was slower, but every now and again, it suddenly increased in pitch and intensity.

Great waves crashed into the bow, producing a hollow boom that made Chadwick wonder how much stress welded steel plate could take. He put on his raincoat and dashed up the steps to the bridge on the port side. Captain Di Palma was standing on the bridge peering through a spinning glass window that flung off the spray slicing up from the bow as the ship shuddered from the thudding waves. The engine telegraph was set to "Ahead Half."

The captain welcomed him to the bridge, saying, "Getting rough, I expected it." As he spoke the engine vibration suddenly increased. "That's the prop coming partially out of the water," he explained to Chadwick. "Dangerous if the engineers don't catch it and throttle down. Could break the shaft."

Chadwick asked if he could visit the engine room.

"Sure," the captain replied. "Just stay on the platform at the entrance. I guess they're pretty busy right now." He gave him directions to the engine room.

As Chadwick opened the door in the bulkhead, a waft of hot, oily-smelling air hit him, in complete contrast to the cold air on deck. The engine room was cavernous and wide, with huge, insulated pipes that led from the boiler to the steam engine, which was not visible from his vantage point.

A watch engineer stood on a lower platform, staring intently at a large dial. As the vessel pitched and the engine rpm increased, he rapidly adjusted a big, red wheel to control steam to the engine. Below him two stokers, stripped to the waist, danced on the heaving plates and shoveled coal from a hopper into the blazing furnace. High, yellow lights illuminated the space with plenty of shadows, which flickered out when the furnace doors were flung open. It was a scene from hell, Chadwick concluded, as he tightly gripped the hot steel piping forming the rail.

At lunch two brave passengers looking very pale showed up to join Chadwick. After lunch he went to lie down. The constant movement to counteract the rolling of the ship was tiring. He woke up in time to catch some coffee and French biscuits in the lounge. The weather was moderating. He read for the rest of the afternoon, enjoyed a well-cooked dinner of steak and kidney pie, followed by apple pie, and went to bed early. Four passengers had dinner with him, but Stefano did not seem to have left his bunk.

After breakfast the next morning, Chadwick tracked down the captain on the bridge, where he was plotting on a chart in the navigation shack.

"Mind if I look?" asked Chadwick, peering over the captain's shoulder.

"Sure. I'm plotting our dead reckoning position. We didn't do too well during the night, but I've just rung for full ahead. We're about three hundred miles from Crete. We'll arrive a day late, typical for a winter passage."

Chadwick looked at the penciled lines on the chart. "I don't see a gauge that measures our speed on the bridge. How do you calculate the distance run?"

"I call the engine room," the captain replied, with a chuckle. "They have a totalizer that shows total engine revolutions. I can convert revolutions between two points into miles quite accurately, less so when the weather is foul."

Chadwick was surprised by the simplicity of the idea. That evening at dinner the captain made a long announcement to the passengers in Italian. Then he made condensed version for Chadwick in English. "We expect to make a landfall in a day and a half. Our port will be Heraklion. We'll discharge some cargo and pick up new goods for shipping to Brindisi. We've received radio messages stating there's been some civil unrest in Crete. Passengers go ashore at their own risk."

The ship tied up at a pier in the inner harbor during the night. In the morning, even Stefano showed up for breakfast. The sea was calm in the harbor. An elaborate structure, clearly ancient, graced the end of the pier. Chadwick climbed up to the bridge. He was interested to see the operation of the derricks, which were busy lifting crates from the forward hold. After a while the captain joined him on the bridge. Chadwick asked him what the old building was at the end of the pier.

"I believe it's a Venetian fortress. Ask at the museum if you go ashore."

"What about the civil unrest you mentioned?"

"I don't think that's here in the capital. The museum is nearby. You should be fine. But please be back by dinner time. The cargo work is going well, and we should be able to push off tonight."

Later in the morning, Chadwick walked down the gangplank and asked a policeman at the dock gate for directions to the museum. The wind still had a northerly bite to it, and he wore his raincoat over his jacket. After a twenty-minute walk he found the museum. A sign at the door in Greek and English stated the museum had been damaged in an earthquake in 1930 and only one wing was open.

Crete was the center of the Minoan civilization; palaces had been extensively excavated. The museum had paintings and mosaics which depicted life over 4,000 years ago, including a cult of bull leaping, in which brave young men leapt over charging bulls, using the horns to get leverage. Chadwick inspected an interesting baked clay disc, which was found in the ruins of a palace at Phaistos on the south coast. Many strange symbols had been pressed into the clay on both sides when it was soft, forming a spiral. Nobody had been able to translate it.

Most interesting of all was a display called the Antikythera Mechanism. About thirty years earlier a sponge diver had accidentally landed on the wreck of a Roman ship, which was full of looted Greek art treasures dating to about 60 BC. The mechanism was named after the location of the wreck, the small island of Antikythera, lying north of Crete. There were numerous photographs showing that it was comprised of several gear wheels, but it was corroded, and parts were missing. A model of the mechanism showed it to be about ten inches high. Its purpose was unknown, but it was suspected to be an astronomical calculator. Chadwick was fascinated to think someone was making what looked like a clockwork gear box more than two thousand years ago. The mechanism itself was in a museum in Athens.

He returned to the ship mentally excited by the ingenuity of man, and resolved to be as good as those old-timers, helping to solve the problems of flight when he got to Farnborough. He had picked up a pamphlet which described the Venetian Fortress. It had been built in the 16th century on the remains of an Arabic fort built about 900 AD. The local name was Koules Fort.

The ship left during the night. Chadwick was not awakened by the blast of the steam whistle as it pulled away from the pier. In the morning the ship was ploughing over a sparkling sea under a wintry sun. No land was visible. Chadwick went to the bridge after breakfast and asked Captain Di Palma if he could look through his sextant and measure the angle of the sun. The captain was only too pleased to talk about celestial navigation. He showed Chadwick how to adjust the glass filters so that he didn't damage his eyes by looking directly at the sun. He threw in the comment that looking at the sun had ruined the eyes of early sailors and pirates, which is why they were often depicted with eye patches.

The instrument was an old one, made in England by the Heath Company. The angle was read off a Vernier. The newer one used a micrometer drum and was much easier to use, the captain explained. Chadwick stood on the bridge and chased the sun, without success. The captain took pity on him and adjusted the angle of the arm so that the sun appeared as an orange ball sitting on the horizon, and then Chadwick found he could easily track the increasing elevation of the sun as it rose in the morning sky. The captain told him that a sight at noon, when the sun was due south of the ship, was a special case and the observer could do a simple calculation in his head and announce the ship's latitude, to the amazement of non-navigators, something Chadwick had already learned by reading Bowditch.

The captain said they should make Brindisi in a little over two days, and in the afternoon the mountains of Greece were faintly visible on the starboard beam. The ship arrived at Brindisi in the middle of an afternoon. Passengers were told they could disembark immediately or stay on board for one more night. Chadwick went ashore before dinner to find the railway station and get a timetable for trains to Rome.

Chapter Thirty-Five

The city seemed to be run-down and was obviously very old, though modern buildings were mixed randomly with ancient Roman ruins. After breakfast on his last day aboard, Chadwick tipped the steward and asked to be shown to the galley. There he congratulated the cook on the excellent meals served during the voyage. To his surprise the cook answered with a strong Cockney accent.

"You're English!" he cried.

"Well, no, guv'ner, I'm an eye-tie. My father was an Italian sailor who married my mother, she's English. I grew up in Whitechapel Lunnon, then we moved to Italy."

"That explains the steak and kidney pie,'" Chadwick said, triumphantly.

Chadwick went to make his goodbyes to the captain, who was in his cabin behind the bridge. Chadwick thanked him enthusiastically for the loan of Bowditch and his introduction to celestial navigation. Captain Di Palma told him it was a pleasure to have a passenger interested in how the ship functioned. He asked Chadwick what his plans were.

"I'm going to take the train and spend a few days in Rome."

Di Palma said, in a fatherly way, "You know, the new government now is fascisti. They tend to be rough, so stay out of trouble."

"Me!" said Chadwick, grinning. "I lead the life of a saint."

He picked up his passport from the purser, who had done the necessary paperwork to get him into Italy, and walked to the station, carrying his suitcase. He bought a second-class ticket to Rome. The train was listed as an express, and he would have to change in Naples. The train wasn't crowded, and he found a seat in a compartment with two other passengers. One was a fit-looking young woman about his age, dressed for hiking. There was a large rucksack on the rack over her seat, which Chadwick guessed was hers. When he noticed that she was reading a book in English he spoke to her.

"Excuse me. I notice you're reading a book in English. Is that where you're from?"

She looked at him steadily for a moment before replying. "Actually, I'm Canadian, but even in the colonies they teach us to read."

Chadwick was taken aback by her sarcastic tone, but persevered. "I'm English, from Liverpool. Have you been hiking in this part of the world?"

"Mostly I've been looking at old ruins. This part of Italy was invaded many times in the past."

"How interesting. I was just in Crete. My name's Allan, by the way."

"How do y'do. Deborah."

Chadwick relapsed into silence and Deborah conspicuously turned her attention back to her book. The other passenger in the compartment hid a sly smile.

"This is supposed to be an express, I believe," Chadwick said, lamely. "Do you know where it stops next?"

"Bari," she said, without looking up from her book.

"And when will that be, do you know?"

"Two and a half hours from Brindisi. After that, Naples."

"That's where I have to change. After that I'm going to Rome."

Deborah looked up from her book. "Lots of good ruins there."

"Are you an archaeologist?" Chadwick asked.

"I'm a student. Maybe one day I'll be an archaeologist."

"I just spent some time in Iraq and Egypt. I was able to visit digs at Ur and Nineveh, as well as tour the great pyramid."

"You do get around. What are you, the scion of a rich family?"

"I wouldn't be travelling second class if I was."

"Good point."

"I'm a very junior officer in his majesty's Royal Air Force."

"Ah, a parasite."

Chadwick wasn't quite sure how to respond to that but continued. "When I was at Ur, I saw a clay plaque of a goddess they had just found. Babylonian, I think."

"Not my period, far too old."

"What are you interested in?"

"Oh, Roman to Viking."

"When I was in Crete, I saw an exhibit about a mechanism they found on an old Roman wrecked ship. It had gears and looked like clockwork."

"Probably an alarm clock that fell off a modern ship."

"Oh, no. It was too big for that—" and then he stopped. Chadwick saw that Deborah was smiling. She was pulling his leg, he realized.

"You know, Allan, you're a very serious young man." Seeing his embarrassment at her remark, she relented and shared that Rome was her destination also.

After that exchange he was quiet for a while. The train was moving along the east coast, and often he could glimpse the Adriatic Sea glinting in the distance. Small towns and villages flashed by at regular intervals. The train stopped at the Bari station, which was in a suburban area, well away from the ancient walled city, and then after ten minutes the train started up again. It turned west and began the climb through the mountains that formed the central spine of Italy. The leg to Naples took two and a quarter hours.

An hour after they left Bari, Deborah pulled down her rucksack and extracted a small, brown paper package. She opened it to remove a sandwich and a hard-boiled egg. She offered the egg to Chadwick.

"Would you like this? The sandwich is quite enough for me."

He hesitated, and then in the interest of making peace said, "Thank you very much. I'm getting peckish."

She handed it to him with a paper napkin and extracted a small salt cellar from a pocket on her jacket. She opened her sandwich and sprinkled some salt on the contents, then she handed the salt to Chadwick, who put a little on his egg.

When they arrived in Naples, they had about forty-five minutes to wait before the Rome connection, so they left the train to find a station bar, where they each ordered a beer. Chadwick would also have liked to order some food, but the menu was written in Italian.

"Can you understand this?"

"Sort of, but I can speak Latin. I wonder if that would work?"

It was an intellectual joke that didn't work. When she spoke in Latin to the counter attendant, he stared at her woodenly. "The language must have changed since the Romans ran this place," she commented with a wry grin.

She ordered a potato salad with some smoked salami for each of them, which Chadwick paid for with lira he had bought from the purser on the ship. He looked at Deborah as they ate. She was tall for a woman and quite thin. She wore wire-rimmed glasses. Her straw-colored hair was cut straight just below her ears. He decided she was very intelligent. They left the bar with five minutes to spare before their train left, and that was a mistake. The platform was crowded, and people were struggling to board. Two members of the Carabinieri, dressed in black uniforms with boat-shaped hats worn sideways, began to herd the last passengers on the train. Allan and Deborah were pushed none too gently into a vestibule at the end of a corridor, a whistle blew, and the train chugged out of the station.

"What on earth are the police doing here?" Allan asked.

"Don't you know? Il Duce has declared the trains will leave on time."

The trip to Rome was uncomfortable. No seats were available. Allan and Deborah sat on their luggage in the corridor. An inspector looked at their tickets without comment as he maneuvered in the crowded space. The train made good time, however. It was dark when they pulled into the Rome Central station.

"Where are you staying in Rome?" Allan asked.

"I dunno. I usually find a hostel in a large city."

Surprised at his own boldness, Allan asked, "Do you want to share a room with me?"

Deborah looked at him warily. "Well, I'm on a budget, but that doesn't mean sharing a bed."

"Of course not. I'm just trying to save money."

"Naturally. You are, after all, an officer and a gentleman."

Allan spotted a large sign over a kiosk, which read "Travelers Aid" in English. They waited their turn behind a German couple, then asked the woman at the kiosk if she could recommend a modest hotel near the center.

"How many rooms?" the woman asked.

"One room. Twin beds," Allan replied.

The woman spoke rapidly on the phone and then passed them a slip with an address. "I suggest you take a taxi. The public system is complicated and slow. This hotel will hold a room for an hour. Mention Traveler's Aid. By the way, there's a good deal of hardship in Rome. Unemployment is high. Be careful on the streets at night. In crowded places beware of pickpockets."

They thanked her and made a small contribution to a tip box. They had no difficulty finding a taxi outside the station, and within thirty minutes they were in the lobby of a small hotel, The Bristol. Allan mentioned Travelers Aid to the clerk behind the reception desk.

"Yes, I'm holding a room. Twin beds. Please give me your passports and sign the register." The clerk glanced at Deborah's left hand.

"Most English people sign in as Mr. and Mrs. Smith. You have Room 21. The bathroom is down the corridor. Your key works both doors." She mentioned the nightly rate, which worked out to well under a pound in English currency.

They took their luggage up a flight of stairs and opened the door of Room 21. It contained only the bare essentials but looked comfortable and had two chairs. Deborah took the key and excused herself to go to the bathroom. Allan washed his hands and face in a small washbasin. He took the chance to strap on the shoulder harness. *Having brought it this far I may as well wear it,* he reasoned to himself.

When Deborah returned, he popped into the bathroom and then they both went back to the lobby and asked the clerk if there was a restaurant nearby. They were directed to a small trattoria three blocks away. It was cold out and they both wore outer coats. The streetlights were dim, but they followed the directions and entered a warm, cheerful room. They hung up their coats and were greeted effusively by the maître de. Allan ordered a bottle of chianti, which they finished while they ate. They exchanged surnames. Deborah talked a great deal about growing up in Ontario. "I'm a Campbell," she said proudly. She was one of the few women to have attended the University of Toronto. Her father was the president of a bank. Allan was more reticent and spoke very little about himself. They were both feeling on top of the world when Allan settled the bill and they walked out into the cold night air.

A block from the restaurant, a man strode past them and then suddenly wheeled round and threatened them with a knife.

"Money, lira," he shouted with a strong accent.

Neither said a word, and then Allan reached inside his jacket as though getting a wallet. The man in front of them reached out a hand. Deborah suddenly gave a startled scream. A second man had come up behind her and put an arm roughly around her neck. Allan smoothly drew out his automatic, thumbed back the hammer and fired a shot to one side of the man with the knife. The bullet struck the paving stones and whined off into the night. The gunshot and ricochet made a tremendous noise in the quiet neighborhood. The two men stood for a moment as though paralyzed, and then took off like startled rabbits. The man in front threw his knife to the ground with clatter.

Allan strode over to pick it up and then said calmly to Deborah, "Are you all right?"

She nodded.

Looking around for a convenient place to discard the knife, he casually tossed it into a street drain, and then took Deborah's arm. "I think we should leg it to the hotel smartly. We don't want to be involved with the carabinieri."

He put the gun away and within five minutes they entered the hotel lobby and picked up their key. Once in the bedroom Deborah, who had not spoken during the whole incident, exclaimed, "My God, what do you do in the Air Force?"

Allan thought for minute, and then said casually, "I kill people."

Deborah's eyes widened. "Oh, no!" she breathed. On reflection, she added, "Really?"

"'Fraid so," replied Allan, feigning nonchalance. "That's what the government pays me for."

Deborah picked up the key and went outside to the bathroom. Allan unlocked his suitcase and put the gun and holster away. When Deborah returned, he said, "You know, those men very likely followed us to the restaurant, and were lying in wait. I think first thing in the morning we should move."

"Do you think that's really necessary?"

"Yes, if anyone reported the shot to the police it would not take a brilliant detective long to find us. Even the robbers themselves could have made a telephone report to just complicate our lives. They almost certainly knew the hotel we're staying at."

"Don't you feel you're being a touch paranoid?"

"Maybe, but without going into details an attempt was made within the past month to kill me and my crew in Egypt." He paused. "We can split up, and you can find a hostel."

"No, you seem like a good fellow to have around."

Early in the morning they went down to the reception desk. A new clerk had taken over. Chadwick paid the bill and they retrieved their passports. He asked the clerk to call a taxi, and when it arrived, he loudly directed it to the central railway station. Inside the taxi as it sped along the streets, he said to Deborah, "If anyone does try to track us, they'll lose the trail at the station."

Deborah shook her head in wonderment, thinking he seemed a bit touched.

Chadwick sensed her mood. "Look, I was in a fracas in Cairo that involved German agents. I don't want my name on any police lists that the Germans may get to see. Of course, we signed in as Mr. and Mrs. Smith. I should thank the lovesick English tourists for protecting my identity. I wonder if the clerk copied our real names from our passports."

After breakfast at the station they returned to the Travelers Aid kiosk. This time a man was answering questions. They made the same request for a modest hotel, single room, twin beds, but near the Vatican. He gave them a choice of several hostelries. Chadwick chose one which was slightly more expensive than the last night's accommodation and they found a taxi.

When they signed in, the clerk copied their names from their passports, commenting, "In Italy it is against the law for a man and woman to share a room, unless they're married, but you are foreign, and times are hard." He lifted his eyebrows and put their key on the desk. "Room 34. The bathroom is next door."

The neighborhood was much busier than the one they had stayed in the previous night. Children were playing in the street and there were two bars and a restaurant in the same block. After they dumped their luggage Chadwick suggested a drink at the nearest bar where they could discuss their plans for Rome. They sat at an inside table and drank coffee.

Deborah said, "I'm pretty familiar with Roman history. Let me work out an itinerary of the best places to visit. How many days have you got?"

"Four, maybe five."

Deborah was as good as her word. She decided they should start off in Ostia, the port of Imperial Rome on the river Tiber. It took them forty minutes to make the journey once they got to the bus station. It was brimming with Roman ruins, many in good condition. Chadwick was amused to see a public lavatory with all the stone one-holers lined up next to each other. "The port dated from the fourth century, BC and had been much improved by the Emperor Tiberius, who built a new harbor on the north bank in the first century, AD," Deborah lectured. They saw public baths, very old apartments and numerous mosaics, and Deborah translated the Latin inscriptions for him.

After two hours Chadwick was exhausted, and they found a small restaurant for lunch. As they finished a bottle of Italian white wine, Deborah regaled him with the history of the early Roman Empire and the Punic wars. Chadwick nodded off in the bus on the way back despite the bouncy ride. Back at the hotel he snatched a nap and they had dinner at a restaurant near the hotel. In the morning they discovered the hotel served a complimentary breakfast of coffee and pastries, which was quite adequate for them. The hotel clerk gave them a map of the extensive tram network and after a couple of false starts they made it to the Vatican.

"Of course," Deborah told him, "There were no Christian churches here until near the end of the Empire. The story of how Christianity was adopted by a pagan country and became one of the world's dominant religions is fascinating."

Deborah clearly felt the Vatican was the ideal locale for the history of the early Catholic church. They found a quiet pew in a small chapel.

"Of course, it all started with the ancient Egyptians."

"They were Christians?" said Chadwick in surprise.

"No, of course not. They started the practice of rewriting history. Often new pharaohs would have the history of the previous pharaoh expunged or changed. Inscriptions on stone were chiseled off. So, it's hard to know the truth of what happened centuries ago. The Romans continued to do the same thing. This is particularly true of the fourth century AD, when Christianity was adopted by the Romans. So, we don't really know the true story. By the fourth century AD the Roman Empire was split into four parts, each run by little Caesars. Constantine's father became Caesar of the western section. He was a formidable soldier—he saved his son from the cruel Galerius and left him in a position to conquer the other little Caesars and again become Emperor of the whole empire. Constantine was tolerant of Christianity, which competed with other religions, mostly pagan. He allowed the Church of the Holy Sepulcher to be built in Jerusalem at the site of Jesus's tomb."

"I've been there—" Chadwick interrupted, but Deborah swept on.

"To achieve the Empire, he defeated Galerius and Maxentius. Both died. It's said he killed his own wife and a son for dubious reasons. There's a statue of him in York, England, where he campaigned. Anyway, in adopting Christianity it left the Romans with lots of problems, hence the rewriting of history."

"Such as?"

"Well," she drawled, "the Romans executed Jesus in a cruel way, didn't make them look good. So, history was rewritten to show the Jews were responsible for Jesus's death, a propaganda victory that reverberates to this day. It's said that on his deathbed, Constantine was baptized as a Christian. The Romans had a great deal to do with what went into the standard bible we know today. It wasn't finally finished until a couple of centuries after Constantine died."

She stood up. "That's enough pseudo history. Let's take a look at St. Peters."

That took most of the day. That night, after dinner and a bottle of good Italian wine, they went to their room. Chadwick was feeling confident and distinctly amorous.

"Deborah," he said, "You're a beautiful woman. Would you mind if I forgot I was an officer and a gentleman for one night?"

"Fiddlesticks. I'm not beautiful, but I do have compensations. Push the beds together and stop messing about. The timing is good. I'm not fertile right now."

He complied with a smile, reminded of a witticism attributed to H.G. Wells, who observed it was much easier to get a female graduate of Oxford into bed than a shop assistant at Woolworth's department store.

In the morning they took a tram to the Colosseum, with Deborah pointing out that, although in its prime it could hold about sixty thousand spectators, not much was open to the public two thousand years later. She told him it was named after a giant statue of Nero, long gone, and was built about 80 AD, funded by the treasures captured in Jerusalem, and using Jewish captives as slaves for the hard labor of construction.

They were both keen to have an early night. They put the twin beds together and turned the mattresses sideways. Deborah was an inventive lover. Allan was hard pressed to keep up with her demands. After one tumultuous orgasm he lay sweating, feeling sleepy but unable to forget the pleasures that could still be had.

"You really are something in bed, Deborah."

"You know what they say. The sweetest meat is near the bone."

In the morning Chadwick reviewed the time left of his leave and decided reluctantly to move on. Deborah planned to visit Florence. Although he had no clear plan of how to get to England, he decided to travel to Germany, and then tour the battle sites in northern France and Belgium. Deborah was amazed he had decided to visit Germany.

"I thought you said the Germans may be after you," she chided him. "It's not logical to put your head in the lion's mouth."

"You're probably right, but friends of mine who ought to know think we'll be at war again with Germany in a few years and I want to see them firsthand before that happens."

They parted as friends and promised to write. He didn't press her to share the hotel bill. Deborah took a bus to Florence, and Chadwick booked a sleeper for that night which would take him directly to Berlin. The journey would take about twenty-four hours.

Chapter Thirty-Six

Chadwick arrived at the central railway station in the middle of the afternoon. He had booked a first-class sleeper which would take him to Berlin via Bologna, Verona, Innsbruck and Munich. The route was though the Brenner pass, and with luck he would be awake when the train cleared customs at the Austrian borders. The station was chaotic. Porters with handcarts weaved between densely packed crowds. Steam engines emitted clouds of vapor and belched foul smelling smoke. There was a constant clamor as conductors made announcements through trumpets and blew whistles.

The conductor guided him to his reserved compartment, which he shared with another man. Later the seats would be converted into bunks. He made his way to the dining car for afternoon tea as the train pulled out. After the noise of the station, it was a quiet haven, punctuated by the click-clack of the steel wheels. Chadwick poured tea into a china cup and selected an éclair from a trolley in the aisle. He spared a thought for Deborah, who at that moment was probably being crushed in a bouncing seat on a bus bound for Florence. He decided she was a woman who knew how to look after herself. He read a book for a couple of hours and then returned to the dining car for dinner, where the waiter introduced the man across the table,

"This is Herr Emsden. You are sharing the compartment."

Chadwick shook his hand, saying, "Allan Chadwick, pleased to meet you." He looked across the table at the man sitting opposite. He was a well-built man who appeared to be in his sixties, with silver hair and a large mustache.

"To where are you travelling. Mr. Chadwick?" asked Emsden in heavily accented English.

"I am going to Berlin, sir."

"Ach, so." Then he added, "I am leaving the train in Munich."

Chadwick ordered filet of sole with potatoes au gratin, along with a glass of white wine. After the entre the waiter brought him a sorbet, and as he toyed with his coffee, he saw that Emsden occasionally glanced at him under bushy eyebrows.

Emsden suddenly said, "You are English?"

"Yes, I grew up in the north of England."

"The English are very lucky."

"Why is that?"

"It is an island. The people who live there feel as, as—" he groped for a word "—one. You share a common—goal. I am sorry my English is poor."

"Your English is very good, sir, but the English are not as united as you think. We have had civil wars."

Emsden dismissed the idea. "A long time ago. Now you have an empire that covers the world. This is only achieved by people with a common— purpose. Ach, that is the word."

After a pause during which Chadwick said nothing, he went on.

"Germany is part of the European continent. We are surrounded by peoples who are not as— as pure. I do not speak well. By people who have not German characteristics. We now have a new Chancellor, who is, himself, an Austrian. But he seems to have a grip on the German problem."

"What is his name, Herr Emsden?"

"Adolph Hitler. He has written a book which gives me hope."

"Ah, yes, I've heard of him. I didn't know he was an Austrian. And what exactly is the 'German Problem'?"

"The problem is that Germany is a proud country. It was humiliated by the Versailles Treaty. The Army fought honorably, and the home front collapsed due to communists and Jewish speculators. In particular, the financial reparations ruined the banking system and the middle class."

"How will Herr Hitler address the problem?"

"Some land traditionally German must be restored. The Danzig corridor and the Rhineland."

"I hope these changes will not lead to war— the last war was terrible."

"I believe they will be negotiated."

"Were you in the army during the war?" Chadwick asked.

"No, I was in the— in the Foreign service. Tell me, what is a young man like you doing travelling around Europe in winter?"

"Actually, I'm on leave. I'm a member of the Royal Air Force. I'm returning home and I had some leave due."

"Very interesting, where were you stationed?"

"Iraq." Chadwick now suspected he was talking too much. "Excuse me, I'm going to read in the lounge car and then turn in. Good night."

In the lounge he looked through the window. Night had fallen, and the occasional lights flashed by. It was rather hypnotic. A waiter asked him if he would like a drink and so he ordered a sherry. He drank it slowly and then made his way to the compartment. The attendant had made up the bunks. Each had a curtain running the full length. He was faced with the choice of undressing in the aisle between the bunks or climbing in, drawing the curtain and being a contortionist to remove his clothes. He climbed in, wriggled out of his jacket and trousers and prepared to sleep in his shirt and underwear. He was soon asleep, as the rhythmic vibration was soothing, and the compartment was hot.

Sometime in the middle of the night, the sleeping car attendant gently woke him, saying, "Herr Chadwick, we have stopped at the Austrian border. Customs officials must examine your papers."

Groggily, Chadwick reached into the inside pocket of his jacket, which was hanging on a hook over the bunk. He passed his passport to the attendant. In a minute or two the attendant was back.

"Herr Chadwick, the inspector wishes to see you. Please put on some clothes and come with me."

Chadwick struggled into his trousers and slid off the bunk. The attendant was waiting in the door of the compartment. He gestured for Chadwick to follow him along the corridor. A man in uniform was waiting in the vestibule at the end. The man looked at him keenly and then glanced at the passport in his hand.

"Herr Chadwick, what is your final destination?"

"Berlin."

"You will not leave the train at Innsbruck, do you understand?" He handed the passport back to Chadwick, who indicated that he understood. The attendant led him back to the compartment.

"Herr Chadwick, we will stop at Innsbruck in about one hour. Please do not leave the train. After leaving Innsbruck we will arrive at the German border. It takes about two hours. There you must clear the German customs. After that we stop in Munich for twenty minutes. Can I bring you a beverage?"

"No, thank you. I'll just go back to sleep."

Chadwick fell asleep in minutes and did not wake up during the stop at Innsbruck. When the train stopped at the German border, the attendant again gave Chadwick a wake-up call.

"Please put on coat and trousers and follow me."

This time he led Chadwick to the dining car. Two officials in black uniforms sat at a table. One man examined his passport, the other had a small pile of passports on the table and was making notes. The official holding his passport addressed Chadwick.

"Why are you visiting Germany?"

"I am simply a tourist, but I particularly want to see the Museum of Antiquities in Berlin."

"In the section marked 'profession' it states you are a commissioned officer. What branch of the military do you serve?"

"I'm a member of the Royal Air Force."

"Are you here on official business?"

"No, I'm a tourist, as I just said. I'm on leave and I'm interested in the ancient world."

"Where will you go when you leave Germany?"

"I intend to visit France."

His interrogator looked dubious but passed his passport to the second man with a whispered comment. This man made some notes and stamped his passport.

"Welcome to Germany. You have two weeks. Do not overstay," he said.

Although the German officials were polite, Chadwick sensed a latent hostility. He went back to the compartment, but he couldn't sleep this time. He noticed that Herr Emsden had not been awakened for the passport clearance. He dressed and went to the lounge. There was a pot of hot coffee on a shelf. He poured himself a cup and added some cream. A blast from the steam whistle echoed through the siding and the train started with a jerk.

An hour later a steward spotted Chadwick in the lounge and told him breakfast was being served. He went back to the compartment and found that his bunk had been converted back to a seat and the curtain had disappeared. He took his razor and shaving soap to the small lavatory. There was plenty of hot water for the sink and he enjoyed a shave.

When he went for breakfast, he hoped he would not be seated with Herr Emsden, whom he had found to be heavy going. The waiter sat him at an empty table, and he ordered pork ribs with sauerkraut. By the time he had finished breakfast, the train was travelling through the suburbs of Munich. When the train stopped, he sat in the lounge and looked through the window. He noticed Herr Emsden stepping onto the platform. Two well-dressed men met him and clicked their heels with a slight bow of their heads. *Clearly a man of some authority,* Chadwick thought to himself.

The five-hour trip to Berlin passed quickly enough. The train stopped twice at stations Chadwick didn't bother to inspect from the window. He tried to read the detective novel he had bought in Alexandria, but the narrative seemed so far removed from the world he knew that he got bored and put the book down. He tracked down the sleeping car steward and gave him a small tip. He asked him in English to recommend a medium-priced hotel near the center of Berlin. He was told to try the Rhinelander or the Bristol.

When the train arrived in Berlin, Chadwick elbowed his way to the taxi stand and stood in a queue. It was bitterly cold, and a brisk wind whistled down the sidewalk. Eventually it was his turn for an empty taxi, and he was soon booking a room at the Bristol Hotel, in British currency. It cost well under a pound a night, and he reckoned he could afford to stay for a week, ten days at the most. The desk clerk copied the details from his passport into a ledger and completed a form for the Gestapo which was sent to Prinz-Albrecht Strasse that night for routine processing.

The next morning, he discovered that the hotel offered a continental breakfast, and when he had finished his coffee, he asked the doorman in English the way to nearest haberdasher. The man didn't understand the word, but he extracted an English-to-German dictionary from his cubby hole and directed Chadwick to a shop three blocks away. Before he left, he picked up a map of the Berlin tram network. When he found the haberdasher, he bought a thick scarf and some gloves, as he was not used to the cold.

He used the streetcars to the Museum of Antiquities where he mainly learned that German teams had been digging in ancient sites for fifty years. By lunch time he was feeling bored. Braving the cold, he made the long walk back to the hotel.

The next day he visited the Museum of Science and Engineering, which he found far more interesting. Early on, the Germans had adopted the steam locomotive and they had a number of early steam engines on view. A German had invented the diesel engine, which promised far better efficiency than the steam engine. Chadwick was interested to discover that the inventor, Rudolf Diesel, had mysteriously disappeared while crossing the English Channel on a ferry. He also found that German advances in chemistry were well represented.

Scanning the notices in the entrance hall he noticed an advertisement by Luft Hansa, the German airline. Sight-seeing flights on board of the new Ju 52 were conducted every day, it said, from Tempelhof airfield, which was near the center of Berlin. The cost was about two pounds in English currency. He decided to take a flight, thinking that knowledge of the new German plane might be useful back in England.

That evening he dropped into a small nightclub near the hotel. Modern American music and scantily clad women dancers went well with several steins of beer. He couldn't understand the jokes, but the audience laughed heartily.

When he got to Tempelhof the next day he joined a long queue for the fifteen-minute flight. It took more than an hour for him to duck under the small door in the fuselage and take a seat, along with about fifteen other passengers. The Ju 52 was an all-metal monoplane with three engines, one in the center and one on each wing. He craned in his seat in order to see in the cockpit, but he was too far back to see much. When they ascended, he figured the plane climbed to about a thousand feet in a little over a minute. The pilot levelled off and made circular flight over the center of the city before making a smooth landing and taxiing to the disembarkation steps.

Chadwick lingered at the cockpit door and asked the pilot if he spoke English.

"Of course," he replied.

"What is your landing speed?"

"Thirty meters per second," the pilot told him, but then Chadwick was pushed away by an attendant organizing the next passenger load. As he walked across the tarmac, he was closely watched by a plain-clothes Gestapo agent.

In the terminal the agent went up to a uniformed policeman and told him to detain Chadwick. The agent then ran back to the plane before it took off again and asked the pilot what he was talking about with the passenger. Back in the terminal he showed his badge to Chadwick and told him to wait. He didn't speak English, but Chadwick remembered enough German to know exactly what he wanted. He sat down and waited until a big man in a black Gestapo uniform approached him.

"Papers" he said brusquely.

"What is all this? "Chadwick asked. "I haven't done anything."

"Papers," the man said again and held out a gloved hand.

Chadwick handed over his passport. He thanked his lucky stars he had not buckled on his gun that morning. The Gestapo agent looked at the photograph in his passport and keenly in Chadwick's face.

"Herr Chadweek," he announced, "you must come with me."

"Just wait a sec," Chadwick protested, "I am a British citizen. Are you arresting me?"

The Gestapo agent seized him by the arm. The other uniformed policeman cleared a way through the crowd, and people looked away. He was led to a low black car, pushed into the back seat and driven to an imposing building on Prinz-Albrecht Strasse, Gestapo headquarters. He was told to wait and seated on a hard bench outside an office. A guard sat with him. After an hour, he was led into the office. A hard-looking man sat at a desk under a large Nazi flag. Judging by the insignia on his uniform he was of high rank. Chadwick was told to stand.

"You have come to Germany to spy, Mr. Chadwick," he said in accented English. "That is a serious offense."

"I am not a spy," Chadwick protested hotly. "I am a tourist, I arrived two days ago."

"Yes, I see that," the German officer said, picking up Chadwick's passport off the desk. "You started work quickly, questioning the Ju 52 pilot about his plane."

Chadwick was flabbergasted. "That was just one pilot talking to another," he said weakly.

"Oh, you are a pilot?" the German countered.

Chadwick felt he was losing a battle of words.

"Who is your contact in Berlin?"

"My contact?" Chadwick repeated. "I don't know anybody in Berlin."

"Come, Mr. Chadwick, you must report to somebody. We know the British have an extensive espionage network in Germany."

"I don't report to anybody in Berlin," Chadwick replied. "I'm a military officer on leave. Travelling for my own pleasure. I am not a spy."

"You know, Mr. Chadwick, in Germany today the police do not have the same restrictive laws that perhaps you are used to in England. There are men in the basement of this building that would have you talking in five minutes."

"I have nothing to talk about," Chadwick insisted, "I am just a tourist. I fly for a living and I was interested in the plane, which is open to the public. If you threaten me, I will report you to the British Embassy."

"Brave words, Mr. Chadwick. Then how do you explain this?" He reached into a drawer and produced Chadwick's automatic.

"Before I came to Europe from Egypt, I was advised to arm myself, as many places are unstable. In Rome I was attacked by a man with a knife and only escaped because I was carrying that gun."

"You also had a book on military tactics in your room."

Chadwick shut his eyes for a moment in exasperation, "That is ancient history. It describes battles in the last war."

"Did you know it is against the law for a foreigner to carry a gun in Germany?"

"I was not carrying a gun. It was packed in my suitcase"

"I shall have to detain you while we investigate the matter further."

"There is nothing to investigate," Chadwick cried. "I want to speak to a representative of the British Embassy."

The official nodded with his head to a guard who had entered the room. He spoke rapidly in German and the guard led Chadwick by the arm down a flight of stairs, along a corridor and pushed him roughly into a vacant cell. It was lunchtime, but he didn't feel at all hungry. He realized he had gotten himself into serious trouble, but he was powerless to do anything, and he didn't understand what had happened.

Suddenly he heard loud voices in the corridor, and some-one started screaming. After a moment there was the sound of a loud "thwack" and then the screaming stopped. By standing on tiptoe he could just see out through a small, barred aperture in the door. A man supported by two guards was abruptly thrown into the cell opposite. There was nowhere to sit in his cell, so he sat on the floor with his back against the wall. His clothes were getting filthy.

At times the corridor echoed to the tread of jackboots. When it was quiet, he could hear sobbing from a cell nearby. After nearly three hours his cell door was opened, and a guard gestured with his head for him to come out. He was led back upstairs and into an office. A tall, young man in an immaculate suit turned to see him.

"Postlethwait, third British attaché," he announced in per-fect Oxbridge English. "Flying Officer Chadwick, I presume. Got yourself into a spot of bother, eh?"

Chadwick started to say something then realized he had a very pressing problem. "Before I say anything, I must visit the toilet" he said desperately.

"Oh," Postlethwait said and he turned and spoke in German to the guard. The guard nodded and led him out, across a foyer and down a corridor to a door labelled "Herren."

Chadwick dashed inside to the urinal, while the guard was waiting for him outside. As they returned across the foyer Chadwick saw a group of men just arriving. He recognized one of them immediately.

"Herr Emsden," he called.

Startled, Emsden looked round and saw Chadwick. "Ach, Mr. Chadwick. What are you doing here?"

"I went for a flight at Tempelhof and now I'm accused of being a spy."

"*Gott in Himmel,* that is serious."

Attracted by the noise, the officer who first interviewed Chadwick strode belligerently up to Herr Emsden. Before he could say anything, another man travelling with Emsden spoke into his ear in German.

"Herr Emsden is head of the diplomatic corps in the Propaganda Ministry, reporting directly to Doctor Goebbels. He has an appointment with Obergruppenfuhrer Himmler in a few minutes."

Emsden addressed the Gestapo officer, "Sturmbannfuhrer—er—"

"Koeppel, Excellency."

"Sturmbannfuhrer Koeppel, Herr Chadwick travelled with me from Rome three days ago. I think I can say without question that he is what he says he is—an English officer returning from his post in Iraq to England. To arrest a serving officer who has spent so little time in Germany would be diplomatically unwise."

"Naturally, Excellency, if you can vouch for him, we will consider the matter closed. I think we can say Herr Chadwick was a little careless, considering the place he was in."

He turned and addressed Chadwick in English, "Herr Emsden has vouched for you and you are released into the custody of the British Embassy. Your gun will be confiscated, and your book returned."

Chadwick turned to thank Herr Emsden, but he was already walking away. He waved a languid arm, not even looking behind him.

Postlethwait grabbed Chadwick's hand. "We should go while the going's good." As they walked down the steps outside, he said to Chadwick, "That's the first time I have ever seen someone get out of the clutches of the Gestapo by taking a piss."

At street level he said, "Mr. Chadwick, if you want my advice, get yourself out of Germany as soon as possible. Whatever you do, you may be under surveillance, remember that." Walking away he shouted, "Good day to you."

Chadwick walked down the street until he saw a bar, where he ordered a beer and sausage with potatoes and sauerkraut. After he worked out where he was, he caught a tram and then walked a short distance to the hotel.

The clerk looked up when he entered. "Man left these for you," he said. He pointed to Chadwick's passport and the book about the Mesopotamian campaign.

Chadwick said, "I may be leaving in a day or two."

He lay on the bed in his room and reviewed the day. He decided he had been naïve, stupid and lucky, all at the same time. He had totally underestimated the climate of fear present in Germany. He had been extremely fortunate Herr Emsden had shown up when he did. He would very likely not be lying on a comfortable bed at that moment if he was still a guest of the Gestapo.

He also realized an almost subconscious desire was plaguing him; he would like to see Lisa Scharf and her son while he was in Germany. Almost certainly, if he was under surveillance, anybody he met would also come under suspicion. He would have to be very careful and lose any watchers if he was to meet Frau Scharf. He knew that Professor Scharf worked at the University of Bonn, but that was the only lead he had as to the whereabouts of their residence.

At the main Deutsche Reichsbahn station he studied a map of the German rail network. If he was being watched, he reckoned the watcher would check on any tickets he bought. He decided to get a ticket to somewhere he wasn't planning to visit right away. That would require cash, and he had about twenty pounds left of the original sum he had put in a money belt. From the map he discovered that Cologne was the nearest main line station to Bonn. Checking timetables, he found that the express to Brussels, Belgium, stopped at Cologne. A plan formed in his mind to book a ticket to Brussels, hop off the train at Cologne and take a local to Bonn. If questioned at Cologne, he would say he was not feeling well on the train and needed a break. Then he decided that ploy would flag the ticket collector at Cologne, who might well alert the police.

In the afternoon he visited the Pergamon Museum to look at the so-called Treasure of Priam, a horde of gold discovered by Heinrich Schliemann in the last century. Schliemann was a millionaire with an amateur's interest in archaeology who believed Homer's Iliad was literally true. Based on the book, he dug in Turkey at a site he thought was ancient Troy. He did find gold, but it was eventually proved to be from a civilization much older than Troy. On the way down to that level Schliemann destroyed much of the remains that were actually from Troy.

The museum took Chadwick's mind off the unsettling events of the day before and his apprehension about the adventure to find Frau Scharf. He knew he wasn't playing with Boy Scouts. If the Gestapo caught him again, he was in real trouble. He went back to his hotel and told the clerk he would be leaving in the morning.

The next day he took a taxi to the station, bought a one-way second-class ticket to Cologne and settled on a bench where he could observe the ticket windows. There were more than twenty windows. He realized he wasn't thinking clearly. A Gestapo agent would simply enter the back of the ticket office to check on his destination.

He got off the train in Cologne in the early afternoon and checked into the hotel next to the station. As usual, the clerk copied the passport details. He dumped his suitcase in his bedroom and returned to the station, where he bought a return ticket to Bonn. Nobody seemed to be paying particular attention to him.

The train to Bonn took forty minutes, and as soon as Chadwick got off the platform, he spotted a public phone booth. He thumbed through the directory and found Professor Dr. Kurt Scharf, but no listing for Lisa Scharf. He called the number listed and a cheerful woman's voice announced, "*Institut für Archäologie.*" He put the phone back on the cradle. The Scharfs apparently did not have a phone at their home.

Chadwick faced a dilemma. He needed Frau Scharf's home address, and quickly. He pulled out a pen from his pocket and dialed the university number again. When the same woman answered he assumed his best plummy English accent and said, "Good afternoon. This is Reginald Smith. I am calling on behalf of Dr. Rawlins. Do you speak English?"

"A little," the woman at the other end replied.

Chadwick went on. "Dr. Rawlins worked closely with Professor Scharf in Iraq."

"Yes, I am familiar with his name."

"Dr. Rawlins wishes to send a private communication to Professor Scharf. Could you please let me have his home address?"

"I can find the professor for you."

"No, that won't be necessary. I promised Dr. Rawlins I would obtain his address while I am in Germany, but I am afraid I'm rather pressed for time."

There was a short delay and then she said, "Kastanie Strasse, number 35, Bonn."

"*Danke*," Chadwick said. "Please give Dr. Rawlins's best wishes to the professor." He rang off and jotted down the address.

There was a street map in the entrance hall of the station. Chadwick studied it carefully and made a note of the nearest major road to the Scharf's address. He climbed into a taxi outside the station and gave the name of the road near the Scharf's address. The driver asked for a number, Chadwick desperately searched his mind for dimly recollected German phrases and said "*Irgend wo* – anywhere."

As they cruised down the road, he looked intently at the street signs, and by fortunate chance caught a glimpse of Kastanie Strasse.

"*Hier*," he cried. "Halt." He paid off the driver and walked back to Kastanie Strasse. It was a typical suburban street with chestnut trees edging the sidewalk. The houses had modest gardens in the front. Chadwick realized if he had been followed, he was leaving a trail a mile wide. He turned to look back down the street. It was empty *Still*, he rationalized, *I've come this far. In for a penny, in for a pound.*

He opened the gate of number 35 and walked up to the front door. His heart was pounding. He lifted the brass knocker and gave two gentle taps. After a few moments Lisa Scharf stood before him. At first, she looked puzzled, and then her face contorted, and she cried, "You!" in German.

"Good afternoon, Lisa," he said as calmly as he could in French.

She pulled him inside, glanced both ways to see if the neighbors were watching and quickly shut the door. He followed her into a room at the back, where a cheerful fire burned in a small grate. A child was playing with a toy on the carpet.

"So," she said, "what brings you to Bonn?"

Speaking in French, he replied, "I'm on my way home. I've finished my tour of duty in Iraq. When I was in Berlin, I got the mad idea of looking you up." He looked at the child. "So, this is your son."

"Yes, mine and Kurt's," she said pointedly. "Kurt was delighted to have a son. He is nearly two."

They both sat down. He looked at Lisa. She had put on a little weight. It had been two years since he last saw her. She looked exactly like what she was—a slightly care-worn middle-class housewife. "And how are things going?" he asked.

"When the baby was born things were wonderful. But within the past few months Kurt has had problems with his work." She looked forlorn. "Things are not the same here in Germany. Since the new leader was elected the atmosphere has changed. Just a month ago the university chancellor called Kurt into his office. He told Kurt that due to pressures completely out of his control, Kurt was going to lose his professorship."

Chadwick was amazed. "How can that be?"

"The chancellor said that Kurt is Jewish. His grandfather was a Jew."

"But Professor Scharf doesn't teach religion," Chadwick said naively. "What difference does it make?"

"Apparently it makes a big difference now. The chancellor advised Kurt to get a job abroad. Kurt fought during the war—he even got a medal. But now he's going to be cast aside, and the chancellor said he feared worse is to come." A tear ran down her cheek.

Chadwick was embarrassed and he felt her sadness engulf him. To change the subject, he said, "Let's have a look at the youngster." He got on his knees and shuffled up to the child. "'Ello." he said, speaking German. "What are you called?"

"His name is Kurt," Lisa said, "like his father."

Chadwick sensed her mood. "Look. I'm sorry to upset you. I just thought while I was in Germany this is my last chance to see you and the child. Let's part friends. I ought to be moving on. Can I get a bus or tram back to the station from nearby?"

She gave him directions and he shook her hand at the door. "Good luck with everything," he said. "I'm sure the professor will work something out."

When the professor was eating dinner with Lisa that evening, he mentioned the odd phone call the department secretary had received from an associate of Dr. Rawlins.

"He wanted my home address. I think I'll write myself to Rawlins just to make sure he has it. You know, a job in Cambridge working on one of his projects is worth thinking about, considering the political climate that is gathering like a dark cloud here. Maybe the timing is right. Dr. Rawlins recently told me that the RAF plans to start construction of an airfield over my digging site soon. I'll have to move anyway."

At the station Chadwick waited thirty minutes and then boarded a train to Cologne. Nobody seemed to pay special attention to him. He managed to squeeze into a seat in a crowded carriage and stared straight ahead. He was emotionally drained. He had no strong feelings for Lisa, but her clear decision to erase any connection he had with her son hurt him. He cursed himself for being a fool. He understood that from her standpoint, the decision was logical, both financially and emotionally. And yet, he was unwilling to accept the fact that he would never see her, or the child, again.

It seemed to take no time for the train to reach Cologne. When he left the platform, he checked the timetable for the first train to Brussels in the morning. His hotel was just a few steps from the station, so he had a simple dinner in the dining room. In the morning he bought a one-way ticket to Brussels, and when he reached the Belgian border, passport inspection seemed perfunctory. He breathed a sigh of relief when he spotted a sign in Flemish at the next station the train passed. In Brussels he also found a modest hotel next to the station. He checked his money belt; he had twelve pounds. He decided to leave the next day for Bruges, which was close to the sector fought for by British and Dominion troops in the last war.

Bruges was an ancient, medieval town. Known as the Belgian Venice it was very touristy, but quiet at that time of the year. Prices were higher than in Germany but for a little over a pound he found a room in a charming hotel and for another pound he booked a tour of the Flanders battle sites by motor coach the next day. The tour guide spoke French, telling Chadwick and the other tourists, "There had been significant fighting for four years to defend a small village called Ypres, pronounced 'Wipers' by British Tommies. The front had ebbed to and fro by several miles with great loss of life. The carnage on the German and Allied sides was unimaginable."

Chadwick saw that some of the trenches had been preserved, but they were too fragile to allow hordes of tourists to tramp through them. At one point the guide showed them a lake which had originally been a crater caused by the British, who mined under the German lines and exploded forty-one tons of TNT. It was claimed the explosion had been felt in London. He realized that the war he had experienced in Iraq was very small potatoes compared to what happened here in 1914 to 1918.

Chapter Thirty-Seven

The next day he took a bus to Ostend and boarded a ferry to Ramsgate, England. The English Channel was very rough, and most of the passengers were seasick. The sailors were busy with mops and buckets keeping the decks clean. Chadwick managed to hold onto his lunch, although he felt a little queasy, a feeling that left him immediately when he set foot on English soil for the first time in nearly four years.

He caught a train to London and checked in at the Air Ministry. The paperwork, sent from Iraq, was up to date, and he was given a rail warrant to Liverpool and told he still had a week's leave. After that he was to report to RAF Farnborough.

He spent the night at a small hotel on Tavistock Square, conveniently near the British Museum. In the morning he took the Underground to Euston station and boarded an express to Liverpool. After so many weeks in Egypt and Europe he took a simple pleasure in hearing English spoken all the time. Before leaving the hotel, he sent a telegram to his parents warning them of his impending arrival.

The train pulled into Lime Street station by midafternoon. As Chadwick walked along the platform, he was struck by how dirty the place seemed. Generations of coal-fired locomotives had blackened the glass panels of the graceful steel arches covering the platforms. He handed in his ticket and walked into the entrance hall and saw that the newspaper placards at the W.H. Smith shop were as he remembered. He climbed into a taxi and gave the driver the address of his parent's house. As they drove down the mean streets, he saw plenty of shabbily dressed men gathered in groups at street corners and outside pubs. The driver noticed him in the mirror looking intently at the scene.

"Them's waiting for opening time," he said.

His remark jogged Chadwick's memory. He had forgotten that the pubs closed in the afternoon.

They soon arrived at Chadwick's home. The street, and indeed the house, seemed smaller than he remembered. His parents were watching from a window and as soon as the taxi pulled up, they came into the small front garden. His father shook hands and took his suitcase, and Chadwick hugged his mother, who had tears in her eyes.

"Welcome back. Oh, you do look fit."

Chadwick still had a bit of a tan left from hours of flying in an open cockpit under the Middle Eastern sun and RAF food had filled out his frame. But the big change was in his head. He felt almost a stranger. The situations he had dealt with and his occasional brush with death and injury had produced a void in their relationship no words could bridge. He had a self-confidence that was certainly not there when he parted from them four years earlier.

They went into the house, and his father produced a bottle of port wine and two glasses for the men.

"Cheers, Allan, here's to your health. You'll have to tell us all about your adventures."

"Oh, there's nothing to tell, just hours of boring flying over the desert."

Chadwick excused himself to go to the bathroom, which was up a narrow staircase. He plonked his suitcase on the bed in his old room, which still had a model Sopwith Camel hanging from the ceiling. The room seemed tiny.

His father shouted up to him, "Aunt May and Uncle Wilfred will be here soon. Come on down and finish your port. There's plenty more."

Downstairs he told them some of the details about his journey home through Europe. They listened, literally agog. They had never left the British Islands. He repeated the story for his aunt and uncle when they arrived. Then his mother started to tell him of the goings-on in the neighborhood—who had died, who was sick, who had been laid off. His father told him that unemployment in Liverpool was terrible—at least twenty-five percent of men on the dole. Chadwick also learned that most of his boyhood friends had married or moved away.

He made no attempt to contact old friends, as he found it was impossible to describe the war in Iraq. Chadwick had no thought of telling his parents or relatives that his shoulder bone had been broken by an enemy fighter's guns. It seemed like an experience they couldn't possibly visualize.

The time passed. He took a tram into the center most days and browsed the stalls in the old market. He watched a film, "A Farewell to Arms," at the Derby Cinema and bought an ice cream in a tub from a pretty usherette during the intermission, while a man played the organ. He left for London a day earlier than he needed to and spent the night there. He enjoyed a show at a club in Soho and the next day entrained for Guildford, the nearest town to Farnborough.

On arrival at the base Chadwick checked in with the adjutant. He was told his kit had been placed in his room in the officer's mess. He had an appointment with the commanding officer, Group Captain Neville Delaney-Jones, at 9 a.m. the next day. He removed his clothes from the tin trunk and tried on a uniform for the first time in many weeks. He asked his batman to press his best blue in preparation for his meeting with the C.O.

Unknown to Chadwick his reputation had preceded him. The British embassy in Berlin had reported the arrest of Flying Officer Chadwick by the Gestapo and his subsequent release. The Foreign Office routinely sent a copy of the cable to the Air Ministry, which was forwarded to the C.O. at RAF Farnborough. The paperwork was, of course, read by clerks in the administration at Farnborough and before long, rumors began to circulate that the officer soon expected to arrive had been on a secret mission who had foiled the dreaded Gestapo. For a mere Flying Officer, he was treated with great deference, much to his surprise, when he arrived at the administration building and asked for directions to the C. O's office.

Chadwick was somewhat overwhelmed by the hearty greeting he received from the Group Captain. He was told he had come highly recommended by his old mentor, Welch. The Group Captain expressed his deepest regrets over Welch's death in combat. The C.O. explained that Farnborough's job was to look ahead, five or ten years, to ensure the air force had the best equipment for the coming war.

"In the past we actually built prototype aircraft," the C.O. explained, "but now we prepare specifications of performance, in cooperation with relevant commands such as Fighter or Bomber and assess the response of aircraft manufacturers and place orders for prototypes. Perhaps even more importantly, we consider the operational needs in the future. How will a bomber determine its position in cloud or at night? How will aircraft find their way back to base in bad weather? There are a thousand questions to be solved."

Chadwick said it sounded fascinating.

"First we have to get you back in flying trim. Report to Squadron Leader Clegg, and get a few flying hours, get to know the local countryside. A pleasure to have you join us, Flying Officer Chadwick."

Clegg ran the flying program. He sat down with Chadwick to learn about his flying experience.

"I see you have 835 flight hours, mostly on multiengine aircraft."

"Yes, sir. I flew on a bomber squadron in Iraq for just under four years. We were equipped with Vickers Vimy aircraft."

"I see you have a wound commendation,"

"I was attacked by a Turkish fighter, probably flown by Germans."

"One doesn't hear much about that side of the occupation of Iraq. What's all this I hear about you being arrested by the Gestapo?"

"Oh, I was returning from Iraq via Europe. In Berlin I noticed that Luft Hansa was offering short joy rides in a Ju 52, so I signed up. When we landed, I asked the pilot a slightly technical question and the Gestapo arrested me for spying."

"How did you get out of that?"

"By chance I happened to run into someone I knew at Gestapo headquarters who outranked the fellow who had arrested me."

"You must have friends in very high places." Legg was of a skeptical nature. "Tell me," he asked, "did you learn anything above what you could just as easily got from 'Jane's All the World's Aircraft'?"

"No, sir, but I was left with the impression that it was a very sturdy plane."

"Very well, get along to stores and draw some flying gear. You're assigned to A Flight. Go and make your number with Flight Lieutenant Codrington."

Chadwick flew several times in various fighters that seemed to be lying around at Farnborough. Then he was asked to pilot a twin-engined all-metal monoplane that was a prototype for a fighter-bomber that was never put into production. He flew with two men who were introduced to him as technicians working on the design of amplifiers for an intercom system. He was surprised by how well the plane flew. It had a comfortable cruising speed of 190 knots. The technicians were taking measurements of sound level in different parts of the cabin.

One day Codrington asked Chadwick if he would like to take part in a development project. Of course, he was delighted to be part of the Farnborough mission.

"We have a prototype of another fighter-bomber that shows great promise. It had one problem, however. At high speed, the controls become very stiff and maneuvering is difficult. One of the boffins from the manufacturer has developed a fix, which has been incorporated in the prototype. He'll be here tomorrow. I'd like you to meet Dr. Ballantyne and go over the problem and the proposed solution. The control system has had static tests but has never flown. That'll be your job."

In the morning Chadwick met Dr. Ballantyne in Codrington's office. He was a tall, aesthetic-looking man with glasses. The top pocket of his jacket bristled with a variety of pencils and a small slide-rule. He had brought along copious drawings and the technician who had installed the new flight control system. He explained his plan to the assembled RAF officers and a flight sergeant rigger. The scientist first proposed to deal with the pitch problem. The cables to the elevators from the control column now passed through a series of pulleys which were connected to a spring-loaded lever. The lever was connected to a small aerofoil outside the fuselage. The aerofoil changed the fulcrum point of the lever so that the mechanical advantage was increased as the speed increased, reducing the force on the stick when maneuvering.

Chadwick thought it looked overly complicated, but kept his mouth closed. It seemed to him that Ballantyne wasn't really dealing with the fundamental problem of *why* the controls stiffened. Codrington suggested bringing along a spring balance for the flight, so that stick forces could be accurately measured at varying airspeeds. It was connected to the column by a small shackle; the other end had a ring for the pilot to grasp.

Chadwick conducted a careful pre-flight inspection. As he ran up the engines, he tested the controls and they operated smoothly. They climbed rapidly to 10,000 feet and then they started the evaluation. Ballantyne was strapped in the navigator's seat behind the pilot. The technician stood behind the pilot or moved to a position where he could observe the control linkage. Starting at an airspeed of 150 knots, Chadwick initiated a climb at 1,500 feet per minute, and then repeated the test at increments of ten knots of air speed. The technician noted the stick force from spring balance.

At 250 knots, the rated maximum speed, Chadwick pulled back on the stick. The plane climbed momentarily, and then there was a loud crack and the stick moved violently forwards. The plane entered a steep dive. The technician was thrown against the overhead, and fell to the cabin floor, bleeding copiously. Chadwick pulled the throttles back and attempted to regain level flight.

The plane continued to plunge earthwards. The stick was shaking violently and Chadwick hardly dared look at the airspeed indicator, which was reading over 300 knots. The altimeter was unwinding rapidly, it stood at 5,000 feet when he glanced at it. The more Chadwick pulled with all his might on the stick, the steeper the dive. Experimentally, he let the stick go forward and the dive angle lessened. In a few frenzied seconds, Chadwick found the pitch controls had reversed. By pushing the stick forward, which was totally counterintuitive, the nose came up and eventually he had some kind of control, and he increased the engine rpm. His instruments told him he was flying at 210 knots about 500 feet above sea level.

The ground was perilously close. He recognized the terrain. He was flying over Salisbury Plain, heading west. The controls were extremely loose. A movement of the stick produced a sluggish response from the plane, which was still shaking violently. He was debating whether to crash-land or attempt return to Farnborough when he discerned an object straight ahead that seemed to be reaching for the sky and approaching at an unconscionable speed. Praying that he was doing the right thing, Chadwick pushed the stick forward and the plane sluggishly climbed. The objects ahead flashed by under the nose, and only then did he realize he had nearly been the man to wipe out five thousand years of English history by de-molishing Stonehenge.

At a thousand feet he risked a turn. It took supreme con-centration to make height corrections that were the reverse of everything he had learned before. Eventually he had the field in sight, and he made a heavy landing. As he did, he repeated the old pilot's joke to himself—*any landing you can walk away from is a good one*.

The technician was still unconscious when they landed. Chadwick opened the side window on his left and called for an ambulance. He noticed Ballantyne had vomited all over his flight suit. He reported the heavy landing to the chief rigger so that they could check the wing struts for cracks, and he asked the engine mechanic to check the engines for over speeding. He was soaked in sweat.

Codrington saw him land and followed him into the crew room.

"How did it go?"

"Not too well," Chadwick said mildly. "I nearly crashed into Stonehenge and we may have killed the technician the com-pany sent."

Codrington slowly digested his remarks and then smiled at Chadwick.

"Welcome to Farnborough!"

Epilogue

The Vickers Vimy was withdrawn from RAF service in 1933.

Iraq was declared a monarchy in 1933 ruled by King Faisal, but he died the same year under suspicious circumstances. He was succeeded by his son, Ghazi, and later his grandson who became King Faisal II. The British still ruled by treaty. In 1941, a pro-Nazi coup was defeated by British troops who occupied the country until the end of WWII. King Faisal II was executed after a revolution in 1958 which ultimately led to the rise of Saddam Hussein.

In 1934 the SD took over military intelligence in Iraq following the assignment of all German intelligence activities in the Middle and Far East to the SD. The Abwehr continued to direct intelligence operations in Britain and the Americas. Herr Weiss, aka General von Hollen, was retired and support of the German dig at Ur was terminated.

Professor Scharf returned to Germany when the dig was shut down. He was fired from his professorship at the University of Bonn in 1934 but managed to obtain a position at Cambridge University and became a naturalized British subject in 1939. He spent the war years interrogating captured German senior officers and was a contributor to the "Double Cross" British intelligence scheme, which used captured German spies to transmit misleading information to their handlers in Germany. Lisa Scharf never had another child. She learned elementary English, but always used German at home. Her son grew up fluent in English and German, which stood him in good stead when he joined the British Army in 1950 in fulfillment of his national service commitment.

Felix Goelz was returned to an Army engineering regiment and was a major when WWII ended. After the war he became a middle-level manager at the Volkswagen plant in Wolfsburg. He never married.

Herr Emsden spent the war years on obscure diplomatic missions. He was cleared by a de-Nazification court after the war and was appointed mayor of a town in Bavaria.

Heinrich Murken returned to Germany in 1937 and transferred to the military arm of the SS, the Waffen SS, fighting in Russia after the summer of 1941. His brutality and sadistic treatment of civilians made his unit a target of Russian revenge and he died of bullet wounds in 1943, rumored to have been shot by his own men.

Schuttzi found her pension was becoming inadequate and emigrated to South Africa in 1935. She married a Boer farmer and lived a blameless but boring life.

Hamid Mustafa continued to cooperate with the reorganized German intelligence operations in Iraq and became a power in Iraqi politics. He died of a heart attack in 1950, aged 60.

Margaret Kaufman married her doctor and returned with him to England in 1935. She retired from nursing but joined the staff of a hospital when war broke out in 1939. She was seriously injured during the Blitz and died of a morphine overdose in 1944 when the pain became unbearable.

Douglas Larson returned to England in 1936. He joined the military intelligence department responsible for domestic security, MI 5, playing a leading role in the capture of several German agents in England, some of which were "turned" and transmitted false information to Germany during the war.

Hiram Leadbetter stayed in Europe until the summer of 1941 when he was deported by the German authorities. He travelled via South America to the United States and later joined the Office of Strategic Services. He played a leading role in operation Alsos, which investigated Nazi efforts to develop an atomic bomb during the war.

Captain Di Palma was in charge of an Italian freighter in New York harbor when Italy declared war on the U.S. in 1940, and the ship was requisitioned by the Americans. Because Di Palma had dual U.S. and Italian citizenship, he continued to serve as captain of freighters crossing the North Atlantic. He did not survive when his liberty ship was torpedoed in early 1944.

Deborah Campbell completed her doctorate and joined the faculty of a small Canadian university in 1935 as an assistant professor. She was denied promotion to associate professor when rumors of affairs with several young graduate students emerged in 1939. She joined the Royal Canadian Air Force and when war was declared, she was posted to England. She enjoyed a highly successful wartime career and had risen to the rank of Group Captain when the war ended. She decided she was bi-sexual in 1945, although the term did not exist then.

Flight Lieutenant Lattimer was promoted to Squadron Leader. He was killed when the Lancaster bomber he was piloting was shot down over Germany in 1943.

Flying Officer Holmes was promoted to Flight Lieutenant in 1933. He parachuted from his burning plane in 1942 and spent the rest of the war as a POW. He rose to the rank of wing commander after the war and retired from the RAF in 1955.

Flying Officer Chadwick served at Farnborough, assisting in the development of navigational aids and bombsights until war started in 1939. He insisted on returning to operational duties and was promoted to Squadron Leader and given command of a Wellington bomber squadron. He was posted as missing in action when his plane failed to return from a raid over Kiel in 1941.

Glossary

Equivalent Ranks

RAF	ARMY
Air Chief Marshal	General
Air Commodore	Brigadier General
Group Captain	Colonel
Wing Commander	Lieutenant Colonel
Squadron Leader	Major
Flight Lieutenant	Captain
Flying Officer	Lieutenant
Pilot Officer	Second Lieutenant
Warrant Officer	Sergeant Major
Flight Sergeant	Staff Sergeant
Sergeant	Sergeant
Leading Aircraftman	Corporal
Aircraftman	Private

Common English and Technical Terms

Aldis Lamp	A lamp with a focused beam used for signaling by morse code
Artificial Horizon	A flight instrument with a display which remains parallel to the actual horizon
Baksheesh	A small bribe
Bank	A flying attitude with the wings not parallel to the horizon, as in a turn
Batman	Military orderly
Blighty	Britain
Boffin	Scientist

Butts	A shooting range with a backstop embankment of earth or sand
Check ride	A test conducted in the air
Chocks	Triangular pieces of wood to block the wheels of aircraft
Crossley Tender	A truck built for the British armed forces by Crossley Motors
Deutsche Reichsbahn	German railway
Dhobi Wallah	Laundryman
Effendi	Arabic term for a man of authority. Generally applied to all westerners in the middle east
Farnborough	An establishment at which experimental development is performed for the Royal Air Force
Fatwa	A muslim religious command
Gestapo	Geheime staats polizei, secret state police, a branch of the SS
H.E.	High explosive
Imam	A muslim religious leader
Keffiyeh	An Arabic headdress consisting of a cloth square secured by a rope band
Knot	Speed in nautical miles per hour (about 15% less than mph over land)
Liebchen	German term for "'sweetheart"
Mufti	Civilian clothes
Mutti	German baby talk for "mother"
MI 5	The British Military Intelligence section responsible for domestic security
NCO	Non-commissioned officer
Nobble	A term derived from horse racing when a horse is drugged to hinder its performance

Peckish	British slang for hungry
Pongo	Army serviceman
Quid	Pound (currency)
Rate one turn	A turn in the horizontal plane with a directional change of 180° per minute
Scarff Ring	A mount for a machine gun that carries the weight and allows it to be aimed
SD, Sicherheist Dienst	State security service, intelligence branch of the SS
Shufti	A look around
Skid[(1)]	A spar on a Vimy to prevent the nose touching the ground on landing
Skid[(2)]	Movement of an aircraft sideways in the horizontal plane, also called slip
Souk	Arab market
SS, Schutz Staffel	Originally Hitler's bodyguard, became the state police of the Nazi party
Theodolite	Precision optical instrument to measure horizontal or vertical angles; used primarily in land surveying
Trilby	Narrow-brimmed felt hat worn by British men
Very Pistol	A large bore handgun that fires flares
Webley	A British armaments manufacturer, famed for their production of a heavy caliber revolver
Wahdi	Stream bed or valley in the desert, dry except in rainy season
Wog	Wily Oriental Gentleman (derogatory name for indigenous native)

Acknowledgements

I want to thank Barbara Flores for some early guidance of the pitfalls that await the neophyte writer. When the first draft was finished, Jody Freeman reviewed the plot and character development and made sage suggestions. My old friends Anne Flood and Lew Schatzer read an early draft and pointed out to me sections that could be clarified. Dr. Louise Hanson gave me the benefit of her wide interest in world history, and in particular her knowledge of German and German mannerisms. Bob Berg is a gunsmith and master machinist who kept me straight on all matters relating to guns during the preparation of the manuscript. Peg Daisley was my tireless editor who reviewed and corrected each chapter as I wrote them. Jay Pizer designed the book and managed to produce a legible map that will be useful to all readers not familiar with Iraq.

Finally, I must acknowledge that I could not have written this novel without having had my experiences in the Royal Air Force. The adventures I had, flying what were at the time some of the most advanced fighters in the world, formed one of the most exciting periods of my life. I hope this has spilled over into authentic realism in the flying sequences. The men I flew with and worked with had experiences that dwarfed my own. Many flew in WWII and some old-timers had flown in Iraq before the war. Their stories, which I still remember vividly, helped me write this novel. Sadly, all of them are no longer with us.

Flying Officer Forsyth at the controls of a Meteor Mark 8, Britain's frontline fighter at the time.

Eric B. Forsyth was born in England and served as an RAF fighter pilot. After Britain reduced her armed forces, he immigrated to Canada and obtained a commercial pilot's license, rated for single and multi-engine land and sea planes. Unfortunately, flying opportunities did not appear.

He enrolled in Toronto University Engineering Graduate School and was later hired to join the Scientific Staff of Brookhaven National Laboratory on Long Island, New York. He worked there for 35 years, eventually being appointed Chair of the Accelerator Development Department, which was responsible for the pre-construction planning and design of the Relativistic Heavy Ion Collider (RHIC), now the most powerful nuclear physics research tool in the United States.

Once established on Long Island, Eric enthusiastically took up sailing. His first sailboat was a 16-foot daysailer, but he soon advanced to ocean sailing. He currently sails a 42-foot cutter, *Fiona*, which he built himself from a bare fiberglass hull. His accomplishments with this boat, which include two circumnavigations of the globe and cruises to polar waters and through the Northwest Passage, resulted in the award of the prestigious Blue Water medal from the Cruising Club of America.

His sailing adventures are recounted in his book, *An Inexplicable Attraction: My Fifty Years of Ocean Sailing* which was included in Kirkus Review's 100 Best Memoirs of 2018.

Printed in Great Britain
by Amazon

10082987R00169